SGT. HAWK

SGT. HAWK BOOK ONE

PATRICK CLAY

ROUGH
EDGES
PRESS

Sgt. Hawk
Paperback Edition
Copyright © 2022 (As Revised) Patrick Clay

Rough Edges Press
An Imprint of Wolfpack Publishing
5130 S. Fort Apache Rd. 215-380
Las Vegas, NV 89148

roughedgespress.com

Paperback ISBN 978-1-68549-095-9
eBook ISBN 978-1-68549-094-2

SGT. HAWK

GUERRILLA WARFARE

Crouching, almost squatting in a cautiously slow advance were half a dozen nearly naked Japanese warriors. For a moment the men felt the thrill of excitement that always followed the sighting of your enemy: alien men in an approaching group, bent on killing you.

Civilization, human reason, these were dead commodities now as two packs of vicious animals faced each other.

"Okay," said Hawk calmly. "Left to right, get your man."

Still the enemy proceeded forward, unaware that their observers were each picking one of them out for slaughter.

1

SERGEANT HAWK

SERGEANT HAWK STARED OUT AT THE PALE POUNDING SEA. The twilight glare from the ocean caused the leathery trails to tighten beneath his deeply set eyes. They were cold blue eyes shot with red, that seemed to reflect all of the horror that they had seen.

Towering white clouds rested lazily on the dim horizon, their proud minarets reaching into an eternal sky. A storm cloud was in their midst, flashing off and on in a brooding rage. The majesty of it all was overwhelming: a tropical paradise, late autumn 1943.

Beneath him stretched the shining white sand, above him were the graceful palm trees that grew almost too tall, their swaying tops containing their only foliage. But Sergeant Hawk felt no majesty. He heard only his breathing beneath the protection of his Marine Corps helmet. It was a somber but comforting sound. Somehow, once again, he was still alive.

At some distance down the beach, the trees were not so tall, they were only charred and splintered stubs. The cracking rifles and screaming men had drowned out the sound of his breathing. The froth on the lonely surf lingered in blood-red bubbles. The smell of freshly slaughtered meat had degenerated into the disgusting odor of rotting death, and Sergeant Hawk had walked away from it.

The countless things that had been human beings, strewn and twisted across the beach, spilled their insides in shocking displays of raw color. It was a sight that burned the soul, as easily as staring at the sun could burn the eyes. His soul had been burned before, but this time he had to turn away.

The sea was peaceful here; if he turned his head far enough to the left, he couldn't even see the landing craft that were still sliding through the waves toward the shore. Men were still racing from their interiors when the ramps dropped open. But now, they dropped open on the white sand of the beach, and the men ran out because they were told to run, not because they wanted to live a bit longer. He watched them drag and stumble beneath their heavy equipment.

Two days ago it hadn't been that easy. A frightened coxswain had tried to unload them in deep water, an eternity from the shore. They would have been carried to the bottom like so many rocks, if Hawk hadn't held his Thompson on the coxswain and forced him closer. As it was, they had had to hit the water half a mile from shore; it was chest-deep and they stumbled over their own stricken friends and shipmates floating on and beneath the waves. The heat from the burning island could be felt even at that distance; their goal was a fiery clump of burning embers, floating in the ocean, a half-mile away. They could do nothing but walk into it, and they did. It had been Hawk's longest walk. Most of them didn't make it.

It was all a game of chance, and he tried to cut the odds, but this time nothing could be done. The vicious geysers caused by crisscross patterns of machine-gun fire had rammed into flesh and bone until the platoon had been reduced to a third of its strength. Both officers lay somewhere in the Pacific. The platoon was little more than a squad—under the command of Sergeant Hawk—when it went ashore. He couldn't understand how even that many had survived.

Just walking and listening to the machine-gun fire, and waiting to die.

Hawk slid a long thin cigar from his shirt pocket and lifted it up to his lips. In one hot day of fighting, the Japanese had been driven from the beach. That night came the inevitable counterattack: a situation gone mad where arms and legs were flying and firearms were discharged at point-blank range.

Now it was over. His platoon was too weak to be effective in the sweep along the eastern edge of the island that was to capture a run-down airfield. There was a break in the constant tension. Tonight he would sleep far enough behind the front line to be unable to hear the taunts of the Japanese. Those guttural, alien sounds. Listening to them was like eavesdropping on the demons in hell.

"What do you say, Hawk, is this the island with the women on it?" The sergeant turned around slowly. The smiling face of Corporal Ralph Armistead confronted him.

"Yeah, this ought to be the one," the sergeant answered, trying to smile. His smile would not appear as quick and readily as that of Armistead. The corporal was a cheerful man, if a man could be called cheerful in such an environment. At least he was an optimistic man who bore the burdens of war with a certain amount of resiliency. A man with such a bright flashing set of eyes and teeth could not take hardship too seriously.

"Well, if you ain't too busy, the captain wants to see you," Armistead said, unaffected by Hawk's quiet presence.

"Okay. All right."

"Beckwith's figured out who all we lost. He said you wanted to look it over. They ain't found half of them."

"Yeah I gotta check that out; I'm in charge of the platoon now," Hawk muttered absently as he walked beside the corporal.

They passed along a leafy trail and encountered the first reminder of the recent conflict. A dead Japanese soldier lay among a cluster of blackened palm stumps, probably a victim of the fierce naval salvoes. The body was bloated until both its uniform and skin were cracked. A green film covered the open eyes, a tangle of red, white and blue entrails festooned the brush.

"I don't know if those bastards smell worse alive or dead," Armistead commented.

Dead, Hawk thought, but he made no reply. The undisturbed greenery ended and the battlefield of the landing beach came into view. Burned machinery and equipment were scattered about so that the scene resembled a city dump. Bodies were still piled along the water's edge, being slowly buried by the creeping sediment the tides had left. Men bustled about, working as if they were on a construction site, or at the scene of a natural disaster that they were attempting to remedy—instead of perpetrate. Men, industriously employed.

You're always a little bitter when you're in the first wave, Hawk thought; I have to shake this feeling off.

The two men saw Joe Canlon at the point where the platoon had been left. It was a line of Japanese foxholes, two of which Hawk had taken by himself, enabling the rest of the men to struggle to the shore. He had shredded the enemy occupants with grenades and leaped into the pit of mangled flesh for cover. His clothing still bore the brown of the dried blood.

Canlon had been with Hawk for several months. He fought and took orders like a robot. He did not seem like an exceptionally bright individual on first meeting, but he had a certain sense of maturity about him, of emotions deeply felt. Few men in the platoon were truly bright, but Canlon was less adept at hiding this fault due to his open and honest ways. He knelt on the sand, his rifle undergoing a rigorous cleaning before him on a blanket.

"Hi, Joe. Anything happening around here?" Hawk asked.

"Naw, not much. I guess I'm platoon headquarters," Canlon joked. His voice was hoarse and deep like that of a caricature of a boxer.

"Where in the hell is everybody? I never can find you sons of bitches," Hawk complained. "No wonder some joker is always getting killed."

"Some major came by and dragged them all off, to go unload some shit. He told me to stay here, so they can find their way back." Then Joe smiled; several front teeth were missing. "Except for Ewell. He told the major he got snakebit and had to have it treated. The guy fell for it."

"That bastard ain't worth a damn," Armistead retorted. "Captain Fankhauser been along here?"

"No, nobody here but me."

"He wanted to see Hawk," Armistead informed him. Canlon said nothing, he was shirtless and the muscles in his thick arms played rhythmically beneath his tough dark hide as he tended to the rifle.

"He'll be along," Joe finally answered after a long silence. "They'll all be back pretty soon."

"Wonder what happens to the captain now that he ain't got a company," Hawk mused aloud.

"What do you mean? What happened to the company?" Armistead asked.

"That LST next to us that caught a knee mortar had two platoons in it. We're the other one," Hawk explained.

"Goddam, it looks like I'm company headquarters now," Canlon exclaimed. Armistead smiled but Hawk retained his expressionless face.

"Go find the captain," Hawk ordered Canlon. "Get the men back here too."

"What about the major?" Canlon asked, working feverishly to assemble his rifle.

"Tell him you're a general," Armistead suggested.

Hawk lay back in the foxhole and removed his helmet. He ran his fingers rapidly through his sandy hair and sighed deeply. His shirt was unbuttoned, exposing a chest covered with dark, dust-caked hair. The arms of his brown-spattered combat fatigues were rolled up over his hard biceps. Already, his beard had grown dark and grimy. The men were lethargically filtering back, and he dejectedly surveyed the remains of his charge.

The men milled about, idly chatting. The sound of combat raged in the distance. These were not the type of men who relished Sitting on the sidelines while their buddies rampaged across the island. Fighting was preferable to the unbearable tension of waiting for it. Sometimes they were afraid, but they liked to fight. Perhaps that was why they were in the Marine Corps.

Hawk accepted part of the blame for the great losses that they had taken. His commanders were to blame also, for the reckless way they handled the platoon, he felt. An operation involving so many lives was worthy of a little study. He had spent his life in awe of men he considered smarter than himself. That awe was gone.

But most of all, the fault lay with the Japanese. An angry sneer touched his frozen features. A sudden urge to be out in the jungle came over him. Hate and revenge had kept him going this long; they would serve a bit longer. Until his time came. These men they were taking from him were all that he had. He wanted to keep them alive. But the Japanese must pay for the ones that they had taken.

He heard Sergeant Beckwith talking, seemingly at a distance, until he saw the round face and plain features inches from his own.

"What?" Hawk asked distractedly.

"...I say that Johnson kid, that seventeen-year-old boy, got it coming onto the beach. I think it was a grenade."

"I'll be damned," Hawk replied sadly, for the lack of anything else to say.

"Yep," Beckwith nodded, "and, uh...Well, here they all are. You want to hear them?"

"No, that's good." Beckwith stood. He was a short, stocky man, almost fat. Hawk had been his platoon sergeant for quite a while. Beckwith was an able and reliable marine, due possibly to his utter lack of any imagination. He was good-natured, for a sergeant, but dull. He had probably gone as unnoticed in civilian life as he did here. The Japanese must not have noticed him either; that was the only way to explain the fact that he was still alive. He was difficult to hold a conversation with, but no one noticed here. He spoke as the situation warranted. No one spoke a great deal on the front line; the individual suffering was done primarily in silence. There was no need to be outgoing to your fellow men at arms, they accepted you more graciously than might your family, regardless of your faults. Yet, he was a boring fellow, suited for such things as compiling a list of dead men.

"Yeah, I don't think they ought to have all these damn young guys over here," said Hawk, when he noticed that Beckwith had not gone away.

"No, I don't either," Beckwith agreed, from the vantage point of his twenty-five years. "It's so damn rough on you, though, the older you get."

"Yeah, but I'd just as soon get a little older," Hawk offered grimly. Beckwith leaned on his BAR for a few moments, reading his list. Finally he walked away. In a few days, he and Hawk would probably have the same conversation again.

Dark came early in the islands, but it was not as oppressive here on the open beach as it would be back in the forest. The men fashioned a cookstove out of a five-gallon can and were making coffee. The few hours' respite from the attack had revived their spirits. The captain did not arrive until after dark. He had no trouble locating the platoon sergeant; there was a lone mirthless figure stretched out in an enemy entrenchment, surrounded by men who would occasionally laugh and joke with one another.

"Hello, Sergeant Hawk. I've been looking for you," the captain greeted him. The sergeant made no attempt to rise; military courtesy was rather lax on a landing beach.

"Yessir?"

"Not much left, is there?"

"Nossir."

"Colonel Hayes has a detail for you, over at battalion CP. He asked me to send you specifically," the captain said enthusiastically. Hawk judged him to be a college kid. They were not well acquainted with one another. "He said to bring the men you have left on over there."

"Tonight?"

"No, no. He's over at Red Beach. They've moved inland and found a good spot for the CP. You'll have to go through the woods to get there. There's still a few snipers between here and there, maybe you'll get a chance to clear out a few."

"Yeah? We may not get that far without some more men. I'd hate to disappoint Colonel Hayes."

"No, it's pretty easy going, tanks have been through there and everything, to link up this beach and Red Beach. It shouldn't be any problem," the captain assured him. "Do you know Colonel Hayes?"

"Yeah, he's a pretty good fella. I've talked to him a

couple times on the telephone. What's he want with me?"

"I don't know. He didn't say," the captain answered, looking away in what appeared to be an attempt to hide his thoughts.

You lying little bastard, Hawk said to himself.

"But anyway, he asked for you and he said he needed you right away. I wouldn't try the jungle tonight, though."

Hawk snorted. "Don't worry."

"Good night, Hawk." The sergeant casually saluted.

Colonel Hayes himself, Hawk thought, what could he want with me? Probably wants to make me a lieutenant since I'm running the platoon now. I won't do it. I have enough papers to fill out as it is. Nobody likes a lieutenant anyway.

The men were preparing for a night's sleep, throwing themselves down in a nearby Japanese anti-tank ditch. Hawk eased himself down onto the floor of his foxhole, it was a hard floor of rock, coral and coconut root. His helmet liner served as his only pillow. He had slept here last night also.

All night the Japanese mortars and artillery had pulverized the marines' beach. The ground rose and fell around them like an ocean in a storm. Hawk had been deafened by the proximity of the blasts, his brain had rattled inside his skull until he was insensible. He had been covered with debris and dirt so that the hole had to be re-dug the next morning. But he had slept. There wasn't much he could do about the falling of the blazing steel.

Thank God that's over, his dozing mind said. Pretty safe tonight. There were always infiltrators to be reckoned with. The Japanese had been known to crawl or swim for miles behind the American lines, merely to stab or grenade a sleeping man. It was very demoralizing. The audacity required for such acts was incomprehensible to the Americans. They considered the Japanese fearless, high on religious fanaticism. Hawk understood fighting men, however. He knew that religion didn't mean much in the face of hot screaming lead. No, they just had guts. Maybe that was part of the reason why he hated them so—the jealousy of competing master-craftsmen. Whatever the reason, he fell asleep with the nagging urge to be out there with them, to fight them, to kill them. And he had no secret reservations of fear. He had become familiar with killing. It was easy now, it was the only thing that soothed his spirit. The war had bought his soul.

2

THE PILLBOX

HAWK AWAKENED A LITTLE BEFORE DAWN. HE LISTENED TO the sea for a moment as he lay there. He wished that he could smell its salty freshness, but the smell of the dead would not permit it. He had become accustomed to the odor yesterday, but it assaulted and offended him anew in the early morning hour.

"Well, shit," he said aloud. He stood up. He felt rested. The dead men were the first sight to greet him. He had more sympathy for a dog on the highway than for a dead Japanese. He could almost rejoice at their gruesome fate. But the Americans. There should be more" dead Japanese, there's too many of us, he thought. Goddam burial detail must be on vacation. That's bad for morale.

"Rise and shine." Hawk nudged Beckwith with his boot. In peacetime it might have given him pleasure to disturb the sleeping lump. Today, he would have preferred to let him sleep.

Beckwith had roused the others in short order. Hawk allowed them to prepare themselves leisurely. As usual, Ewell's loud voice dominated every conversation.

Ewell was very tall, somewhat corpulent, a huge man. His personality was that of a high-pressure sales-man. He had a tendency to be convincing or impressing someone at all times. In this world of men who seldom spoke, he was the exception. He was not well liked. Hawk did not care for him because he feared that he could not bear up his end of the fighting. He knew that Ewell was well versed in avoiding his share of the labor.

Ewell had met his match, however, for he was engaged in an argument with Private Alois Lundstedt, a griping, cantankerous malcontent, who was equally disliked.

"I tell you, the little bastard bit me right there on the wrist. It's a wonder I'm alive," Ewell exclaimed in his characteristically too-loud voice. He was referring to one of the black and yellow striped snakes that infested the beachhead. The order had gone out to kill them, so they were assumed poisonous.

"You're so fulla shit, Ewell. I saw you get cut on the Higgins boat," Lundstedt replied.

"I heard them things wouldn't even bite," Joe Canlon jumped in. He never took the other two men seriously.

"Well let's get one and see if you let him chew on you, Canlon," Ewell said excitedly, adjusting his glasses. Joe roared at the other's reaction. His laugh was akin to the braying of a jackass. It was a contagious laugh, and soon everyone was laughing. It was difficult to tell if the group was laughing at the raucous noise Joe emitted or at Ewell.

"All right Ewell, knock off the horseshit," Hawk interrupted in an annoyed snarl. "We're headin' over to the CP so everybody get your shit and let's go." Ewell fell silent; he was afraid of the sergeant. But excitement was still in his face. Lundstedt was far from subdued, and he continued to curse as he picked up his equipment; somehow his attention had been diverted from Ewell to life in general.

"This is a hell of a place to die in," he ranted. "A rock ten thousand miles from anything, nobody knows or cares where in the hell you are. These damn shittin' islands ain't worth a goddam for nothing."

"They need 'em for airfields or something, don't they?" Joe asked seriously.

"Shit no! If they wanted to end this war, we'd be fightin' in Japan, not way the hell out here," Lundstedt raved. "After we get blown to hell they send the goddam army in for a *garrison* unit. Goddam army, *garrison* unit, ain't that some shit. Buncha yella draftee winos..."

"Ah for chrissake give it a rest, Al," someone said. Lundstedt was undeterred.

"When they get enough islands to garrison all the army, safe and sound, they'll turn us loose on Japan— you wait and see, goddam it."

"We're assault troops," Ewell explained. "The army uses tactics and strategy; their strategy is to let us take the islands." Ewell left a pause for a laugh after his comment, but no one was accommodating, so he supplied it himself. "Our strategy is to charge everything in sight."

"Move out," Hawk ordered. He led the men up the beach, beyond the point where they had been relieved from front-line duty. They passed the various rear-echelon men, hard at work. The noncombatants eyed them quietly. Hawk's platoon, now a squad, slouched by, ignoring them. Inside, every one of the squad swelled with pride. That's right boys, you're looking at combat infantry, and we're going back out there.

The squad entered the awesome depths of the dark forest. There was no trail to the CP, as such, but a path had been beaten through the jungle by the passage of men and machines.

They paused suddenly as if by unspoken accord. Hawk waved Pogue Gist to the head of the single-file column. Gist and Private Quiroz were the two scouts left to the squad. Their extraordinary courage stood out, even among these hard and brutal young men. Courage was the primary prerequisite for a scout; the admirable skills came later with experience. Gist and Quiroz had guts and experience.

The sun filtering through the dense treetops played across Gist's large, flaring jaw muscles. The large face looked like solid rock, perched on his big neck and shoulders. Gist nodded without speaking and took the point. The men waited for him to get a lead on them.

Armistead set down the light machine gun he had been carrying, one of the benefits of being the remnant of a company. Most of the men carried the new Garand rifle; the conservatives still lugged around their .03's. Sergeant Hawk began walking again. Armistead let everyone pass so that he might rest a bit longer. He smiled occasionally as the men filed by. That Armistead, he's a good old boy, several of them thought.

Snipers loved treetops. The offshore and aerial bombardments had shattered an occasional giant of the woods, but most were intact. A network of interlocking ferns, elephant ears and leafy shrubs covered the earth.

Vines and creepers encircled every plant. Steam rose from the ground as the sun dried its soggy surface.

At night, or after a rain, the temperature would sometimes fall to or below a chilly 60 degrees. Now the atmosphere was sheer simmering humidity, filled with the scent of exhaling vegetation. Hawk rolled up his sleeves and unbuttoned his shirt.

The platoon sergeant kept his head constantly in motion, his eyes always searching, always narrowing and shifting. You never see the one that gets you, and Hawk believed that. If he saw everything at all times, no one would ever get him. Behind him walked Cal Brock who had just the opposite attitude. Brock didn't give a damn whether he lived or died. He hardly even watched where his feet were taking him. He was resigned to die in this war; sooner or later, it didn't matter. He just wanted to take a few of the enemy with him. He had spent hours on the beach, gloating over their rotted remains. Brock was only twenty; he spoke in a kind of a nasal mumble. Hawk suspected that he had mental problems far beyond the realm of the usual despair or shellshock, for he never exhibited the slightest fear of anything. He was a very strange fellow, with small brown eyes and a receding chin.

Ewell was sweating profusely; being quiet made him nervous. Lundstedt was becoming angrier with every leaden step be took, though if one asked him, he couldn't have said why.

Gist suddenly appeared around a turn in the path. Hawk held up his hand for the men to stop, and walked forward to join the scout.

"Better have a look," Gist said, in what was the

closest he could come to a whisper. Hawk nodded and followed him. A few moments later they returned.

"There's a pillbox up here, so keep your traps shut. The sons of bitches must have put it up last night to cut off our beach from the CP," Hawk said unemotionally. The men shuffled anxiously. Hawk noticed Private Gaedcke's eyes growing big and white. The sergeant quickly looked away from him.

"We're going around it, ain't we?" Beckwith asked, certain that they would.

"Nope." Hawk looked at the ground as he drawled the single syllable. There were a few muffled gasps. "C'mon," the sergeant said in a low voice.

They walked carefully over the crunched vegetation of the trail, avoiding the jutting roots and stubs left there. The path widened a bit, and then quite a bit. Evidently tanks or bulldozers had been turning around here. They hadn't done so this morning, however, for a coconut-log fortress was placed at the edge of the forest, covering the clearing with an excellent field of fire. Sand was piled on top of it, giving it a conical appearance. Sunlight glinted off of the funnel-shaped flashguard of a muzzle that rested in the large rectangular opening serving as a gunport. It was a 7.7 millimeter heavy machine gun. The men crouched around the bend in the trail while Hawk craned his neck at the enemy emplacement. A metallic escape hatch on its roof betrayed it in the bright light of the morning's rising sun.

"The flanks out in the woods are booby trapped," said Hawk. "We'll have to go up the middle." Gist nodded in agreement. Private Gaedcke looked at the dread-inspiring space of coverless ground in front of the machine gun. He thought that the two men were mad.

Gaedcke knelt beside Hawk. He cleared his throat. His mouth was so dry he could hardly speak.

"Sergeant Hawk, I'm supposed to be a radio operator. Maybe I shouldn't be here," he said. Hawk looked over his shoulder at the wide eyes in the baby face.

"I'm supposed to be in the navy," Hawk replied. "Don't worry," he added with a wink, "it's gonna be all right." For some reason, Gaedcke wasn't frightened anymore.

The usual procedure was for one man, a demolition man, to carry a satchel charge up to the gunport and toss it in. An easier procedure still, was the administration of one good shot from the tank cannon. The squad had none of those things. Hawk slipped a fragmentation grenade from his belt and pulled the pin out, holding his thumb down on the safety lever.

"If I get nailed, go back to the beach," Hawk told Beckwith. "Okay, I want some cover now, goddam it. Don't go shittin' your pants as soon as they open up." He looked out at the pillbox again. Beads of sweat covered his face; the straps of his helmet swung free, like the ears of a cocker spaniel. "There ain't nothing to this, now, so take it easy." He slipped the strap of his Tommy gun over his shoulder with the muzzle pointing down. "Now get in the woods opposite the gun and get set up."

The men crawled through the tangled maze of forest along the edge of the circular clearing. Twenty yards from the bare turn around they found good cover where the earth sloped down into a swamp. Hawk patiently lit a cigar and waited.

Armistead quickly set up his thirty-caliber machine

gun. Lundstedt lay beside him on the slope, preparing to feed the belt of cartridges through the weapon. The other men watched them silently, their weapons pointed at the pillbox. Armistead's lips tightened, his hands had run out of things to do. He was ready.

"I guess that's it," he whispered. He adjusted the front and rear sights until the enemy gunport fell within them both simultaneously. Lundstedt nodded his head. Armistead smiled nervously and held down the trigger.

The sharp, vicious spitting report split the morning calm. Hawk first saw the ferns vibrating around the American gun muzzle, then he looked around and saw the white spewing splashes dotting the front of the pill-box. Beckwith's powerful BAR opened up. The serrated barrel and funnel-shaped muzzle of the Japanese machine gun swung back and forth before it replied, as if it were looking for its challengers. Then it fired, its voice of a distinctively lower pitch seeming more than the American barrage. Hawk stood, poised and holding his breath.

The American shots grew more accurate. They began mercilessly drilling the vulnerable viewport. The whining ricochets from within the fortress were clearly audible. The enemy fire grew more sporadic. Then it stopped.

Hawk's swift reflexes carried him rapidly across the clearing. He ran in an arc along the edge of the clearing, avoiding direct exposure to the viewport. He could only hope that the tape-measure mines that were strewn throughout the nearby forest did not lie buried here under the open territory that served as the machine gun's field of fire.

His sudden dash carried him safely across half of

the open space. His heavy boots pounded the earth. He knew that any poorly negotiated step upon the rubbish beneath his feet would be his last. To trip was to die, to drown in a fiery sea of lead. His eyes were glued to the viewport, though his vision was blurred by the vigorous running and outpouring of adrenalin. Stay down, his mind screamed, stay down, Jap. But the evil-looking barrel began to swing again; it was a snake preparing to strike. Breathing through his mouth, Hawk's lungs burned and his gullet constricted, but he only ran faster toward the threatening shaft of hollow metal.

The Japanese now bravely dared the American cover fire. The enemy machine gun ripped off another burst. A trail of ferocious explosions squirmed and twisted their burning way across the clearing, the dust from each shell blowing to the height of a man. The shots stabbed at Armistead's position, rather than at the charging sergeant. But without hesitation or warning, the berserk stream of shells then crossed the open space in search of Hawk. He heard the waspish buzzing and slapping all around him. The ground churned and flames sprouted on his right side, forcing him away from the edge of the clearing and toward its center. His plan had been to skirt the bunker and come up on its blind side; that was now virtually impossible. Stranded directly in front of the enemy gun, he knew that he could forestall his fate only momentarily.

His legs felt tired and shaky, but he had to go forward; there was no alternative. He was close now; he could see the excited faces of the Japanese gunners; he knew that he was blocking his own cover fire. The chain of erupting shells followed him like an express train chugging down the track. Realizing that it was hopeless, he suddenly stopped and feinted back quietly, allowing the raging geysers of smoke and metal to fall harmlessly in front of him. The Japanese fought the barrel of their overheated weapon in an effort to swing its spurting death across his path. Hawk ran directly in front of the stuttering monster and again the blasts followed him, this time seeming to pass over and through him. The men in the woods now saw their sergeant jump the sizzling muzzle and land squarely on top of the pillbox. The leap was nearly impossible and he appeared to have taken wings to accomplish it.

Hawk's helmet went clanging down the front of the emplacement as he climbed the sand piled on its roof. He seized the escape hatch with one hand and tugged powerfully at it. In the other hand he still held the primed grenade. The round iron portal would not budge.

"You bitch!" He wheezed, tugging at it again, the sweat cascading down his face. The Americans resumed their cover fire and it fell all around him. Shots rang off of the metal hatch, the smell of burning metal, of welding, filled Hawk's nostrils. He had to trust the marine sharpshooters, though they were avoiding him by mere inches. He sat up on the hatch, unshaken by his predicament, catching his breath. The squad watched him in utter fascination; he seemed to be moving in slow motion as he jumped to the ground, on the blind right side of the enclosure, where he had originally intended his charge to take him. He leaned on the log wall there, again trying to pull air into his lungs and push air back out.

Brazenly, he swung around the corner of the bunker to its front wall. He flattened against it and edged toward the swaying muzzle that peered out of it. His thumb slipped off of the safety lever and the lever sprang free. The grenade snapped and the fuse began to hiss. He flung it inside.

The grenade clattered heavily against the back wall of the pillbox and then erupted. The stinging black blast belched from the opening. Hawk held his mouth open so that his eardrums would not burst, but he was still nearly deafened. He could not hear the protracted, haunting wails from within the death trap. Dazed, he shook his head angrily. Smoke billowed from the hole in thick puffs, as if it were being exhaled by a giant mouth. The sergeant unslung his machine pistol and pulled back the bolt. Blindly he stood in the choking cloud and scoured the floor of the pillbox with a long, .45-caliber burst. He stepped away and shook his head violently once more. He could not hear the anxious scampering of feet, but be finally looked up and noticed a small uniformed man escaping from the rear of the emplacement, running swiftly for the forest. His flat brown helmet fell from his head.

Hawk watched him for a moment, then he leveled the Thompson and squeezed its trigger. A jagged flash leaped from the muzzle and three neat red spots appeared diagonally across the broad little back of the Japanese soldier. He was pushed forward, falling flat on his face. Hawk's iron nerves were not startled when he turned and found himself surrounded by the squad— although he did blink twice at them, for he had not heard their advance. The voices of the men sounded as if they were at a great distance. He was annoyed by the discomfort. Armistead was smiling. He saw that Hawk had not been hit.

"Good job, farm boy," the corporal said.

"That wasn't so goddam easy." Hawk coughed, and coughed again.

"Naw, them bastards wouldn't stay pinned down like they was supposed to," Gist said. "I thought they had you there, Hawk." Gist offered the sergeant a block of chewing tobacco. Hawk accepted, taking it and placing the entire block in his shirt pocket. Under the circumstances Gist could not ask for its return.

"Did anybody get hurt?" Hawk asked, looking around.

"No. Pulled it off without a hitch," Beckwith said. Hawk sat down in front of the pillbox, leaning against its front wall, beneath the twisted barrel of the captured machine gun. He uncapped his canteen and took a long drink. He held the container in his lap for a moment and then took another long swig.

"Go get the machine gun," Hawk finally ordered Armistead. "Let's get the hell outa here, before anything else shows up." The squad filed behind the corporal and returned to the forest to pick up the gear that they had left there. Gaedcke remained behind. He went to one knee in front of Hawk.

"That was really something, Sergeant Hawk."

"Damn sure was. It wasn't supposed to happen that way. You'll see on the next one. We'll crack it a lot easier. Them damn mines and trip wires in the weeds had me skittish. We shoulda just crawled through 'em. Shit, I like to got killed," Hawk commented, taking another drink. Gaedcke smiled and shook his head in admiration. He then heard a groan behind the bunker. Hawk could still not hear very well. Gaedcke stood and walked toward the rear of the fortress.

There lay the man that Hawk had shot; he had rolled over on his back. He grimaced in pain. He had a smooth face; it was a young, almost feminine face.

Upon impulse, Hawk decided to see what Gaedcke was getting into. The young marine was approaching the stricken man; the Japanese was crying, begging for help in his own tongue. Hawk entwined his hand in the rear of Gaedcke's collar and snatched him roughly back.

"Just what in the goddam hell do you think you're doin'?" Hawk screamed.

"This one is still alive. He's hurt," Gaedcke explained. "I guess we should go back for a corpsman." Hawk allowed a disgusted expression to contort his usually expressionless face.

"This is how you take care of a Jap," Hawk snarled. Holding his Thompson in one hand, he squeezed the trigger. The loose grip caused the weapon to lurch violently, but it performed the task effectively. Hawk disliked killing unarmed men, but he never hesitated to splatter the brains of a pleading and dying man. This was no place to be sentimental, he reasoned. Usually such things were done while the adrenalin was high, when they seemed more appropriate. Gaedcke jumped back in shock at the discharge into the wounded man. It had been done in cold blood. He could not understand how familiar Hawk was with such things, how meaningless they were to him. He could not know that he himself might do the same thing after he had practiced a bit in righteous fits of anger.

Gaedcke stared in horror at the gutted skull.

"Don't ever go up to no Jap," Hawk reprimanded. "Them bastards commit suicide and take you with 'em. I seen a corpsman and four stretcher bearers get killed that way. That son of a bitch is probably layin' on a grenade right now."

Somehow, Gaedcke doubted it. His admiration of Hawk was tempered now. Hawk smiled one of his rare grim smiles. He turned the man away from the sight and slapped his shoulder.

"Where you from boy?" Hawk asked.

"Kansas."

"Yeah? You wanta get back to Kansas? Don't think about nothing you see here. Keep puttin' one foot in front of the other, one day at a time, and it'll get over with. If you get nailed, you'll never know the difference anyway. Keep killin' Japs, that's the answer to it. Remember your buddies and keep killin' Japs." Gaedcke looked into Hawk's deep eyes. He saw all of the pain and misery, the horror of loss that he had yet to experience. "Don't worry about no goddam Jap. Worry about marines."

"All right, Sergeant Hawk." Hawk retrieved his fallen helmet, and dropped it on his head. Gaedcke watched him sling his Thompson dexterously over his shoulder. Hawk did everything dexterously. Everything associated with fear and death anyway. Even his voice was deep and terrifying.

"Sergeant Hawk? Are you from Georgia?" Gaedcke asked in reference to the thick Delta accent that Hawk bore. Hawk didn't know why he had asked.

"No. Mississippi. And I wanta go back there."

3

THE MISSION

THE MEN CAME DRAGGING BACK SLOWLY FROM THE FAR side of the clearing. Their pace belied their feelings, however, for they were overjoyed that no one had been hurt. Suddenly, Canlon came skipping lightheartedly from the pack.

"Hey, Ewell shit his pants," he cried in his dumb voice. "Hey everybody, Ewell shit his pants!" Ewell looked indignantly down at the other man dancing around him.

"I did not. I most certainly did not," he protested.

"Yes you did, Ewell," Canlon persisted.

"Somebody did," Lundstedt said amidst a stream of curses and obscenities.

"It was Ewell, it was Ewell," Joe brayed. At that moment, with everyone gathered near the pillbox, Private Bertoni made his appearance from the far edge of the clearing. He was wearing a fresh pair of dungarees. The crowd of men roared in derision. The culprit had been discovered.

"Hey, Bertoni, you'd think you took that pillbox," Ewell shouted, feeling vindicated.

"I helped take it," Bertoni grumbled sheepishly as he walked toward them. This only caused another outburst of laughter.

"That bastard didn't do a *goddam* thing," Lundstedt said under his breath, and then added in a louder voice, "except shit his pants." The release of the recent tension caused the laughter to reach hysterical proportions. Neither Hawk nor Brock took part in the hilarity. Hawk might have felt sorry for Bertoni, if he hadn't been such a big talker aboard ship. Instead he felt nothing.

"We'll see how funny it is next time," said the surly platoon sergeant. He eyed the men meaningfully until the laughing stopped. When they had regained their composure, he swung into the lead on the path toward the CP. Quiroz already had taken a five-minute head start. Beckwith fell in beside Hawk.

"Hey you know, I wanted to talk to you, about that..." Beckwith looked over his shoulder,"...Brock guy. I think he's outa his mind or something. He sat up there shooting at the pillbox without even taking cover."

"So what?" Hawk said. "Maybe he'll get a medal someday."

"That guy ain't got good sense. I can't understand a word he says. Maybe we oughta try and get rid of him."

"Yeah? Why don't we get rid of everybody but me and you?" Hawk asked, irritated. "He's okay, forget it. How'd the rest do?"

"Fine, just fine. Ewell was all shook up, but he did fine."

"Now Ewell *is* a jerk," Hawk said.

* * *

IT TOOK another hour and a half of walking to reach the battalion CP. Quiroz was there, sitting under a coconut tree, waiting for them. Rows of neat tents were being set up in a nearby meadow, but the officers still had enough respect for Japanese artillery to use the captured entrenchments for their headquarters. They would wait until the front was driven north to a safe distance before occupying the tents. Hawk pushed back his helmet and searched for someone that might be Colonel Hayes.

Hawk knew that Hayes was a good man, from the few times that he had spoken with him; the commanding officer had seemed amiable and concerned. He had a good record too.

The sergeant was a little ill at ease about meeting with him at this time. His recent losses in the landing preyed upon his mind. Why a colonel would want to see him was a disturbing question for which he had no answer.

Hayes and his staff were bustling about a semi-mobile command post. A tarp was thrown over an ammo crate that sat before a bombed-out bunker; on this a map of the atoll was spread out. Hawk had never seen the man, he had only spoken with him. The sergeant recognized the voice from within the confines of a crowd of gesticulating officers surrounding the ammo crate. It was a quiet firm voice. The colonel was tall, with silver hair and angular features.

"Colonel Hayes? Sergeant Hawk reporting, sir." Hawk saluted properly.

"Oh?" The colonel looked up from what he had been doing. "Yes. Dave, this is Sergeant Hawk. He's the one they always call for on the telephone when they get into trouble." Another, hefty officer looked at Hawk and smiled. He admitted to having heard of him. "Okay then men," the colonel spoke again, "get to work on that. I have something to discuss with the sergeant here." The herd of officers dispersed magically; they knew that the colonel would not be talking of tactics and logistics to the sergeant, but that some emergency was on the front burner.

The two men were left standing there for a moment, alone and speechless. The slouched, dirty, medium build of the noncom contrasted sharply with the straight, tall, crisply immaculate superior.

"I hear your platoon has been catching hell, Jim?" The intonation was that of a question. Hawk disliked being called Jim; he had always been known as James. Still he could appreciate the friendliness of the gesture.

"Yes sir, it looks like everywhere we go, we get the crap beat out of us."

"Well, that's the way it goes sometimes, that's what it takes. But you're a good marine, one of my best, you have quite a reputation. I know it hasn't been easy running that outfit by yourself. You push hard, but I know that you're always out front." Hawk, didn't answer. He didn't know where the colonel had attained this omniscience but he was flattered. "Some days you're lucky, and some days you aren't. Don't you think?"

"Yes, sir, that must be it."

"Look here, Jim. You know what this is?" The officer stepped back so that he might look at the map. Hawk glanced at it.

"Looks like a map of the island."

"That's right. Here we are. Here's Green Beach. How is Green Beach?"

"Fine. It'd be a lot better if they'd shovel some sand over the dead guys."

"Yes, things are still fairly chaotic. Anyway, here's the front, moving east. That's where all the Japs are, we're backing them toward this old airfield. Things will be winding up once I get that corduroy laid and get some tanks through here." He gestured toward the eastern swamps. "The Japs really don't have a chance, you know. They don't know how to use artillery or armor, their air and naval support is medieval, they're outnumbered—it's all a question of time."

That ain't all it's a question of, Hawk said to himself. The colonel ran his finger across the laminated paper to the northwest corner of the island.

"We've got a little problem over here, though. There's a Dutch plantation out near this peninsula. We're not headed in that direction, but we might drive some Japs over there during the campaign, you understand?" Hawk nodded in assent; he knew that the enemy would eventually collapse and scatter everywhere, having to be blown out of every cave and rabbit hole on the atoll. "I can't leave those people out there unprotected. I'm told that there are women and children with them. We don't really know how many people are involved, but the Dutch are our allies, you know?"

Hawk nodded affirmatively; he wasn't sure if he was aware of that or not, but the answer must be yes.

"What I'm getting at is," Hayes continued, "I want a man with a little savvy to take a squad or two over there and watch out for them, just to scare away any runaway Japs that might get driven that far. I doubt that any will

—there are so many natural barriers cutting off that corner." The colonel smiled at Hawk. "Want to tackle it?"

"Well, yessir. But if they're on the coast, why don't the navy just evacuate 'em?"

"That's another problem, there's a bad run of reef up here. The navy won't even consider it. I've already had a little falling-out about it with them. They're afraid of getting hemmed in up there. It looks like it's up to us, and time is running out."

Hawk shook his head and sighed. "Wonder why them folks wanted to get in such a spot," he said, making the question sound rhetorical, so as not to offend the colonel by making him think he wanted an answer.

"Oh, I'm sure that their presence there has to do with the plantation. It's for certain that nothing will grow on this end of the island. We had to land here because of those rough northern waters. You'd have to hoof it across the island, this way," Hayes said, pointing to the vast, empty western half of the map.

Goddam, was Hawk's first impression, that's a long haul. But he said nothing, his gaze riveted to the map.

"It might take a couple of days, I'm hoping that they'll be all right until then. The flyboys tell me they're okay for now," the colonel went on quietly, inconspicuously awaiting a more enthusiastic response from Hawk.

"What's out here, sir?" Hawk pointed to the blank, white left side of the paper that he was expected to traverse.

"We don't know," the colonel said frankly. "Swamp, rivers, ridges. The jungle is so thick that we can't really tell. There doesn't appear to be any Jap concentration there, but I wouldn't swear to it. The pilots have reported a few sightings of natives; the Japs have probably worked them over pretty well." Hawk studied the blank spot stoically. In his mind it was alive with forest, reptiles, insects, muck, a few scattered Japanese—and dead Americans. "Now you don't have to remain there long, just a few days. We'll link up with you as soon as we secure a substantial part of the island."

The colonel's inquisitive staring at the sergeant increased in intensity. "You don't have to do it. I can get somebody else, but I wanted someone that I knew would be looking out for his men. I don't want to lose anyone at all on a two-bit operation like this." Hawk nodded. He didn't want to either.

"Okay," he said simply, "we'll handle it."

"Good. You're a good man," Hayes said with relief in his voice. Sometimes these taciturn front-line NCOs were hard to deal with. "Now let me stress, time is of the essence," Hayes admonished now that Hawk was safely in his web. "You have to get there before the Japs. Any casualties or injuries will just have to be abandoned. Clear? That means any."

Hawk acknowledged the order with one dark raised eyebrow. "When do we start?"

"As soon as possible. Oh, the morning's all right. We're running a spearhead off to the west, just so we'll have a line of defense. They might put up a fight to draw us to the western flank, but we know that it'll just be for show. Our western flank is going to swing east eventually in a pincers move. Anyway, you'll have to cross the front and head northwest to this little river—then the rest of the island is all yours."

"Good deal, then. Oh...uh, will I get any more men?"

"We'll see. Good luck, sergeant," the colonel saluted casually. The conversation was at an end.

"Thank you, sir."

As Hawk walked back to his men, he considered what he had gotten himself into. He wasn't sure whether he had drawn the hardest or the easiest duty of the campaign, but he had a strange feeling that it was either one or the other. There was that quality of the extreme about it. His mouth made an expression equivalent to a shrug. So what?

The sergeant rejoined the squad, they seemed not to notice. They were joking with one another. The men could laugh quite a lot when their spirits coalesced into anything approaching normality. They were very young. Hawk preferred that they have a few years on them, but he had a high turnover in his inventory; the Japanese were oblivious to his preferences.

Ewell was busy ridiculing Canlon; he made the perfect butt of a joke. Canlon didn't care, he liked to laugh whether he was the butt of a joke or its maker. Hawk sidled up to Canlon.

"What's the latest?" Joe asked upon seeing him.

"They want our squad to cross the island tomorrow, to protect a Dutch plantation," Hawk said, looking at his orders. The colonel had given him a copy in English and a copy written in Dutch, so that Hawk's intended beneficiaries could understand the situation.

"Dutch, huh?" Joe said, a mildly puzzled expression upon his rough, nearly comical face. "What kind of people is that?"

"Shit man, Dutch. Wooden shoes, windmills. Kinda like Germans, I guess."

"Oh yeah, I've heard of them," Joe said; the wooden shoes had done it. "Don't know much about them, though. How'd they get way out here?"

"I don't know. Do you think it'll be rough crossing the island?" Joe looked at the relentless terrain and nodded.

"I think you're right. The colonel don't though. He called it a two-bit deal."

"But he don't have to do it," Joe suggested. Hawk smiled. A smile on his face was as out of place as a debutante in a waterfront dive. He liked old Joe. Joe had a way of going right to the heart of a matter.

Beckwith grew curious and joined the two men. Hawk filled him in. Hawk ordered him to assemble the men. He wanted to get to the front that night, so that they could get an early start on crossing the island.

Hawk wanted to find Captain Fankhauser again. As far as he knew, the captain was still his company commander. He should be told about these special orders. Hawk's primary concern was getting more men, replacements, to take across the island. A few questions put him on Fankhauser's trail. He was at the new western front, with a fresh company. Hawk steered his men down one of the debris-covered roads to the front.

Mute wounded lay along the road. Many watched the men pass through one eye. They held their red-soaked bandages and waited patiently to be carried back to the aid stations. They appeared to be so much forgotten garbage lining the road. The haggard, hollow-eyed men returning from the front passed them as if they were invisible. Orders were to ignore the wounded. They were someone else's responsibility.

Nearby, machine guns rattled angrily and cracking

rifles answered them. Sharp grenade reports, the pounding of mortars, and bellowing of artillery could be heard in the farther reaches of the forest. Smoke blocked the sun; dark wings of death seemed to beat overhead. There was a haunted hush every now and then while the weapons of war took a breath. The quiet made Hawk's skin crawl. Clouds were low in the sky, causing weird echoes. A light drizzle began to fall. Whenever they reached a lonely stretch of the muddy road, they could almost hear the mourning of the newly made ghosts, beckoning the living to join them, to give up this earthly struggle. They were relieved when the road ended in an open area occupied by a Japanese village that had been constructed there.

Construction had not yet been completed when the marines struck. There was a concrete canteen, living quarters and even a temple, partially built. Most of the walls and all of the roofs were caved in and blackened. Orange flames, capped by plumes of black smoke, were scattered about the little town. Marines were cautiously going from door to door in quick, nervous dashes. A Japanese tank, one tread blown away, was lying at an awkward angle. Three Shermans were parked idly in the town's main street. Hundreds of little motionless heaps were all that was left of the defenders. A score of bodies were lined up between two of the tanks; they were carefully covered with ponchos. A boy was on one knee, his hand to forehead, grieving over one of the covered marines. Beside him stood Captain Fankhauser. Hawk went up to him and saluted.

"Hello Captain," Hawk said self-consciously. He spoke in a low voice so as not to disturb the man on one knee. He informed Fankhauser of his special orders.

"So, I was wondering if you couldn't get the platoon back up to strength. We gotta leave in the morning," Hawk concluded.

Fankhauser did not seem sympathetic. "I can't spare anybody," he said coldly.

"We can't do those people out there much good unless we got a few more men," Hawk persisted.

"All right. All right, Hawk. I'll see what I can do. They're your orders. If you can't do it, why don't you ask to be relieved. There's only two can'ts around here: If you can't get it, you can't stay."

Hawk bristled, but he held his tongue and clenched his fist. He felt entitled to more men, but he was not one to beg. After that last comment, he was not even going to ask again. He turned without a word and rejoined the men that he had left.

"Well, we gettin' some replacements?" Lundstedt asked.

"I doubt it," said Hawk, lighting a cigar.

Lundstedt cursed and screamed, caught up in a tirade. Once he even slammed his helmet to the ground. Hawk ignored the outburst, but Lundstedt was going to need toning down soon. The sergeant was getting a vicarious release of his own rage by watching him. Hawk noticed Brock, stretched out on the ground, utilizing a Japanese corpse for a pillow. He chose to ignore such ghoulishness, lest he encourage it by letting Brock know that it rankled him. Beckwith noticed it at the same time.

"Shit! Brock, get the hell off there!" Beckwith shouted. Brock slid back his helmet with which he had been shading his eyes and mumbled something inaudible. Slowly, he complied with the order. Joe Canlon walked over to Hawk and spoke confidentially.

"You know, we gotta have more men."

"Yeah, I'll shit around here a while and see if that son of a bitch sends me some. He oughta send a couple more squads at least. That's what we're supposed to have."

Hawk's new men found him there at the edge of the village, late in the afternoon. He didn't recognize them as his new squad at first. Four men in torn bloody combat gear came dragging up to him.

"Sergeant Hawk? I'm Staff Sergeant Mayeaux, anti-sniper platoon. This is your replacement squad. They didn't have any place else to stick us. I guess there's not enough of us to do anything with." No emotion showed in Hawk's tired face. He had hoped against something like this, but he was not surprised. It was typical. Lundstedt was not so long-suffering. He paced and cursed Captain Fankhauser. The new men eyed him as if he were a circus freak.

"What the hell do they expect us to do with one squad?" Lundstedt asked Hawk. He had worked himself into enough of a frenzy to confront the sergeant on the issue.

"Ah, shit on it," Hawk said, as if that settled the matter.

"No, really, I'm serious..." Lundstedt insisted.

"Shit on it," Hawk repeated impatiently. Then he looked up at Mayeaux. "Y'all ready to head across the ass end of this island?"

"Yes. To a Dutch plantation, I'm told," Mayeaux replied.

"Yeah, I don't know what them people been doin'

since Pearl Harbor, but all of a sudden we got two days to get over there and protect them," Hawk said.

"How do you know they're even still alive?" Lundstedt interrupted.

"I just do what I'm told, Lundstedt. I ain't like some people. I don't give a goddam if they're alive or dead—I'm gonna protect them." Hawk's grim demeanor cooled Lundstedt's ardor. He knew that he had pushed the sergeant far enough.

Thus ended any debate about the wisdom of the mission or the size of the party. A little later a messenger came up and told Hawk that that was all the men that the captain expected to be able to spare. Hawk made no protest; it would do no good to register a complaint with a messenger. He was resigned to his task and the men would follow him. They camped by the little river that was the gateway to the unexplored half of the island. Hawk planned for an early departure. Hawk sat alone in the dark that night. Armistead threw himself down beside him, a cigarette dangling from his lips.

Neither man spoke for a long time. Everyone else had gone to sleep. Hawk and Armistead were of two completely different personalities, one incurably happy, the other guarding his brooding solitude with miserly diligence. But it was Hawk who finally spoke. His words were heavy and ominous, articulated clearly, untinged by his harsh accent.

"You know? We're going to get into trouble with no more men than this." Frogs trilled in the background.

"We been in trouble before," Armistead answered at last, turning his brilliant, ain't-life-grand smile toward the sergeant. Hawk couldn't help but smile back at him.

4

CROSSING THE ISLAND

THE DARKNESS OF EARLY MORNING WAS STILL DEEP OVER the Pacific when a sudden noise caused Hawk to sit up. Combat had rubbed his nerves raw and he always slept lightly, subconsciously listening for an out-of-place sound. He never awakened groggily, no matter how exhausted he might have been, for alertness was equivalent to longevity. Reflexively his hand went down for his submachine gun and slid it into his lap. He heard the sound again. This time he was able to identify it as the raucous laugh of Joe Canlon. Hawk sighed deeply and fired up a cigar. It sounded as if some of the men were playing cards in the. darkness. The time for departure was fast approaching and the early risers were already awaiting it. The sergeant listened mutely; he heard the loud mouth of Ewell making jokes at Canlon's expense. Armistead was laughing too, but he would laugh at anything. Hawk slowly got to his feet. His movements were almost lethargic usually, until he was being chased by Japanese fire: then none moved more quickly or with greater agility. It was as if combat was his reason for living and he lay in suspended animation waiting for it. He picked his way through the encampment, to find the three men sitting on the ground in utter darkness playing knock poker.

"About dark this evening, you guys are gonna be wishing you'd done more sleeping and less card playing," said Hawk.

"Probably," Armistead answered, his teeth shining in the dark. Ewell's face was invisible under his helmet and he fell suddenly silent. Joe sat there in his underwear, shuffling a deck of grimy cards.

"Just woke up," came Joe's dumb, boxer voice from the dark, "Couldn't get back to sleep." He was probably smiling, but the few teeth that he had were too brown and black to see in the dark.

"I guess we might as well saddle up and ride. Get this shit over with," Hawk suggested.

"Sit down and play a hand. It ain't gonna be daylight for a little while," Joe told him. Hawk slumped down beside them, insisting that he cared to participate only as a spectator.

"Are you guys playing for money? Shit, I can't see my nose, it's so goddam dark," Hawk said. Joe roared in amusement.

"I am," Joe answered. "I don't think this shittin' Ewell has put a nickel down since we started. He thinks I'm as blind as he is in the dark."

"I been puttin' in what I think I can afford," Armistead laughed. Ewell said nothing as he held his cards to within inches of his eyes, trying to make them out. Hawk's presence had definitely put a damper on him. Ewell loved to make fun of Canlon and his crude ways. The sergeant listened as the men drew cards. Eventually they all conceded that Armistead had won the hand. Tiring of this, Hawk began making a round of the camp, stirring up the men who were not troubled with insomnia. Some were sent for ammunition, food, and supplies; others simply tried to get their aching limbs into motion.

By first light, the small contingent was ready. No additional men had been sent by the captain and the sergeant was too stubborn to ask him again. Quiroz led the way with a fifteen-minute head start. The men watched his short, thin figure wade into the shallow river and clamber up the bank on the other side. The terrain beyond the river was a mystery to the men, because their map had no entries pertaining to the area. Probably one or two pilots were the only human beings that had ever seen this land, and seeing and crossing were two entirely different matters. With a silent wave of his hand, Hawk led the way into the cold water of the river, up the bank, and into the towering, emerald temple of the forest.

The sounds of battle were far away now, almost inaudible. The hacking of machetes and the scurrying of the small animals were the predominant sounds in this sector. The scope of their task became a reality to the men now. They had visions of miles of this back-breaking chopping and stumbling. It was not until midday that the sergeant allowed them a break. The feast of K-rations and hot canteen water was a welcome change of pace.

"What's your platoon sergeant's name?" one of the new men asked Armistead.

"Hawk, James Hawk," said Armistead lighting a cigarette.

"He looks like a hawk," the other observed. The new man's name was Fine; he diligently kept a journal or diary, and this new bit of information went into it.

"Yeah, that bastard's got a belly full of guts, I'll say that for him. He's as cold as ice. Not crazy or wild, you know. He knows what he's doing. Mean and gutsy. Nice guy, too."

"He doesn't mind working, that's for sure. If I was in charge I don't think I'd be swinging an ax with the rest of the peons," Fine chuckled.

"He's like that. He's kinda funny some times. Kinda moody. I guess he's got a little bit of a temper. I'd like to see you find somebody who don't act kinda funny out here," Armistead laughed. He looked about the forest reflectively. "Yeah, this is the shits. Man can't live like this for too long at a time," he added. Fine wrote something down. Armistead looked at him, a little irritated at the constant scratching of the pencil. Yeah, he thought, try to find somebody who ain't a little funny.

Armistead stood up and stretched. He offered Fine a cigarette, but the other refused and continued writing. The corporal shrugged and walked away. Lundstedt was standing up eating and Armistead sat down beside him, commenting that it would be more comfortable and sensible to sit down. Lundstedt, who seldom accepted criticism gracefully, cursed him and proceeded to finish his meal standing, though he would have preferred to sit had someone else not suggested it.

"Maybe you'll go down in the new guy's book. The jerk that eats standing up after working all day," the. corporal continued to chide Lundstedt.

"I don't give a goddam what some sorry Jew bastard writes about me," Lundstedt growled.

"Is he a Jew? How do you know?"

"Shit, man, look at that beak. He's kinda sneaky looking, you know," Lundstedt said, as if it were obvious.

"Oh," Armistead laughed, "now I see. He seems all right. Kinda nutty, though, all that writing. If I was you I wouldn't go calling him a Jew. You never know when you need somebody out here."

"I don't need nobody and especially no Jews. Anyway, I ain't goin' around calling nobody nothing. What are you, my daddy? You don't just call somebody that," Lundstedt munched with his mouth open. "Shit, you might hurt his feelings," he said, looking over at Fine.

Hawk unfolded his worthless map. He snorted contemptuously at the vacuum it contained on its western half. In about a month or so, he thought, we *might* be able to cut our way through this. He had visions of walking out of the jungle in a couple of months and finding that everyone had gone home and left them there. Everyone but the Japanese. They would all be dead. He looked down at his compass and up at the tangled nightmare of undergrowth. He would have to bear down on the men if they were to ever make it. It would probably be impossible to overwork these rough characters, so he might as well drive them to the limits of their endurance. The repast completed, Hawk gave the order to continue the journey. There was a change in tactics now. Rather than hack away at the eternal vegetation, the men tried to snake their way through it. They did not need a highway to get across the island. They crawled and ducked, hacking only when it was necessary to free themselves from the network of impeding plants. Hawk had them alternate in taking, the lead, because invariably the men at the end of the column would have a much easier time of it than the men in front. The ground covered by use of this new method doubled their morning efforts.

By dark, however, they were not only exhausted but thoroughly lacerated from crawling-through the thorny bushes. Their clothes were ripped, soaked with blood and sweat. The knees in everyone's pants were gone. With virtually no camp preparations or precautions, Hawk allowed the men to fall down on the soggy earth and sleep for the night. The mosquitoes hovered in for a feast on the defenseless men. No one was plagued with insomnia that night. No one kept watch. The sun had been burning into Hawk's face for an hour before he awakened the next morning. No one else was up.

He got up slowly, his muscles loudly complaining at the disturbance. He found himself covered with hundreds of insect bites. He popped an atabrine pill into his mouth and shook himself to loosen his aching joints. The night before, he had considered the possibility of an enemy ambush way out here almost ludicrous. Now he had nagging pangs of guilt about not posting a guard. He must not overlook this necessity again, no matter how tired the men were, or how remote the Japanese seemed. The island was not that big that a wandering patrol or deserter couldn't stumble onto and slay them in the night.

He gruffly awakened the marines with kicks and shouts. The thought of a mutiny never crossed his mind, so confident was he of his mastery over these surly warriors. Another man might have had considerable trouble managing such a crew in such a remote locale, especially with such a small gap in their ranking. But the most irascible of the men would not long contemplate challenging Hawk's authority—due in part to his dark and menacing presence, but just as largely due to their like and respect for him. He would not order anyone to do a thing that he himself shrank from doing. He was in the forefront of the combat or the labor. Yes, and he was unpredictably dangerous. There were rumors that the Japanese were not the only men to face the muzzle of his submachine gun.

The day got off to a slow beginning. After expending all of their strength the day before, the men were not sure they could dredge up any more. It was midday before they got their second wind, when their bodies realized that their minds would not permit a rest. Their faces were contorted with strain when Hawk stopped them in midafternoon for a break. It was absurd to hope that he was anywhere near the plantation; Hayes had simply underestimated the trip, the sergeant thought. He had probably done so in order to spur the patrol to greater speed. "Time is of the essence," Hawk recalled. There was no sense worrying about it, he shrugged to himself; they would get there when they got there.

They hadn't got there by the end of the second day. That night Hawk drew a line on the map to the point where, by the most optimistic estimate, he was located. It was still two or three times that far to the other end of the island. Taking off his helmet, he ran his fingers through his sandy hair. He folded up the map. They might make it in a week, he concluded.

He certainly hoped that there were no Japanese awaiting him at the end of the grueling journey. His men would be in no condition for any life-and-death struggles after a week of this. They would be ready for someone to put them out of their misery. And the Japanese would doubtless comply.

The next morning the men were inured to the hardships of the trip. Rough-going was second nature to the Marine Corps, and after a couple of days' practice they took to the jungle with a passion. There were no wasted words or actions. The Japanese had been forgotten. They had one enemy now—the endless wasteland of tropical verdure.

A few hours after sunup, the lead man halted. It was Private Gist. He hailed back for the sergeant to come have a look. Hawk crawled over each man from his position at the end of the line. When he got to Gist, a breathtaking view came into sight. The ground dropped away for a few hundred feet and below, acres of jungle rooftop swayed in the cool Pacific breeze. Hawk's eyes had been used to focusing at the close-up plant life, and they now twitched in complaint at the panoramic view. There was no end to the expanse of green; it just faded away into a distant haze. The view gave first-hand credibility to the blank map that Hawk had been carrying.

"That's a lot of weeds," was the sergeant's assessment.

"Yeah, and that's a lotta climbing," Gist reminded him, with a thumb aimed down the wall of the plateau. Hawk peered over the edge. It was a nasty drop with few handholds. Hawk muttered a long-drawn-out obscenity as he pulled his head back. He gathered the men together on the edge of the cliff. Their first impression was gladness, at the prospect of breaking the routine with a little mountain climbing. That impression had changed by the time the last of them reached the base of the slope. There were several complaints of twisted and sprained limbs, but none were granted any solicitude.

There was noticeable slackening in the density of the vegetation for a few hundred yards from the base of the slope. The earth was rocky and hard, supporting only wiry grasses. Then the soft moldy soil returned, and with it the riotous greenery.

A brand new natural discovery was made just before dark, however. It was made by a man named Claiborne, who had been with Hawk for months, but had never spoken more than two words to him during that time. There in the choking thicket was a motionless body of water. It was a stream or bayou, with foliage draped over it on either side so that it was almost invisible. A canopy of trees covered it from the sky, making it shady and gloomy. In the late afternoon light the water looked black and forbidding.

Hawk and Claiborne waded out into the narrow little ditch, finding it only two or three feet deep. Hawk checked his compass for the thousandth time. The bayou seemed to be running due northwest.

"We'll bed down here for the night," the sergeant told Claiborne as they stood in the murky water. "I think we'll follow this bastard tomorrow and see where it goes. I think it's going where we're headed and that's gonna be the answer to a prayer. Lord, forgive me my sins!" Hawk almost broke into a smile. "Go tell the guys, that's it for today." Claiborne never said a word, but only turned slowly back toward the patrol. Hawk knew that he hated to talk, so he stopped the man. "That's okay, Claiborne, I'll tell 'em." Hawk liked Claiborne; he didn't want to badger him with an unpleasant task. Marines had to fight, but they didn't have to talk. Hawk took a last look at the unimpressive little ditch. Columbus could not have been more happy at the sighting of San Salvador.

Beckwith divided up the watches, as usual, but this time Hawk paid more attention than usual. Claiborne was taking the middle watch, which was particularly undesirable because it tore a hole in a man's sleeping time. There was nothing remarkable about that, except that it seemed Claiborne always had the middle watch. Hawk mentioned this to Beckwith.

"The guys work it out among themselves. I guess he volunteers for it. I don't know how they do it," said Beckwith.

"I think I know how it's done," Hawk said sarcastically. "Claiborne's kinda bashful and he gets stuck with it."

"Well, he's a grown man, he can take care of himself," was Beckwith's reply. Hawk could never be close friends with Beckwith. He was too dull and unimaginative. He felt a greater liking for Canlon and the mute Claiborne, though he spent most of his time with Beckwith. Armistead was a good friend, but he was friends with everyone.

"Yeah, well I'm gonna see that he takes care of himself tonight," said Hawk. He looked about the crude encampment. "Ewell!" he screamed. "Get your fat ass over here!" Ewell came running up dutifully.

"How many watches have you had so far, Ewell?"

"You mean since we hit the island or…"

"You know goddam good and well what I mean," Hawk snapped.

"Well, my turn hasn't come up yet on this patrol,"

Ewell said hanging his head, avoiding the sergeant's steely gaze.

"Well, it just came up. The middle watch tonight. Tell Claiborne. Ewell, why are you always trying to put something over on somebody?" Ewell fidgeted like a scolded child. Finally he shrugged. Beckwith laughed.

"Because he's a no good son of a bitch." Beckwith answered for him.

"That must be it. You're sneakier than a damn Jap."

Hawk snorted. "Go away." He waved his hand disgustedly. "Ewell's a jerk," he said, once the man had left. Beckwith agreed. Sergeant Mayeaux fell down beside the other two sergeants. He propped his M-3 up on his leg.

It was a fairly new, mean-looking machine pistol, known as the "grease gun", because of its tiny, cylindrical shape and wire, paratrooper stock. Hawk had been offered one, but he preferred the solid wooden stock of his Thompson. They were both .45-caliber weapons of little use in firing over long distances. Like Hawk though, Mayeaux seldom fired over a long range; he was usually face-to-face with death, and he wanted enough firepower to make it a good contest. The M-3 came with an interchangeable barrel to fit German ammunition. The only problem was that it was in the middle of a Pacific island occupied only by Americans and Japanese. And one Dutch family. Beckwith fondled the shiny little weapon.

"I think I might get me one of these things," he mused. "I'm sick of lugging this bastard around." He gestured to the bulky BAR lying on the ground. Hawk and Mayeaux entered a conversation dealing with their respective homes back in the states. They were almost neighbors, one from Louisiana, one from Mississippi. Hawk asked Mayeaux to identify his men—he had never gone to the trouble of introducing himself to them.

"That's Klazusky," Mayeaux said, pointing. "That's Fine, and there's Marks." Each man raised his head when his name was called. Hawk waved and nodded to each.

"They look like they been around," Hawk said.

"They have," Mayeaux answered simply. To be the sole survivors of a platoon, they had to be very lucky or very skillful.

The next day the men took up the journey by wading into the bayou. The bottom was gummy with silt and fallen leaves, but the pace of the trip was greatly increased. The shallow water dragged at the men's legs, but this was a welcome impediment after fighting the choking vines and creepers with their entire bodies. The one drawback was the thick black water snakes that slithered about when disturbed. Most of the men could not have cared less about the evil-looking reptiles, but Ewell and Canlon had a phobia about them. They seemed to have composed a chant of revulsion as they alternately shuddered aloud in disgust. It broke the monotony quite well for everyone else, however, because it was always entertaining to see Ewell uncomfortable, and Joe's deep voice shrieking was hilarious. This was the first time Hawk had ever seen Brock laugh.

Joe had been slapped on the backside by a trailing branch and he looked behind himself to make sure he hadn't been snakebit. Brock, who was wading in front of him, scooped up a snake as big as a man's leg and held it writhing by the tail. He dangled it in front of Joe, who just then turned around into it. Joe dropped his rifle and sucked in his breath in horror; with arms outstretched he stood paralyzed, vibrating rhythmically as if he were being electrocuted. Brock tossed the snapping reptile up into a tree amid the roars of laughter. Brock fell down in the water laughing, his lips pulled back over his teeth like a snarling wolf. Hawk thought it a most peculiar smile, but maybe that was because he had never seen the boy smile before. Tears rolled down Beckwith's cheeks as he steadied himself on Hawk's shoulder. Hawk didn't laugh, however. He had seen many horrified men in the last two years and the sight held no humor for him. He solemnly watched Joe with an almost compassionate expression on his expressionless face.

Joe recovered himself and roared as loud as the loudest of them. He bent down and fished out his rifle from the muck. Brock was lucky, Hawk thought. If that had been Lundstedt or even Gist, Brock might have received a belly full of lead for his little joke.

"All right," said Hawk, when the laughter had died down, "we'll stop here while Joe cleans his rifle." He lit up a cigar and sat on a thick tree limb that grew inches above the surface of the rivulet, his legs still in the water.

"You oughta beat the shit outa that punk," Gaedcke told Joe. Canlon had to clear a place up on the dry land to clean his rifle.

"Yeah," Bertoni said, "I wouldn't let him get away with that."

"He's a wise ass," Bertoni continued. "I'd like to see somebody whip his ass." Joe looked up from his work.

"Then why don't you do it," he suggested, and then,

raising his loud voice. "Hey, Brock, Bertoni wants to whip your ass." Joe laughed at his own glibness. Brock glared across the bayou at them and slid back his helmet.

"I ain't hard to find if anybody wants me," he said finally. A chorus of hoots and howls went up.

"I got five bucks on Joe," Ewell shouted.

"It ain't me fightin', you crazy bastard," Joe laughed above the roar. Brock stared at Bertoni, who was the first to turn away. The shouts died down and the matter resolved itself for the present.

"Why'd you do that?" Bertoni asked Joe. "Now you got that loony bastard layin' for me."

"You wanted to see him get his ass whipped," Joe said seriously. "I was helping out. He ain't gonna do nothing. Forget it—Hawk'd probably shoot anybody who started a fight."

It was not long before Joe's theory was tested. Hawk gave the order to pull out and the men filed back into the bayou. Bertoni made the mistake of falling in in front of Brock. Out of the corner of his eye he saw blurred movement and simultaneously heard someone shout, "Look out!" He heard the air above his head whir as he reflexively ducked. Brock was holding his rifle like a baseball bat and had swung with all his strength at Bertoni's head. Both of the men's helmets fell into the water.

"You want some shit, dago, and now you got it!" Brock hissed, saliva dripping from his mouth. He took a step forward and Bertoni turned and ran. Brock reared back to brain him from the rear, but before it connected Hawk was between them. Brock's arms slammed into Hawk as he clubbed at Bertoni, knocking the rifle from his grasp. Hawk kicked the boy savagely in the stomach. He doubled up in pain and Hawk kicked him again full in the face. Brock fell back into the water and Hawk stomped twice at his defenseless back.

"I'll kill you," Brock gasped, sputtering water. Hawk kicked his face again and he lost consciousness. Momentarily he revived and Hawk was standing over him, aiming his submachine gun down at the fallen man. Up to his neck in water, his face a bloody pulp, Brock squinted up at Hawk.

"You got five seconds to give me one reason why I ought not to kill you," Hawk said unemotionally. His head reeling, Brock just stared into the muzzle, speechless. Hawk pulled back the breechblock of the weapon and aimed the barrel carefully at the bloody forehead.

"'Cause I'm one of your men," Brock gasped quickly.

"That ain't good enough," Hawk answered.

"'Cause I won't give you any more trouble," Brock gasped.

"You goddam sure won't," Hawk said, lowering the sights, "or anybody else either. You better make sure you kill me before you ever try some shit like that again. Now get your ass up. You done had your break." Hawk turned away to the circle of stunned men. "See what you started," he said to Joe. "Stay away from that guy, and that punk Bertoni, too. Let 'em kill each other if they want."

"I'll watch him for you Sarge, and make sure he don't try that on you," Joe said.

"I said stay away from him. I watch out for myself," Hawk replied. Joe nodded, thoroughly ashamed of himself. "You're a good marine, Joe. Those guys are scum and they'll get you hurt," Hawk advised. The episode raised a few eyebrows and reinforced the men's opinion of Hawk. Now they had tangible evidence of his ability to enforce his authority.

But Hawk had made an extremely dangerous enemy. Brock pulled himself out of the water and fell behind in agony for the rest of the day. Whenever he paused, he would glare ahead at the back of Hawk, his finger tightening on the trigger of his rifle. The only thing that stopped him from murdering the sergeant was the fear that he couldn't do it in one shot. He would rather face a wounded Satan than a wounded James Hawk.

Brock had showed his hand now, however. It was obvious to everyone that he was slightly off the beam and capable of making an unprovoked attack. Someone would always be casting a stealthy glance at him, and thus Hawk was relatively safe. At least he must have thought that he was safe, for he never looked again in Brock's direction. Actually, it was only contempt that prompted the sergeant to ignore him. He hoped the boy had learned a lesson, but if he hadn't, another class would have to be held. There was only one way to straighten some men out, and Hawk felt that any man could be straightened out. The almost effortless way in which Brock had been summarily dealt with out left the patrol silenced for most of the day. They did seem to move a little quicker when Hawk issued an order. Bertoni stayed close to the sergeant, but he knew that he was a marked man as long as Brock was around.

Not long after the Brock incident, the men halted in mid-step at the sound of a groaning engine. Everyone froze, thinking that at last they had come out of the woods and back to the war. They quickly recognized the noise as that of an aircraft, approaching from some distance.

"Whose is it?" Joe asked Hawk. Hawk removed his helmet to eliminate the distorting echo it caused. He looked like a dog pricking up his ears, though perhaps a bit more hairy and dirty than the average canine.

"It's a Jap," Hawk nodded, as if he had suspected that fact all along. "Yeah it's a Zero, just buzzing around— looking for something." Hawk listened for another few seconds. All eyes were upon. him. "Okay, get under these branches along the bank. He's headed this way," was Hawk's prognosis at last. The arching trees effectively covered the stagnant bayou from aerial view, but Hawk wanted to make doubly sure that his men were invisible. The engine grew louder until it was right overhead. Then it went away, but returned—it was circling them, it seemed.

"What is that son of a bitch doing?" Beckwith whispered.

"I don't know why, but he's looking for something," Hawk replied as be replaced his helmet. He pulled the map out of his shirt pocket; his shirt was open and he had to struggle to get the piece of paper free of it. "They know something, that's for damn sure. We ain't very close to that farm yet. They gotta be looking for us."

"Must of picked up a radio message about us, reckon?" Beckwith asked. Hawk nodded in agreement, but be was a bit uneasy about that suggestion. This mission wasn't exactly the attack on Fortress Europe; it hadn't been bandied about the air waves that much. He jammed the map back into his pocket. Ten minutes later, the last strains of the Zero's engine died away.

The men came out of hiding and Hawk pensively

ran his hand across his wet, hairy chest. He ran his fingers through his scalp, letting his helmet float beside him.

"If they were just patrolling, that'd been a recon plane," he mused aloud. "That sucker was looking to nail somebody. He had to be after us." The men stared mutely at him, as if he were the brain and they were the body. A snake broke the silence when he came swimming at Joe, who danced out of the way.

"Mmmmm, I wish those babies would take a break," Canlon whined. There was nervous laughter; the Brock incident was still fresh in everyone's mind, with the possible exception of Joe Canlon's. His memory span was shorter than most.

"Keep your ears peeled for another plane," Hawk announced, ignoring Joe's snake. "They might be back; we're the only thing on this end of the island that they could be after." The sergeant replaced his helmet and the journey resumed.

Progress was much greater than Hawk had estimated, here along the course of the little stream. The snakes, leeches, and eels that languished in their motionless slime were welcome neighbors after the miles of thorns and brambles. The terrain eventually became sandy and the banks of the gully rose higher on each side with neat step-like layers of sand cut into the earth. They seemed to be walking in a miniature Grand Canyon, the various layers of sediment rising above them on each side. The canopy overhead remained; it was an altogether beautiful spot, with flowers, leaves, and feathery dandelion-type seeds sailing on the shimmering surface of the still water. There was now a sandy beach that could be walked upon, giving the men a chance to dry out, and greatly speeding up their pace.

It appeared that things were finally settling down to the minimum of hardship, when a wail went up from the end of the column. Ewell had stepped in some animal's burrow that had been covered with matted leaves and twigs. Had the injury occurred to anyone else, Hawk would have immediately inspected the leg and done what was possible to ease the pain. Instead he cursed Ewell for a full five minutes while the other lay on the sand, his pained face aimed at the ground. Regaining his composure, Hawk pulled up the pants leg and unfastened Ewell's boot. Before the incident, success had been within his grasp.

"Well it's swelled up real nice, Ewell," Hawk said with disgust. "I hope to hell you're satisfied, you goddam oaf." Ewell cringed as Hawk removed his helmet. He expected him to fling it angrily into the woods, but instead he set it down gently. "You know I got orders to leave behind any three-legged oafs that hurt theyself," Hawk growled as he felt the giant leg. "It ain't broke. If it was broke I'd leave you layin' here—you can't even screw yourself up right."

"Let's just shoot him," Joe gibed.

"This ain't funny, goddam it. Ewell, can you walk?" Hawk asked. The lumbering man was helped to his feet and he tenderly tried his leg. He winced and shook his head negatively. "I mighta known you'd say no. You're the goddamest, most shiftless son of a bitch I ever seen. Why the hell ain't you in the army?" Spurred on by the sergeant, Ewell tried the leg again and nearly fell. Hawk's anger eased a bit at the effort. "It would have to be the biggest, dumbest ox in the whole outfit," he observed.

"I hate like hell it happened, Sergeant, I just didn't see that hole," Ewell explained.

"How many men went past that hole without stepping in it, Ewell?" Hawk waited for an answer but none came. "I'll tell you. Every goddam one of us. It took a cross-eyed hippo that weighs more than three men to find that damn hole. All right, I guess we gotta take turns draggin' this worthless bag of shit around. Let's go."

"What should I do about this leg, Sergeant, put a splint on it or something?" Ewell asked timidly.

"Don't do nothing. You can't do nothing with a sprain anyway," said Hawk, gesturing to the black-and-blue limb. "All it can do is slow the absolute shit out of us—you'll be great in a couple days and we'll still be stuck way the hell out here in the weeds."

Gist was selected to aid Ewell first. He was as tall as the latter, but of a slimmer build. Gist was a carpenter from Texas. He was probably the strongest man there. His veins stood out on his long arms as if he had no skin on them, as he effortlessly pulled Ewell along. Ewell put an arm over Gist's shoulder and hopped painfully forward, but did not dare complain or cry out. The pace was slackened, but not terribly. Gist and Ewell were allowed to fall behind, with Lundstedt assigned to follow them up at the rear position.

Hawk had chosen Lundstedt for a very good reason. He ceaselessly heaped invective curses on the hobbling Ewell, because no matter how slowly the injured man advanced, the ill-tempered Lundstedt had to march even slower. Ewell was a natural goldbrick and this ailment would have been a godsend under any leader other than Hawk. The sergeant knew him too well and was suspicious of even a genuine injury. The result was that the injured private kept testing the leg and gradually putting more weight on it, in hopes of assuaging his outraged noncom.

5

THE VAN SPEER PLANTATION

GRETCHEN VAN SPEER RAN THE BACK OF HER TINY HAND across her forehead to remove the yellow hair from her eyes. The climate on the Pacific atoll was a temperate one—entirely pleasant, until one spent any length of time working out of doors. The girl was seldom called upon to work, but today she was cultivating a garden near the edge of the forest. She had never considered herself a gardener, but one runs out of things to do on a lonely island and it becomes necessary to develop new interests.

She set down her bag of seeds and took a deep breath of fresh air. Pausing to rest, she looked back over the expansive cleared field that served as her family's front yard; it surrounded her father's plantation house, which was a low rambling adobe-and-rock structure that looked sturdy and white in the sunlight. In the distance she could see her brother, Moritz, and one of her father's hired hands, Ernst, bringing in the rubber that they had collected from the forest.

She waved to Moritz, who had awakened early that

morning; this was the first that she had seen of him today. Even at this distance she could see a smile appear on his handsome face as he returned her wave. Ernst, the helper, gave no sign of having seen her; he knew that Gretchen would be wasting no courtesies on him. Ernst was a recent arrival and he and Gretchen had come to terms rather quickly.

Ernst had fallen under the spell of Gretchen's charm right from the beginning, and unfortunately, she had done little to discourage him. He mistook her lonesome offer of friendship for something more. The Van Speers considered the hired hands to be of a lower station in life and preferred that they keep a distance suitable to that station.

The family had two other helpers at this time, neither of whom caused them any problem. Klaus, also a recent arrival, ignored Gretchen's existence, possibly in deference to Ernst. The other servant, Rolf, had been with the family for years and treated Gretchen as he might his own daughter.

Gretchen's father, Rudiger Van Speer, had had words with Ernst over his daughter. Moritz had ,spoken with the man also, but it was obvious that the helper was still very much smitten with her. The Van Speers would have liked to have been free of the young man's company, because of late, he did not mix well with them. Such an eventuality was unlikely under the present circumstances, however, and so they all lived out their peculiar relationship in this last outpost of civilization, thousands of miles from anything.

Gretchen rubbed her hands on the leg of her dungarees and picked up her hand spade to resume the planting. Under her breath she hummed a pleasant melody, popular in Europe several years earlier. In those days she had begged her father to let her stay in the old country and go to school, where she could have an endless social life and droves of friends her own age, for she was very attractive. Dances and parties were more compatible with her lively personality than was the austere life of pioneering on a rubber plantation. Now, she could see that her father had been right in refusing her. Europe was a shambles.

This was not a time to be young. She was especially glad that Moritz was not in Europe, where young men were being slaughtered by the truckload and trainload. He was only twenty-one, a perfect age for cannon fodder.

Gretchen was the oldest of the Van Speer children. She was two years older than Moritz. They had a younger sister also, Ilse, who was only five. Rudiger Van Speer's island provided all of them with a safe refuge from the war, but if also provided incredible isolation.

Still, Gretchen knew that the war would not last forever, and neither would her imprisonment on this forsaken South Seas atoll. The tune she sang made her think of Europe, nevertheless—the old Europe, as she remembered it. The music was quite beautiful and it went we'll with her intent tilling of the soil.

Her task was so engrossing that she did not see more than a dozen grisly creatures emerge from the depths of the gloomy rain forest. There were no rubber trees there and no one ever entered or left the plantation from that end of the field. The crack of a twig caused her to lift up her little oval face. The sight that met her eyes startled her into dropping the spade and gasping in horror. Her senses were so shocked at first that she thought that a herd of mangy gorillas had swung down from the trees and were now loping across the open ground toward her. But upon-further inspection she saw the remnants of clothing hanging from the beasts; they were in fact, men. She jumped lightly to her feet, unable to tear her eyes away from them. One was almost upon her, while others still slouched boldly out of the jungle. She had made up her mind to flee for her life when the closest one stopped. He held a wicked-looking weapon across the front of his hairy mud-caked body.

In his mouth was an unlit cigar and he seemed to be smiling without baring his teeth. Gretchen's smooth brow wrinkled in fear at the savage countenance. She stood frozen for a moment, as if hypnotized by the flashing blue eyes that shined through a mask of whiskers and helmet.

"How do you do, ma'am? I'm James Hawk and..." The deep growling voice jarred her into action again. She tore her eyes from his and ran as fast as she could for the plantation house. She looked over her shoulder once but the man didn't pursue her. The other men were gathering around him and the entire group just stood there in the field watching her run.

"Now ain't that a pretty little thing," Hawk commented, as Armistead stopped beside him, resting his light machine gun on the ground.

"Mmmm, hmmm, ain't it, though? This ain't gonna be such a bad mission after all," Armistead said with a low laugh. "Wonder how many of them I got to pick from?" The rest of the men were forming a disorganized semicircle with Hawk in the middle. They watched the retreat of Gretchen's shapely figure until she disappeared into the house. Then Hawk spoke again.

"Now I don't want nobody giving these folks any trouble. We all got plenty of trouble without cookin' up some more. Ralph, you can keep your dirty hooks off that kid," Hawk admonished, running what was left of his sleeve across his forehead.

"Yeah, but can she keep her hooks off of me?" Armistead replied. There were a few laughs.

"Wonder why she took off like that?" Hawk asked innocently.

"'Cause you're so goddam ugly," Canlon called from the edge of the semicircle. "That's the same thing those girls in Mississippi used to do. It's been so long though, you just forgot."

"Ah, that's a crocka shit," Hawk retorted, a bit embarrassed. He realized that his appearance must have had something to do with the lady's sudden departure, and that was not a flattering realization. He felt like an animal, or the ogre under the bridge. He certainly knew that he smelled like an animal, clad in bloody, mildewed rags. Yes—then came the final admission—he did look like an animal. Matted hair extended from his cheekbones to his waist. He looked around and snorted. "I don't look no worse than anybody else," he protested weakly. "Let's go."

"MOTHER! MOTHER!" Gretchen cried as she ran across the moat and into the dark interior of the plantation house. She managed to pause long enough to close the heavy wooden door behind her and bar it. Trudchen Van Speer came into the front living room and breathlessly asked what was wrong. "Soldiers, Mother, a whole army of brutes are coming for us," she said excitedly. Her mother peered out of the open window, her startled expression turned into a worried one. They were definitely a vicious looking band of cutthroats. Mrs. Van Speer deftly slid open the drawer of the bureau that sat beneath the window. In it lay a loaded Webley revolver, but she did not take it out.

"So they have come at last," the mother whispered. "They are the Americans, Gretchen. Try to stay away from them. Send Rolf after your father, and send Ernst in here."

"Moritz is back, Mother," Gretchen offered.

"Send in Ernst. Tell Moritz to stay in the smoke-house with you. Hurry now, they are almost here." Hawk's grim and forbidding figure was already casting, a long shadow across the barred door.

"Hey, in there," he called. "We're the Marine Corps. We're on y'all's side." The men behind him chuckled and traded jokes. "Come on now." Hawk turned to the men and smiled self-consciously. "We're gonna protect you, whether you like it or not."

Mrs. Van Speer stepped back from the window and studied the rough crew arrayed before her. They would have been truculent enough in appearance without weapons, but each seemed to be armed to the teeth. She made no move for the door until the tall, gaunt Ernst entered the room from a rear door. He carried an Enfield rifle and placed it behind the door.

"Now if you don't open up..." Hawk drawled.

"I'll huff and I'll puff..." Canlon shouted. There was a roar of uncontrolled raucous laughter. Even Hawk laughed.

"No, now, if you don't open up," Hawk continued,

"we're gonna set up camp right here in front of your door."

"Should I open the door?" Mrs. Van Speer asked Ernst.

"Yes," he answered. "I will talk to them if you like."

"No, I suppose I can do it." She lifted down the bar and then as an afterthought turned to Ernst and asked, "Are my children safe?" He nodded his head. She swung open the door and stepped timidly out onto the bridge over the shallow moat. The marines eyed her silently.

"How do you do, ma'am. I'm Sergeant James Hawk, United States Marine Corps." He politely removed his helmet. "We were sent here to look after you." Then he looked into the open door for the girl. "And yours."

"How do you do, sir. You are on the Van Speer plantation. I am Trudchen Van Speer, wife of the owner, Rudiger Van Speer. We are very grateful for such...able protection, but there is nothing to protect us from. I hope you haven't gone to any great trouble for nothing."

"Oh, no, ma'am. They made us come here. It don't matter none how worthwhile it was—we had to come and we gotta stay," said Hawk, fumbling with his shirt pocket. He produced a set of filthy papers.

"Here's a copy of orders they gave us. They got a little dusty on the way out here," he apologized, handing her the papers. "They're written in your language. The CP didn't know you folks spoke English." She took the proffered documents with two fingers, and gingerly opened them.

"Nice place you got here. We had the goddamnedest time finding it, begging your pardon, ma'am," Hawk said, surveying the white adobe-walled house. Mrs. Van Speer ignored the remark as she read the orders. Hawk noticed that she was reading the English orders. Somebody had gone to a lot of trouble for nothing, he mused.

"Oh, it is written in Dutch also," she finally said.

"Yes ma'am. Like I said, they didn't know y'all spoke English."

"Yes, I was confused. Do you speak Dutch, Sergeant?"

"Shh...heck, no, ma'am, I can't even speak English hardly."

"That is a pity. What is your native tongue?"

"Uh, well, it's English. I just meant I don't talk the way they teach you to in school."

"Ah, I see. Well, someone speaks and writes very good Dutch. I would very much like to meet him."

"Well you'd have to cross the island to do that, ma'am. Us and the Japs are fighting it out over there. I don't even know the fella that wrote that."

"I must do that someday soon. One meets few Dutch, living out here. I would like to hear of my homeland."

"That sounds like a nice idea, but I'd hold up on it for a while, till the fightin' dies down. The marines and the Japs got kind of an understanding. We don't ever take each other prisoner. The winners get the island and the loser gets dead."

"I see. Would you mind waiting here until my husband comes in from the forest," she said.

"No ma'am. We got nowhere else to go," answered Hawk. Before he had finished speaking, she had returned through the huge door and shut it.

"Well, she's okay, but if I got my choice I'll take that other little lady," Armistead commented.

"Something tells me that she didn't take much of a

shine to us," Hawk observed, rubbing his scraggly beard. The marines sat down on the ground. Their idleness reawakened the sense of leadership in the sergeant. "Brock, Gaedcke, Bertoni, let's get some foxholes dug. There, here and there." Hawk pointed out toward the edge of the field, a few yard from the woods. "After stompin' a circle around this place we know there ain't no Japs out there, but that don't mean they can't pay us a visit later."

* * *

"GOD, I WISH HE WOULD HURRY," Mrs. Van Speer said to Ernst.

"There is nothing to worry about," Ernst assured her. As if to reinforce that assurance, the sound of boots could be heard in the kitchen. Klaus, Rolf and Van Speer came striding into the room, red-faced with exertion. Rudiger Van Speer was a square-jawed, broad-shouldered man of less than medium height. His presence inspired confidence in his wife; she had seen him capably handle adversity before.

"Rudiger, it is an army of goats, right in our flower bed. Their leader is a half-wit, with the accent of an American Negro. He says they will stay whether we want them or not," she said, concerned but not overly excited, perhaps even a little angry now that she was safely under his protection.

I will speak with them," Rudiger said simply.

The door swung open and Hawk wheeled around to face it.

"How are you, sir? I'm James Hawk and..."

"Yes, you are here to protect us. But as you can see,

there is nothing to protect us from. I won't let you leave without serving your entire...contingent a home-cooked meal, however."

"Well, thank you, sir, that is mighty nice of you—but we really can't leave here. We have to wait here until our battalion links up with us and that might take a little while. They might drive a few Japs over this way, too, and then y'all would be in a hell of a fix, you see."

"There are five men here, Mr. Hawk. They are well armed. We have been here for years before your arrival and we are not in need of your services. That is not to say that we are not grateful for the offer, but...we have almost as many men as you, already. Would your men care to clean themselves up a bit before you leave?" Hawk sighed deeply. Protection was certainly a difficult commodity to peddle.

"That *is* mighty nice of you, sir," Hawk began slowly, "and I can appreciate your spirit, but I'm just a poor old sergeant that has to do what he's told, and I'm told to stick right here."

"I see. Well, I suppose there is no need in discussing it further. Forgive us if we seem rude, but your presence will complicate our lives, much more than lessening our anxieties. You have already frightened my wife and daughters out of their wits."

"Well I hate that, and we certainly don't mean to be no trouble. You don't have to be concerned with us at all. I mean we'll sleep out on the ground and hunt our own food if you like. You won't even know we're here." Hawk tried to be apologetic. He turned to the marines. "And don't nobody even speak to the ladies here, or go killing any chickens or. any shit like that." Hawk's tone changed to a loud snarl.

"Now, we're gonna have to dig a few holes here and there," Hawk continued, in his conciliatory tone. "Marines can't go nowhere without digging up a few holes." His attempt at getting a smile from Rudiger Van Speer failed miserably. "But we'll fill all of them back in when we leave and we won't dig anywhere that you got something planted."

"I hope that we can remain on courteous terms with one another, Sergeant. Your men may sleep in that barn over there. I don't think we have enough food to supply all of them for long, however."

"Like I said, don't you worry about us. We can shift for ourselves." There was an awkward pause. "How far is the cotton patch? Must be a good ways because we been all around here."

"Cotton? We have no cotton here. This is a rubber plantation. We have a few garden vegetables also."

"Rubber? Well I'll be god... Back home the only kind of plantation we got is cotton." Van Speer did not seem to think that was especially remarkable, for he said nothing. "Well, I guess we'll get the lay out here and I'll come and talk some more with you later on tonight."

"Very well, if you must."

Hawk led his men into the field, halfway between the house and the forest.

"Shit on that old buzzard. We oughta let the goddam Japs have that son of a bitch," was the sergeant's critique of the conversation.

"Yeah, he's all pissed off, just because we're here," Canlon joined in. Gist spat a stream of tobacco toward the plantation house.

"Well, I guess he's thinking about his wife and daughter. We don't make a very pretty picture. But if them Japs get over here they'd string 'em up like hog meat, so he oughta be damn glad to have us. Now I'm telling you again, this guy don't like us—in fact he'd rather face the Japs than us, it looks like, so no chicken killing, or burning up the furniture or raping the women." Hawk shouted.

"Can we burn the women and rape the chickens?" Canlon asked.

"I'm serious," Hawk said, making his voice deeper in proportion to his sincerity. "Don't give these people no shit. If no Japs show up, I don't want 'em to be able to say that they're worse off for our being here."

* * *

VAN SPEER RETURNED to the interior of the house. Every inhabitant of the plantation was there in the spacious living room, awaiting his opinion on the situation. Moritz had an arm over Gretchen's shoulder. Little Ilse sat on her mother's lap, bored with it all.

"I tried. The man is following orders and I cannot persuade him to do otherwise. He is short on intelligence but evidently is a loyal soldier. If their leader is the wisest among them, the rest are to be feared. They must be dangerously stupid. They are all crude, lower-class Americans—if there is any other type, I have not met them. Avoid them as much as possible, Trudchen and Gretchen. Let the men tend to them."

"He said they would stay here until they have killed all of the Japanese on the island," Trudchen said.

"He was telling the truth. The marines are vicious swine that kill everyone in their path. They take no prisoners. Of course, the Japanese are forced to treat them the same way," Rudiger explained.

"God! I hope the Japanese don't mistake us for them!" Gretchen exclaimed. She ran to the window and looked out at the milling band of brutish men. Turning away, she was convulsed by a shudder. What new horrors had entered her peaceful pastoral life, she could not imagine. The leader of the men was bellowing and they would scatter at his gestures. He removed his helmet and she could see his dark, brooding brow, scowling in the sunlight. Without the martial headgear, he looked a little better, she decided. He might even look human, were he clean-shaven.

That evening, Hawk knocked on the plantation house door. His appearance was as unkempt as ever, but he at least made an effort to look presentable by buttoning his shirt. The door opened only a little crack and then it was flung open. A tall, hatchet-faced man stood facing him. Hawk politely introduced himself, but the man only motioned for him to enter. He led the American through a large living room and into a den that also was in the front of the house. It had a large window that could be opened onto a veranda. Rudiger sat there at a huge wooden table, alone. Hawk commented again on what a fine place the Dutchman had.

Ignoring the banalities, Van Speer bade him be seated.

"How did your forces know that there were Dutch people here?" The older man reached behind him and took a small, odd-shaped glass from the hutch positioned against the wall. He poured the sergeant a drink of clear liquid that the marine's taste buds identified as gin. Hawk shifted uneasily in his chair as he thought of an answer. He had been called upon to do more talking than was his custom of late. Leading thirty or forty men into combat was more his specialty than were diplomatic relations.

"I honestly don't know, Mr. Van Speer. They had 'Dutch Plantation' written in on the map. There's not much they don't know about these islands, I guess."

Van Speer grunted. "There was a Canadian ship that came by, almost two years ago. They had been sent to evacuate all of the allied nationals that they could on these islands. We refused to leave, naturally." Hawk could well imagine the experience of the Canadian captain trying to pry Van Speer off of the island. He almost laughed aloud at the thought, but instead studied the furnishings of the room. There were many fine old European antiques in the den, and throughout the house. The home was rather cozy, all but actually crowded with priceless belongings.

"They eventually tired of my stubbornness, and sailed without us. I thought Trudchen and the girls would be better off here anyway. That was before I became aware of the fact that the Japanese were bent on garrisoning these valueless islands, or that anyone would be foolish enough to try and take them back."

"Yessir," Hawk admitted. "It's all pretty stupid."

"Be that as it may, they did leave us some British weapons. A Bren machine gun, a Sten gun and three Enfields. They are at your disposal, should you ever need them, God forbid. But I am sure that the Canadians are the ones that alerted your commanders to our presence here, and I only wanted to see what you knew about the matter." Rudiger licked the liquor from his lips.

"I don't know how it came about, sir, or who you have to blame for us being here, but I think you'll be glad to have us as time goes on."

"Well, the war had to come here, too, I suppose, and my lot is better than most. I only wanted you to know about our little arsenal."

"That stuff'll come in handy if we're ever attacked. I appreciate your telling me about it. You certainly didn't have to."

"Yes, but it's time I realized that this is my war, too, Sergeant."

"Yessir," said Hawk quietly. "How long have you been out here?"

"I have been here most of my life. My family was begun in Europe during a brief absence, when I thought that I had moved back there permanently. They returned there every year for a few months, until the war broke out. I am an islander, however. I haven't left in ten or fifteen years. The children don't like it here. Too dull for young people, you know."

"I expect so. I can see your reason for staying though. Sure is beautiful country, and weather. I imagine your family will come back and settle down here, once they get past the age of running around and all."

Van Speer nodded. Perhaps Hawk wasn't as stupid as he seemed. The sergeant pulled out a cigar, but the Dutchman offered him one of his own.

"So you ain't had no trouble with the Nips yet?" Hawk asked, as he lit the thick cigar.

"Not at all. As you know, this end of the island is

rather difficult to reach. They have probably written it off as uninhabited. We can't reach them; maybe they can't reach us. Perhaps your patrol was unusually persevering. I believe that is the reputation of the Marine Corps. We have three sailboats down in the inlet along the coast. We can circumnavigate the island, fortunately. The Japanese have not been here long. In fact I believe that they could not have arrived more than a week or two before the marines."

"Sons of bitches are sure dug in good, though. Another thing I wanted to ask you about. I see this big antenna wired up in the top of a dead tree. Y'all got a radio here?"

"Yes, an excellent radio. Lately all we have been able to pick up is Japanese gibberish, I'm afraid."

"I'll swear. I got a guy that knows how to work radios pretty good. If you don't mind, we'd like to fool with it a little." Hawk spoke courteously, knowing that he intended to commandeer the radio, regardless of Van Speer's wishes. Van Speer knew this, too.

"Of course. You have the run of the place. You, personally, and perhaps an aide, are welcome to stay here in the house. Obviously we cannot accommodate all of your men here." Actually the huge old house would have held them all, though not comfortably.

"Well, that's mighty nice of you to offer and I might take you up on it. I hope we get along, me and you. I know we got off on the wrong foot, because of us scaring your family and all. I guess we've forgot how to act. It's been so long since we been around civilized folks."

"We were all taken aback, I assure you. But I intend to run business as usual here. I would greatly appreciate it if you would caution your men on the subject of frightening my wife and daughters."

Hawk stood and shook Van Speer's meaty hand. The old Dutchman had a powerful grip.

"I've already done that, Mr. Van Speer, and if you have any complaints, come straight to me and I'll kick some ass quick. These are pretty good boys, most of them, but you gotta be kinda wild to be a marine. If you need any help on your place here, you just grab one of my boys like he was your own and work him."

The two men parted, this time with a better under-standing of one another. Rudiger watched as the young sergeant returned to his men in the barn. He puffed thoughtfully on his cigar. The sergeant was likeable enough, in a crude sort of way, he thought.

There were three men on watch and the remainder were gathered in the barn, some on the floor and some in the loft.

Canlon was astride a cow that was tethered in a stall. In the center of the men sitting on the earthen floor was Rolf, who was a bit older than Mr. Van Speer. He was passing out little wooden bowls, then pouring a steamy liquid into them from a huge pail. Hawk asked what was going on, and received a bowl of his own in reply.

"This is *erwtensoep*, delicious Dutch soup," Rolf clucked. "It will cover those bony ribs," he added, thumping Hawk's tight stomach with his finger. "Tomorrow we will try some island dishes, and maybe a stein of beer for everyone."

"Yeah, break out the suds," Canlon called from the back of his trusty steed. Rolf waddled over to him with a bowl and the entire pail of soup. "Hey, this shit's pretty good," Canlon exclaimed as he drank it down in a single gulp. Rolf refilled his bowl.

During the process of feeding the marines Rolf discovered Ewell's injured leg and ordered the big man to follow him back to the plantation house. At a nod from Hawk, Ewell hobbled after the old man.

The next day Hawk, with Gaedcke in tow, inspected the radio. It was housed in its very own radio shack and was a very sophisticated piece of equipment. There were several outhouses behind the plantation house, including a shack to smoke the latex gathered from the rubber trees. But beyond all of these buildings and near a little path that led to the -ocean on the island's northern coast, was the radio. Gaedcke carefully placed the earphones on his head and seated himself amidst the humming machinery. Hawk cautioned him not to break anything, as this was not government issue. After about fifteen minutes, Gaedcke announced that it was a helluva radio, but that all he could get were various Japanese broadcasts. Hawk ordered him to keep trying to reach the battalion, or any Marine receiver, for that matter. He leaned on the door of the ancient shack and absently listened to Gaedcke's exhortations. As if in response to the thought then crossing his mind, Gretchen Van Speer came skipping out of the back door of the farmhouse with Ilse.

The two of them crossed his field of sight and entered the corral surrounding the barn. He thought that perhaps Gretchen had seen him watching her. If Gaedcke's babbling hadn't been so irritating, he probably would have not done what he did. But it was, and so he headed out of the shack toward the rear if the barn. As he approached the chicken coops at the rear, he heard voices.

"There's no need to rush off, honey..." It was Brock's voice.

"Ilse only wanted to see of the eggs had hatched yet, sir. We must go back now," Gretchen explained. Hawk didn't wait to hear any more; this was close enough for him to the makings of an ugly scene.

"How are you, ma'am," said Hawk, rounding the corner. Now surrounded by two of the American beasts, Gretchen lost her modicum of poise. She clutched Ilse to her and backed away a step. "Beat it," Hawk said to Brock, whose departure was swift. "Can I walk you back to the house, ma'am?"

"Yes, thank you," she answered, once she was safely around him, with a clear path between her and the plantation house.

"I know you ain't too fond of us, Miss Van Speer, but you ain't got nothing to be afraid of, except..."Hawk looked straight ahead as he spoke but the girl was fascinated by the magnetic eyes hidden in his hideous face. She stared unabashedly at him.

"Except what?" she asked quickly.

"Well, I'd stay away from that fella there. He ain't quite right in the head. I wouldn't get off by myself with just him around."

"I see. Then I shouldn't want to, either." Ilse jumped in front of Hawk and asked his name. Hawk slung his Tommy gun over a shoulder and scooped her up into his arms.

"James. What's yours little lady?"

"Ilse—that's Gretchen, my sister." Hawk smiled, for

the first time exposing a row of even white teeth. "Why do you have hair on your face?" Ilse asked.

"I'm part dog. It just grows there."

"No you're not. You're a man and you could shave it off if you wanted to. That's what Gretchen says. She says you want to look ugly and scare people." The beard came in handy for Hawk. It disguised the deep crimson color in his flushing cheeks. He set the child down.

"Well, I guess I'll have to do something about that, then. I want Gretchen to like me." They stopped at the back porch steps of the farmhouse. Gretchen stepped up on a level with the sergeant's eyes.

"Thank you, James," she said, with a broad smile, and, pushing Ilse before her, entered the house. Hawk stood there for a moment, then turned and walked back toward the radio shack.

"James?" he muttered. His head was aimed at the ground but all he could see was the radiant smile of Gretchen Van Speer. Gaedcke was shouting at him but all be could hear was a musical Dutch accent, speaking his name.

"It's Colonel Hayes himself, right here on the goddam radio!" Gaedcke screamed. "This thing don't pick up good, but it's got a hell of a transmitter. Hurry, hurry, you can hardly hear him. It might be the wind."

Hawk put one earphone against his head and identified himself.

"Good to hear you, Jim." It was Hayes, all right. "We've been receiving you, but I guess you can't hear us very well!" He was screaming. Hawk thought he could hear combat in the background. "I hear you made it without any trouble!"

"Yessir, none at all. These folks don't especially want us here, though."

"What they want and what they're going to get are two different things, Jim. We've run into some terrible opposition, Jim. It might take us six weeks to two months to get over there. I'm almost positive you'll be getting some backwash over there. There's just too many of them to keep penned up over here."

"Pretty rough going, you say?"

"Oh, hell yes. Worst ever. We're always moving in on them, you know, but it's costing us. We've already lost twice as many casualties as we expected. It's like they're sending in those troopships on cue. We'll have to have some reinforcements of our own if this keeps up. What we need is a couple of Jim Hawks over here."

"I'd like to be there, too. By the time I got there, y'all'd already have 'em cleaned out, though."

"I hope you're right. Well, you're doing a good job. Stay with it and keep in touch."

Hawk handed the earphones back to Gaedcke and commended him for his successful connection with the CP. At least now they could tell Hayes about any trouble that might arise. It was not as lonely out here with the huge pulsating radio in operation.

"Why don't you come out here and tell 'em we're okay every few hours," Hawk ordered Gaedcke. "Just so they don't forget about us. You don't have to wait for an answer. They can hear us good enough, and we may never pick 'em up again." Gaedcke acknowledged that as a good idea.

There were three guard posts: a foxhole directly in front of the plantation house, another on the left side, and another on the right side. The rear was unguarded;

it was considered safe due to its proximity to the ocean. The Japanese hadn't landed by sea as of yet; it was doubtful that they would do so in their waning hours. Any stragglers were expected to come stumbling out of the jungle.

Hawk magnanimously assumed a watch in the left foxhole and approached it just before dark that night. The lights were on in the plantation house, giving it a warm and friendly glow. Hawk felt like an outcast on a cold night as he passed by the brightly lit apertures. The lights seemed to have an emotional effect upon him; he felt almost human again. The cold machine of death that he had become was ' thawing out. If he could keep .from being shot at long enough, he might have a complete recovery, he thought. He settled down in the foxhole and stared dreamily back at the house, rather than toward the grim jungle. His numbed human urges slowly returned after weeks of suspended animation.

A tropical moon bathed him in a blissful silver sheen that he thought beautiful, where before he would have only thought it dangerous. Then he thought of the war raging across the other end of the island, of the men he would never see again. Narrowing his eyes, he faced the jungle. And then Ewell relieved him—the time had passed so quickly he could not believe it.

"Hey, Marks, let me see your razor," said Hawk. He was sitting against the front of the barn, behind a helmet full of water. In his hand was a jagged piece of glass that was apparently to serve as a mirror.

"I don't have a razor," Marks answered.

"Don't give me that shit. I ain't seen a whisker on your goddam face since you joined up with us."

"I don't shave." Hawk dropped the glass and jumped

to his feet. He grabbed a handful of the boy's face and pulled it up to his eyes. The pores were empty of stubble.

"How old are you, Marks?"

"Seventeen."

"You're a lyin' son of a bitch. You're just a little kid. A big little kid. What are you, fifteen, sixteen?"

"No, Sergeant Hawk, I'm seventeen."

"Yeah, and I'm forty."

"I didn't know you were that old, sergeant."

"I'm not, you crazy little bastard! Do I look forty! Who's got a razor in this crazy-ass outfit?"

"I believe Corporal Quiroz has a straight razor, but I don't think he uses it for shaving," Marks reported.

"Go get it and go get Sergeant Mayeaux. I want to know what a damn twelve-year-old is doing in my outfit." Marks came back with the razor and without Mayeaux. Hawk was willing to settle for half of his order for the present. The razor was plenty sharp for Quiroz' purposes, and plenty dull for shaving. Hawk hacked and chopped and scraped and bled for forty-five minutes. Canlon walked up from a stroll that he had just taken down to the seaside.

"Cleaning up for that babe, eh?" he quizzed.

"Shit, no. Can't I even shave without somebody giving me some shit?"

"So this is why you didn't want anybody talking to the women. What do they call it, privileges of rank?" Canlon asked.

"They call you a nosey New Yorker son of a bitch." Hawk never slowed in his efforts. In two years of war he hadn't been wounded this badly or lost so much blood.

"Okay, Hawk. By the way, you got more hair on your

neck there than I got on my ass." Hawk adjusted his looking-glass and realized that Joe had been right. When he looked up to curse him again, however, Canlon was gone.

The morning sun was high in the sky before Hawk had mowed away enough fur to recognize the face in the broken glass. He splashed the cold water on his lacerated flesh and sat back against the barn with a certain pride of accomplishment. The garrison duty at the plantation was growing into a colossal bore and the men were looking for any diversion to occupy their time. At least that was what Hawk told himself. It was boredom, rather than the comment by little Ilse, that caused him to shave. With no particular plan of attack, he found himself walking in the direction of the farmhouse. The bony face of Ernst met him at the door. Hawk had an instinctive dislike for Ernst, but he was ever polite to him.

"Mr. Van Speer in?" Hawk asked, but Ernst only shook his head. "Uh, Mrs. Van Speer?" Ernst waved him in with his head and told him to wait there, in the foyer. Trudchen Van Speer came out of the kitchen with a towel in her hands. She smiled broadly.

"Sergeant Hawk! Is it you?" Hawk smiled and nodded his head sheepishly. "Well, there is a marked improvement. I had no idea that you were a handsome man."

"Yes ma'am, it was one of the best-kept secrets in the Marine Corps," said Hawk, trying to survey all of the rooms casually. "I...uh...wanted to talk to Mr. Van Speer about the...uh...plantation and all."

"What about it? Perhaps I can tell you. Sit, please."

"Uh, well." Hawk pricked up his ears. Someone was

in the kitchen. "Well, I was kinda thinking. They spend a lot of time out there in the woods and that's kinda dangerous. Maybe I oughta send some guys out there with 'em. I think I'd feel better about it if I did. It wouldn't look too good for me if anything happened, you see. What do they do out there all day anyway?"

"I don't think Rudiger would hear of that, Sergeant Hawk—he is very self-reliant. There was a time when he alone would be the only man tapping the trees."

"Yes, ma'am, but that was before the island was full of Japs. The Jap's go nuts if they knew there was an Allies' rubber plantation here. They think they got the market cornered. They're rollin' in the stuff and we can't get it back in the States. I guess 'cause they got all these islands."

"Well, you can ask him. But don't be surprised if I'm right. You wouldn't like it out there, anyway. I know. I've done it. There are over fifteen acres of cultivated trees and more growing wild that are spread out in the jungle. They go to each tree in the morning, cut it, equip it with a spout and collecting cup, and then go to each tree in the afternoon and collect the rubber. It is liquid. Then they put it on paddles in the smokehouse and harden it into biscuits. It is dreadfully boring."

It was difficult for Hawk to disagree, but he had to appear interested if he wanted his visit to continue. Mrs. Van Speer went on about the price of rubber and the Japanese monopoly, but he scarcely heard a word. His hearing of the sounds in the kitchen was much more acute, however.

"What's cookin'?" Hawk finally ventured.

"*Nasi goreng*," she answered, a smile crossing her face at the sight of the blank expression on his face. It was difficult not to like the simple fellow, she thought; he wasn't a bad looking specimen, now that she could see him. "It's an Indonesian dish. I don't know how American tastes run, but I believe that you will like it."

"Oh, they run to just about anything and I'm sure that I will. You got your daughter in there working?" Hawk wasn't aware of being just a little too obvious.

"Yes, she does most of the cooking. Rolf is making her do it this time. He says he promised your men some authentic island cooking, and I'm afraid it has kept her rather busy this morning."

"Oh, well don't go to no trouble for them son of a... guns. They'll eat sh...slop. That Rolf is a pretty nice old coot. He got the swelling down on Ewell's leg. I thought I was going to have to cut it off."

"He is a thoughtful person, but that's because he has been a servant for so long. Now, you must stay and eat with us in here. Rudiger will be back soon; we can't wait for him though. He doesn't feel obligated to follow any schedule." She rose to her feet and returned to the kitchen. Hawk heard the back door open and Gretchen's voice call to Rolf, who was working outside. Trudchen came back with a tray and put a dish of fried rice and meat in front of Hawk.

"Sure smells good." Gretchen came in with a pitcher of beer and Hawk stood up in mid-sentence. "And looks good, too." The girl smiled at him. He could tell that she was impressed with his new shave, but of course it wouldn't be proper for her to mention it, he supposed.

"You look a hundred percent better than the last time I saw you, James," Gretchen said, turning her back to him and returning to the kitchen. Hawk's bronzed face turned several shades of red.

"James?" Mrs. Van Speer arched an eyebrow at Hawk from her seat across the table from him. He opened his mouth and spread his palms, as if to explain, but nothing came out. Fortunately Gretchen came back and took her seat, next to her mother.

"Yes, James," she said. "Ilse and I met the sergeant yesterday, when we were checking on the eggs." The mention of her name brought Ilse into the room along with Rolf. Both of them had complimentary observations with regard to the newly visible Hawk.

"Yeah, the kid wanted me to clean up and I aim to please." Hawk smiled. Gretchen studied his face as she gracefully handled her fork. The flashing blue eyes had a sad look to them. His smile looked out of place. It was an exercise that Hawk was not used to—nor were his facial muscles. Nevertheless there were dimples far back on the side of his face; he would look quite merry if he held his smile long enough, but he never did. It just flashed across his white teeth and then fled, as if it had made a mistake in appearing there. It was a manly, even an intelligent face.

"Good looks must run in your family, Mrs. Van Speer," Hawk said suddenly, after quaffing his beer. "I can see where your daughter got to be so pretty." There was a pause in which no one spoke. "This one's gonna be a knockout, too," he added, placing a thick hand on Ilse's blonde head. "All your kids blond?"

"Yes. Gretchen, Moritz and Ilse—quite a coincidence isn't it?" Hawk was about to agree when Rudiger and Moritz came in. He could hear feet shuffling in the kitchen and could only assume that Ernst and Klaus would soon appear also. Mr. Van Speer commented immediately on Hawk's face—before he even sat down. Again, Hawk blushed.

Hawk again made his proposal concerning the accompaniment of the plantation workers by marines. Rudiger gave his characteristic, curt grunt in reply, which meant no thanks. Hawk didn't pursue the matter; he was only making conversation anyway. The meal completed, the guest of the Van Speers stretched and shoved his dish away.

"That was the best meal I ever ate, I swear if it wasn't. You have an awfully nice family, Mr. Van Speer. I'm grateful for your kindness. It's good to be around regular folks again."

"Do you have a family, back in America," Trudchen asked.

"None to speak of," Hawk replied.

"Are you married?" Gretchen elaborated, in hopes of a more lucid answer.

"Naw. I was doing good to take care of myself before the war. Times were pretty rough back home, and I never did much socializing. Seems like I always been stuck off somewhere with the menfolks. Never got around the ladies too much. I guess that shows. My manners are pretty rusty."

"Not at all," said Gretchen. "You are much too critical of yourself." She and her mother were bustling about clearing the table, and Hawk joined in the work until they made him stop. "This is not work for a man, but you can do me a favor," Gretchen said with a smile. Her small frame came close enough to him to make a delightful chill run through his body.

"You name it," he choked.

"I would like to go down to the sea, to see how my

boat is faring. But I do not want to go alone. Would you mind walking with me?"

"Moritz will go with you," Rudiger grumbled. "Sergeant Hawk is much too busy for anything so foolish."

"Naw, I ain't got nothing to do. I'm about to go crazy here doing nothing. I'd be glad to go," he protested.

"Yes, father. I don't want to take Moritz away from the fields, and the soldiers wouldn't bother me with James there."

"They won't bother you with Moritz there, either," Rudiger said.

"It might be better if Sergeant Hawk went," Trudchen suggested. "He has control over the men." Rudiger grunted a nondescript reply. Hawk suspected that the grunt was negative in intent but that Rudiger knew that he had been strongly outvoted. Gretchen motioned Hawk out the front door. He hesitated, then picked up his submachine gun and followed her out. They circled around to the back of the house in silence.

"This way," she said, leading him to the narrow path that led to the sea. They had to pass Lundstedt, Ewell and Canlon on the way. They were sitting there on the ground, idly chatting. Canlon broke into a wide grin at the sight of the man and woman.

"I gotta go down to the water. Be back in a few minutes," Hawk mumbled to Canlon.

"Hell, you don't have to go, I'll do it for you," Canlon needled. The pair kept walking. "It's a hell of an outfit when the sergeant's gotta do everything himself," Canlon called after him. Hawk only glared over his shoulder, which caused Canlon to roll over on his back giggling.

The trail was a rocky, sandy corridor through dense

leafy forest. Gretchen led the way, holding the springy boughs lest they snap back and hit the man. The path led ever downward and soon the roar of the sea was audible. There were flowers growing in profusion along the narrow way. This led Hawk to believe that at some time there had been an attempt to cultivate the area, but that the jungle had reclaimed it. Gretchen's feet made no sound as they trod the rugged terrain. Hawk let his boots crunch heavily in the gravel, for his gun was slung over his shoulder. He was on a vacation from the war.

The half-grown palm trees and tangled growth abruptly ended; the vast, compelling seascape filled the limits of Hawk's vision. The white beach was breathtakingly beautiful. Perhaps it was the same as the one that he had landed upon, physically, but it looked entirely different, because he was somehow different. The rippled sand was dark where it met the peacefully lapping waves; beyond the waves the water was clear and blue. Not far distant, the sharp reef stabbed the surface and he could hear the ocean pounding it heavily. In a sandy cove below them, the masts of several boats were visible, barely rocking on the calm surface of the lagoon.

"That's quite a view." Hawk raised his voice above the sea.

"This is nothing. You should see the western shore —it's like paradise," Gretchen answered, trying to keep her windblown hair out of her face. "Come on and see my boat. It's the little one." She ran down the slope and onto the deck of the sloop. The man followed, moving a little less lively.

"Do you sail, in America? Did you live by the sea?"

"I never did. We got a little stretch of beach along

the Gulf there. The sand is white, just like this." Hawk climbed aboard. He looked out at the white sand. He saw it turn blood red and saw heads snap back under the impact of bullets. His entire body flinched.

"What's wrong?" The girl asked.

"Oh, I thought I was somewhere else there for a second." He shook his head. He had heard of such flash-backs occurring to men, but this was his first. He felt cold sweat on his forehead as the wind blew in his face. Perhaps these were the withdrawal symptoms that accompanied the transition from combatant to semi-civilian.

"Home? You thought of home?"

"Yeah," he lied. "Mississippi." He eased himself down on to the deck, laying his weapon beside him. "No, I've never sailed...a sailboat. Been oh a few ships, though."

"I can teach you all I know—in about two minutes. This is the mainsail, this is the jib, that's the tiller, and" —sliding a rudder looking affair from a slot on the deck —"this is the centerboard. Isn't that interesting?"

"Yes," he lied again. He feared that she would continue teaching him, and though she was the most charming of teachers, he was in no mood to learn. "You like it here, don't you?"

"It's all right, sometimes. Sometimes I would rather be elsewhere, around people. I would like to live here during the week and in Europe on the weekends." She laughed. Hawk smiled. "It is very lonely sometimes. I feel as if I am wasting my life here. Time goes by and nothing much happens. Do you k-vow what I mean?"

"Yeah, I think so." Hawk stared at the deck. He real-ized that he was much older than she—not so much in his years, but in what had happened during those years. Especially in the two last years on the brink of eternity. He vaguely remembered the feelings of which she spoke, but he couldn't bring them back with any degree of clarity. Of late, he hadn't been worried about life passing him by; he had been worried about hanging onto it. That was easier to worry about, he decided; you could discern when the worrying was paying off.

"Your old man likes it here, I know that much," he said suddenly, never betraying his thoughts.

"He loves it, but he's old and settled. He's done everything he wants to do with his life—he doesn't mind being stuck out here." Hawk smiled again as he looked into her eyes. They were three shades bluer than the sea, here in the glaring sun.

"Well, maybe he's been around and this is the best he's found. It's nice country." Then he thought of Rudiger Van Speer. "Well, maybe we oughta be getting back before your father sends the marines after us. Did you do what you came here for?"

"I came here to talk to you," Gretchen said, standing up on the gunwales and balancing herself with a hand on the mast. They stared at each other for a long moment, the wind whipping in their ears.

"Why?" he finally asked. There was a serious expression on his face.

"I don't know. Because you have an unusual voice and beautiful eyes. Because you're a soldier. Because life is passing me by every time I meet someone without knowing them. You'll be gone soon and I wanted to talk with you. That's why."

"Oh. I'm glad you did." He slowly got to his feet and lifted her hand from her side. He pressed it gently.

"Thank you," he said in a low voice. Then he stepped off of the boat and offered her his hand. She took it and jumped to the sand with a laugh.

"Someday, I will take you to the western shore. It doesn't take long to sail over there. I love to sail, and I want to show you the lagoon over there."

"Sounds good to me. Just say when. I guess this end of the island is pretty safe."

"Soon. I have to decide whether I'm going to tell father or whether I have to sneak out. I don't think he likes the idea of me being around the...Americans, very much," she said. But more importantly, she continued to hold his hand after they had climbed up out of the cove and all the way down the path.

"I expect not," said Hawk.

6

GRETCHEN AND HAWK

GRETCHEN RETURNED TO THE HOUSE AND HAWK wandered aimlessly between it and the barn for a little less than an hour. He spied Joe Canlon taking up a post in the central foxhole and, putting on his helmet out of force of habit, he meandered out to him. Joe had a wad of chewing tobacco in his mouth; when he saw Hawk approach, he handed him up a plug. Hawk silently took it and sat down on the ground with his legs dangling in the hole, his body propped on one arm. Joe finally spat down into the floor of his foxhole and broke the silence.

"Well, what happened?" asked Joe.

"What do you mean? Nothing happened."

"You two were gone for a long time for nothing to happen. Come on, what happened?"

"I don't know. I guess I fell in love with the kid."

Joe hooted and nearly swallowed his tobacco leaves. After gagging for a moment, he found his tongue among the tobacco leaves.

"I knew that babe was hot to trot when I first seen her," Joe rasped.

"Aw, shit, you ignorant son of a bitch—I said nothing happened." Hawk spat out onto the ground and scowled out toward the forest. "You try to talk serious with some-body and they give you a buncha shit." Joe's big smile faded.

"Kinda sudden, wouldn't you say?" Joe tried to sound serious, but the close observer would have heard the beginnings of a chuckle in his throat.

"Yeah, I know. I'm a stupid jerk, but it's too late to do anything about that. You know..." Hawk paused and looked around at Joe. "I don't know much about women."

Joe nodded, expecting more than that simple state-ment. When nothing more came, however, he was forced to speak.·

"Yeah, so?"

"I think she likes me, you know. I don't know why, or what her angle is. I mean, I been watching her and thinking about her ever since we got here—I just wanted to talk to her at first, and now...I don't know. She said she wanted to talk to me—ain't that funny?"

"I guess. You ain't making too much sense. What's the problem? Sounds like things are going pretty smooth to me."

"Well. Say I was to get...mixed up with her, or even married, maybe, after the war...I never figured on coming out of the war, to tell you the truth. I don't want anybody worried about me, and I don't want to have to watch myself. You know?"

"I guess you'd have to slow up a little. The way you been fighting them Japs, I don't figure you'll come out of the war either." Joe laughed.

"Yeah, that's what I mean. It'd kinda take the edge

off me. That's always been my ace in the hole. I been just like a Jap. If I get killed, so what. Who cares? I mean I try like hell to stay in one piece, but in the back of my mind...I've just seen too many guys get nailed to think that it can't happen to me."

"Look here, Hawk, I don't think that kid wants to get *married* or anything, not already anyway. I think maybe you fell kinda hard for her and you're afraid she don't like you as much. I think you're cookin' up a reason to stay away from her. So you don't get disappointed, maybe?"

Hawk spat thoughtfully out onto the ground. What Joe had said sounded good, perhaps even right on target.

"You ain't as dumb as you look, Joe. But still, the day's coming when we gotta go back to the battalion. If she did like me, would it be fair to her?"

"Fair? No. But what man ain't fighting in the war? What woman ain't waiting for somebody? Forget about that shit. Make your play and if she don't go for you, shit on it. There's plenty of other women in the world. Some are gonna like you and some ain't. You picked out a kinda fancy one there. I ain't never had much luck with that type. If you want her, take your best shot. But all I'm saying is don't get set up for a big fall. We're in a pretty rough business to go feel like shit and maybe walk out into a bullet. Forget about her and start thinking of yourself." Joe spat again.

"You're right. I'm afraid of losing her and I ain't even got her yet. I already feel like shit. Maybe that's just the way I am. I ain't ever been much fun to be around. I got a bad temper. I like to work, off by myself." He mumbled a few more words to himself. Then he shook his head and repeated, "You're right."

"If it was me, I'd forget that crazy stuff about getting married, and just see what happens. Just have a few laughs with her and stop thinking about what's gonna come of it." Joe laughed and slid his helmet back. "I guess that's easier to say than to do. I'd probably flip out, too, if that babe looked my way." Hawk stood up.

"Yeah, this damn sitting around doing nothing has a lot to do with it. That'll make you crazier than anything. I been jumpier here than I ever was on the front line."

"I'll take this dump over the front line," Joe said in a low voice, and then with a laugh: "And I ain't got no girl." Hawk walked back toward the barn. He turned and waved at Joe as a sort of afterthought. Joe was still watching him and he waved back. He had seen a different side of his sergeant, very different. James Hawk and tender emotions seemed somehow incompatible. He didn't give the love affair much of a chance at success.

Hawk was a cold-blooded killer of men. He faced flaming steel with ice in his veins. He cursed and beat his own men as readily as the enemy. He sat in trenches for days at a time without a single thought seeming to pass through his thick skull. He was a crude, hard, vicious man who had never expressed feelings of any sort other than anger, hatred, and their by-product revenge. Romance and James Hawk? Not likely! This was probably the first time that any female had ever spoken to him, Joe thought. He'd get over it.

That night, just before dark, the crowing of the roosters reminded Hawk of the eggs, whose hatching Ilse waited upon. Should he discover some chicks, it would give him another excuse to return to the plantation house. He left a circle of card-playing marines and directed his steps toward the rear of the barn, where the chicken coop stood. His keen hearing picked up voices coming from the coop, but this did not slow his walking until he identified one of the voices as that of a girl. He leaned silently against the edge of the barn, listening. Slowly, he removed his helmet, so that it would not bump against the wood and give him away.

"Really, Ernst, it's none of your concern." It was Gretchen's voice. It had an authoritative tone in it that Hawk had never heard.

"Then you would prefer an American chimpanzee over one of your own countrymen?" Ernst snapped in his quick tongue.

"Certainly over you. Now if you would permit me, I must return to the house." It sounded as if she had taken a step and then be had blocked her path. "Really, Ernst, isn't this a bit silly?"

"No. I consider it a very grave matter when..." Ernst was interrupted by the crunch of boots behind him. There stood the object of his jealousy, the unsmiling marine.

"Evening, all," he said. "Looks like we're meeting here pretty regularly, Miss Van Speer."

Ernst drew back his long arm and drove his fist full into the American's face. Hawk never blinked as the blow glanced off. His eyes were two satanic orbs, glowing in the twilight, but he kept his hands at his side. Ernst took a step back, regretting his temerity. Hawk's fiery gaze seemed to slacken and he sighed deeply.

"Now that you got that outa your system," growled Hawk, "maybe you got something to do somewhere else." Without a glance back at Gretchen and giving the marine a wide berth, Ernst stalked off. Gretchen had been holding her breath. She now released it.

"Are you hurt?" she asked, looking up into his face. There was no evidence of any mark caused by the punch.

"Naw, I didn't even feel it. Kinda made me mad, though. I'da come up sooner but I thought I was interruptin' something."

"No. I liked Ernst when he first came here... So few people come here. But he was a little forward and, I suppose you heard, a little possessive."

"Yeah, he's a hothead all right. I guess you were just...passing the time with him and he took it the wrong way." Hawk slid a cigar between his lips. Perhaps it was the smoke that caused his narrow gaze to narrow a bit further.

"Yes," she said, nervously, and turned toward the henhouse. "Look. This is why I came out here. Isn't that the cutest little baby?" Beneath an angry hen, the rounded bottom of a chick was barely visible. Hawk stepped over to the mother and child.

"Well, I don't know," he snorted. "Let's have a look-see." He grabbed the hen by the back of her wings and raised her up. The bird cursed him resoundingly for his audacity. There was only one chick and several cracked eggs.

"Yeah, they oughta keep you in drumsticks a good while," he theorized. Gretchen reached over and picked up the infant bird as he held the angry mother. She rubbed the tiny feathered creature against her face and laughed her frail, irresistible laugh.

"Ilse will love you. Do you think it'll be all right if we take it in?"

"Yeah. Chickens are stupid, they don't know the difference." Gretchen fairly ran to the farmhouse door with the tiny bird while Hawk sauntered slowly in her wake. She waved him in and they entered through the kitchen. Before they went into the living room, they could hear Rudiger reading aloud, but Hawk couldn't understand the language in which he spoke. Upon entering, they saw Ilse seated upon her father's lap, listening to a child's story, perhaps. She squealed in delight at the sight of the chick. After paying his respects to the family, Hawk followed Gretchen to the front door and stepped out onto the moat.

"I must tell father about Ernst; he has had words with him before," she said from the doorway. Hawk shrugged; it was none of his affair, he supposed. "And Rolf and I will prepare the boat tomorrow, so that you and I can go sailing the day after. Will that be agreeable to you?"

"Sure will."

"But don't mention that to Father," she added. He nodded, hesitantly, and stepped back into the front yard. "Good night," she called.

"Night," he answered, and turned toward the barn, adjusting the strap of his submachine gun. He walked, lost in thought, with his eyes aimed at the dark ground.

"Do not call out, I want a word with you," came a voice from the corner of the plantation house. Hawk's eyes had not yet adjusted to the dark, but he thought that it was Ernst. He directed his steps toward the dark corner.

"Yeah, what you need?" Hawk asked innocently. His

eyes finally focused on Ernst in a black turtleneck shirt; beside him stood Klaus, who was a little shorter but twice as wide.

"You must stay away from Miss Van Speer, dog," Ernst commanded.

"Yeah? Why's that?" Hawk asked, apathetically.

"Because we are going to beat you to within an inch of your life every time we catch you speaking to her," Ernst explained as both of the Dutchmen advanced on the marine. Hawk ran his fingers along the strap of his machine pistol.

"Yeah? Startin' when?" Hawk watched as they split apart and continued to come toward him. He wriggled his shoulder so that the strap was about to slide down his arm.

"Starting now!" Ernst lunged for his left arm and Klaus reached for his right. The Thompson slid down Hawk's arm and he seized it by the barrel. Before Ernst touched him, the marine had swung the weapon powerfully, catching him on the side of his head and driving him, like a nail, into the ground. Klaus froze for a moment but continued forward—to his misfortune, for in one continuous movement Hawk brought the stock backhanded into his face. Klaus staggered back a few steps and fell flat on his rear, to sit there on the ground, bleeding profusely.

"Now I got fifteen mean sons of bitches sittin' over there in that barn," drawled Hawk. "If you boys don't want me to take this up with them, you'd best stay outa my way." It was doubtful that Ernst heard his words, but Hawk was confident that Klaus would relay the message. He shouldered his gun and proceeded to the barn.

Hawk reached the barn door and leaned against the wall, watching Ernst and Klaus pick themselves up. He really couldn't blame Ernst, he supposed. He might even be doing the same thing if Gretchen had jilted him. He fired up a half-burnt cigar. Armistead and Beckwith came strolling out of the poorly lit barn door. They sighted the slowly moving, groaning Dutchmen.

"What are those two up to?" Beckwith asked.

"Ah, they got their shit hot for me. Over the girl, I guess," Hawk mumbled. "Better watch out for 'em. That Ernst has a mean streak up one side and a sneaky streak down the other."

"What'd they do, jump you?" asked Armistead. Hawk nodded. "I bet they don't make that mistake again. You want us to beat the shit out of 'em?" Hawk shook his head.

"Naw, I think we understand each other now."

GRETCHEN RETURNED from the front door, humming her favorite song of the moment. Rudiger called her into the den, where he sat with Trudchen and Ilse. He rolled a glass of gin around in his hand.

"You have become quite friendly with the sergeant." It was a simple statement from the father to his daughter.

"Yes," she smiled. "Isn't he wonderful?"

"He's an American," answered Rudiger.

"Yes, but isn't he sweet. Isn't he...virile?" Rudiger seemed to shudder in lightly restrained rage at such foolishness. He composed himself and chose his words.

"We must be practical. It is not possible for you to

develop any fondness for him." She hung her head. Then she told him about the incident involving Ernst.

"Yes," he said. "We have trouble with our own people, but that makes no difference. I will admit that Hawk is a head taller than other men, in his world, this world into which we currently find ourselves thrust. It is a temporary world where violence and brutality rule. The man is an ignorant savage who would have no place in a world at peace, in the world in which you must live. And he is an American." Rudiger added the last sentence as if it were of equal or greater weight than the others, as if the man's nationality was an incurable deformity. He said it as if he were ashamed to mention the fact, to admit to himself that his daughter liked an American.

"He isn't ignorant," Gretchen whispered.

"No, dear," Trudchen interjected before Rudiger could launch into a demoniacal tirade. "But he is... uneducated, uncultured—don't you think? Certainly, he's a nice fellow and, nice looking, but he is an American. You can overlook that for the present, but it is going to become a problem..." Trudchen looked to Rudiger to end the sentence.

"There is nothing more to discuss. You must go nowhere near the filthy dog, ever again." Rudiger could control himself no longer

"I'm twenty-three years old and I'll do as I please."

"You are my daughter, on an island in the middle of a war, and you will do as I say. Do your loyalties lie with your family or with some stray dog?" Rudiger looked self-consciously toward the window; his words had been rather loud. Gretchen cringed a bit at his shouting, but she managed to meet his flaming gaze briefly before turning and leaving the room.

"We must watch her closely," Rudiger told Trudchen at the end of a deep breath. "She has temporarily lost her senses." Trudchen said nothing. She knew that her daughter had lost her senses, but she could not be sure that the affliction was a fleeting one. "Why did those swine have to come here?" Rudiger asked rhetorically.

* * *

GRETCHEN WENT to her room at the rear of the house, across a hall from Moritz's room. She would have liked to discuss the matter with her brother, but she knew that he would not understand either. She laid her head on the bed and sighed. If an army of American women had landed here, she thought angrily, then he would understand. If a woman wanted to court a man, she was forbidden, disloyal; and the man was a dog, a savage. But if a man wanted to pursue a woman, look out, love conquers all. Gretchen grew more and more angry as hot tears streamed down her face. No one here could empathize with her; they were simply not in her position. She had to do what she thought best. The first "best" thing to do was to go down to the beach tomorrow with Rolf.

* * *

OLD ROLF PAID Hawk a visit the next day, handing him a note from Gretchen. Hawk opened it and squinted at the message.

Tell father you are going into the forest tomorrow for some reason. Meet me at the beach after breakfast.

Hawk folded the paper back as it had been and looked at Rolf, who raised his eyebrows in a questioning expression.

"Tell her that I'll do it," said Hawk, the question of Rolf's role in all of this temporarily occupying his mind.

"Mr. Van Speer would not like this," said Rolf, in reply to the unspoken thoughts. "And he would like my part in the matter even less. Do you understand?"

"Yeah. If we're captured by the enemy, don't spill our guts out all over you?"

"Yes, I believe that's precisely what I mean. Daughters and their lovers may leave their troubles behind, but old servants must stay and live with their problems." Then Rolf left. Hawk felt a sudden affection for Rolf. He realized that the man was more loyal to Gretchen than to Rudiger. He thought for a moment. He would have to pay Rudiger another visit in order to comply with Gretchen's wishes, and he dreaded it. He would have to cook up a good story.

* * *

A HEAVY KNOCK at the front door, later in the afternoon, brought none other than Mr. Van Speer to swing the massive barrier open. There before him stood Hawk, slouched and unsmiling. Rudiger lifted his chin and stared coldly back at the expressionless American without speaking. The marine spoke first.

"Some of the boys heard a lot of rustling around last night. They figure it was the Japs, doing a little recon. I'm gonna take out a patrol and do some scouting tomorrow. I figured I oughta let you know what's going on."

"My God!" exclaimed Rudiger, visibly shaken. "They are here! Ilse must sleep in the cellar tonight, in case there is any shooting." Hawk immediately regretted the ruse that be had chosen. He fully expected Rudiger to drop dead on the spot, judging by the white color that he had turned.

"Oh, it's probably nothing but some animal," said Hawk, trying to soften the first impression that he had given. "I just want to check it out. Nothing much to worry about." He had little practice at the art of lying and this was going badly; the effect of his lie was going to be worse than the exposure of the truth, he feared.

"We must take no chances. There may be shooting. The cellar will serve as an excellent bomb shelter. Trudchen and I must sleep with Ilse." Rudiger waved his hand and looked somewhat ashamed. "Otherwise she will not go to sleep." Unfamiliar with the difficulties of child rearing and, knowing how unnecessary the whole thing was, Hawk only nodded. He couldn't protest too much, he decided. Rudiger would get suspicious. He must now just go along with the crazy story.

"Well, okay. I'll put a man down there with you. That place is out back in the open, ain't it?"

"Yes, but that won't be necessary; there isn't that much room," Rudiger answered impatiently.

"Well, he may have to sleep out on the ground, but I'm gonna let Corporal Armistead watch over the cellar for you." Hawk scarcely suppressed a smile now at Rudiger's reaction to his innocent story. As he spoke, Trudchen came up behind her husband, and Hawk again regretted the severity of the stratagem that he had chosen. He was spared repeating the tale to her by Rudiger, .who thanked Hawk and shut the door.

"They are here," Rudiger gasped as he embraced Trudchen. "It has begun!"

* * *

HAWK RETURNED to the barn and gave Ralph Armistead his new orders. The corporal was a bit mystified about the whole thing until Hawk confided in him, telling the entire story. Hawk also instructed Sergeant Mayeaux and his squad, Fine, Marks, and Klazusky, to follow him into the woods the next morning. They were to camp out there and circle back later in the day, their return preferably unseen. The entire clandestine maneuver was becoming more and more elaborate, with the deployment of troops on two fronts. Because that was what Gretchen wanted and because there was little else to do for diversion, Hawk had few misgivings concerning the plot. A hike in the rough would do Mayeaux's men good. Perhaps Ralph would become friends with Rudiger, and then he could serve as the mediator with the Dutch, relieving Hawk of that duty. Armistead was a rather jolly fellow who made friends easily; perhaps he would be more compatible with the stubborn Van Speer than the brooding Hawk had been.

Hawk went to sleep with a light heart that night, with the prospect of a glorious day to come. He longed to see Gretchen again and to bask in the magical spell that she held over him. Still, he had no trouble sleeping. Joy could not forestall sleeping habits gained during artillery bombardments, Miss Van Speer's charms notwithstanding.

* * *

GRETCHEN WAS ALREADY on the deck of the sloop when Hawk came down the path to the cove. She was startled at his appearance, but on recognizing him, broke into a wide smile and waved. He had an almost intuitive moment as-he looked down at that smile. One way or another this day would change his life. It already had, actually, for suddenly his life meant something, other than merely being a poker chip to bet on a contest with the Japanese. He rocked his helmet back and returned the wave.

She was beautiful. She wore her dungarees and blue shirt that he had seen countless times before. Yet she was lovely to a marine on a Pacific atoll. But she would have been just as lovely to anyone, anywhere. He had discovered her when her splendid beauty was at its age of perfection. He smiled down at her yellow hair, her azure eyes and her full lips that rested so evenly on her shining teeth. He knew that he must confess his love to her today. He knew that his life was in her tiny white hands. Even at that, he was ecstatically happy. His life had been put on the line too many times—when there was *no* prize to be won—for him to be afraid now.

Hawk leapt aboard and removed his gun and helmet. He admitted that he knew little about sailing, but that he was willing to serve as her crew. He was soon taken full advantage of as he unfurled the two sails. He managed them, awkwardly, while she steered. The boat sailed the calm waters along the coast, between the reef and the white beach. There was little danger of capsizing at the leisurely pace, and even if they had, the bottom was only a few feet away and clearly visible. The shore curved gradually so that the cove was soon out of sight.

They were now sailing into the wind, so that it became necessary to sail a zigzag course. The angle of this maneuver brought them close to the shore, and they could observe it quite easily. The terrain and the flora were growing progressively more outrageous; it was the most rugged territory that Hawk had ever seen on the island, and he had seen as much of the island as any man. It would have been impossible to traverse that land, even with two squads of marines. It was just as inaccessible by sea due to the treacherous reef. It was doubtful that anyone had ever set foot on the island here and, according to Gretchen, only she and Moritz had ever seen it. The big ships could send their little boats through the rock and coral near the plantation, but here even that was not possible.

The giant orchids and other flowers of every conceivable color climbed each tree and rock in a spectacular display. The scene was almost unnatural, so perfect was the massive arrangement. The land was rocky and riddled with small bodies of water, visible from the ocean.

"See, I told you that it was beautiful," said Gretchen proudly, the wind almost pulling her hair straight back. But Hawk was looking at her only, when he shook his head in agreement; she looked like a Viking princess there at the tiller, voyaging to the edge of the earth. He saw the youthful strength and character in her face as she intently studied the wind. When he looked at her, he felt a dull ache in his stomach; God, but he loved her, like a schoolboy, he loved her!

"There is the most beautiful spot of all," she shouted

above the wind. "This is as far as I usually go. This is the most beautiful place in the world."

It was indeed, even to a marine sergeant's untrained eye. A little stream ran right through the beach and perhaps fifty yards back was a tall waterfall, the water so pure it seemed as if diamonds were spilling down from its heights.

The sails were deflated and they cruised into the quiet of the lagoon at the mouth of the stream. A gentle backwater prevented them from entering the rivulet, but from this vantage point they had a splendid view of the falls. The big-leaved and big-flowered plants almost hid from sight the peak of the cascade, so that it seemed to flow directly from a wall of vegetation. Gretchen leaned against the stern, and after securing the sails, Hawk stretched out amidships. The boat creaked soothingly.

"Shall we go ashore?" She asked. The boat rocked gently, swaying to the rhythm of the rushing water. Hawk peered over the gunwales. The white sand was the first thing to catch his eye. It reminded him of things best forgotten.

"No, let's stay here a while," he suggested. She smiled across the deck at him. "You know," he said, "I hated to tell your father about the Japs like I did, but that's all I could think of, as a reason for disappearing all day."

"It served its purpose," she said. "He'll think nothing of it, when nothing happens. Nothing ever happens here." She looked out at the primeval wilderness. "It's been exactly like this since the beginning of time, I think."

"I guess it hasn't changed much," said Hawk reflectively. "It takes people to change things." His words seemed to fall into a vacuum; it was an acoustical effect produced by the surface of the water and the nearby cascade.

"That's why my life hasn't changed. It's too much a part of this island. Your life can't change without some intrusion." Gretchen was far away somewhere, as she spoke.

"Yeah, the war's the only thing that ever came here; it sure is the most important change," he said. The sun beat down upon them but the island air was pleasantly cool.

"The war and James Hawk," said Gretchen, returning from her reflection. "Those are the most important changes in my life." As she spoke, she crawled across the deck to him. The hull gently nudged the sandy bottom of the lagoon. He sat up slowly, and she sat beside him, leaning against his solid frame. Hawk eased his arm up from his side and placed it across her shoulder. Gretchen sighed mournfully and there was a long pause between them. Finally she broke the silence.

"When do you think it will end?"

"The war? Oh, I don't know, at least another couple of years, if they intend to take back all of these islands."

"Isn't it strange that two countries, a world apart, fight for so little. One would have to want something very much to fight for it, wouldn't he?" she asked.

"No. Not if you can tell somebody else to go out and do your fighting for you—you don't have to want it quite so bad."

"There's nothing I want badly enough to fight and kill for, or even badly enough to order someone else to fight for—I certainly could not do that. I can't understand it all." Emotion rose in her voice. "Why are they so angry? What do they want?"

"They never asked me what I wanted. I just fight to be fighting, just for meanness, I guess. I wouldn't even know, if someone asked," Hawk laughed ironically.

"Even if I ask?" She tilted her head back to look up into his face. "What do you want?" She gazed into his eyes with her moist lips parted.

"All I want...is you." He struggled within himself for the words and the strength to say them. "I want you to love me, the way that I love you." He placed his large hand beside her face and pressed his lips to hers briefly, and then he drew back. Then tenderly, he embraced the fragile girl and held her in a long and lingering kiss.

"That is one thing you will never have to fight for, James Hawk. I love you." She reached behind his head and caressed the long, sandy hair. She pulled him down to her and again they kissed.

Gretchen sighed deeply and Hawk settled back against the gunwales.

"I've never had much, or even wanted much out of life, and now I find you, in the middle of all of this. This just doesn't seem like me. It seems like I'm watching someone else. But I know that it's me that needs you, Gretchen. I don't believe I could go on without you." Hawk spoke matter-of-factly, very serious, with little expression on his face. It was as if emotions buried deep within him were battling valiantly to escape one last time, before the death of his youth killed them also.

"You do not ever have to go on without me, nor I without you. There is a lot between us now, but that will not last forever."

Hawk listened thoughtfully to her words, and then spoke. "Would you be worried about me, being in the war and all?"

"Yes, of course, but you will come back."

"Maybe not."

"Let's not talk of the things that we can't change or the worst of the things that might happen. We have each other today and, God willing, we will have each other tomorrow. We both have our lives and our problems that we must untangle for each other." Gretchen was almost pleading and Hawk had the distinct feeling that he was missing her meaning.

"You mean the war?" he asked, his confusion apparent.

"Yes, the war and us and my family."

"Yeah, I guess that'll take a lot of untangling."

"I don't think so," said Gretchen, looking out toward the open sea now. "They've never seen you, this way, the way I've seen you all along. You are gentle, but you are strong. Strong enough to do anything."

"Well, I hope I don't disappoint you."

"You won't," she laughed. The laugh broke Hawk's somber meditations. He could not long stay lost in solemn pensiveness when beckoned by such a joyous sound. • He reached over and held her to him again. Her sweet warmth melted the icy wall that his distorted emotions had built up around him. By mutual assent, they leaned down and stretched out along the deck of the boat. The ever sure and coordinated movements of James Hawk became hesitant and awkward. She was very delicate and he feared hurting her.

"I'm sorry," he said once.

"Don't be. It's all right."

He closed his eyes and the falling of the water was all that he could hear, echoing again and again, each time deeper into his mind. The buoyant little sloop did not resist their soft easy motions...and then it was over. Hawk felt very different. Watching the torrid ochre and blue of the setting sun, he felt alive.

The white sand, the clear blue water of the lagoon and the cataract, the lush green of the forest and the pinks and oranges of its flowers, all of the fiery colors of the tropical day melted slowly into twilight shades of grey, before the tiny sloop lit its lantern for the return voyage.

If RUDIGER VAN SPEER suspected a rendezvous between his daughter and the marine, he never let it be known. As far as outward appearances were concerned, they had pulled off the artifice nicely. The day was not quite so nice for Rolf, who had to sit alone all day in the cove, in dire dread of being discovered there, alone. Sergeant Mayeaux was not as conscientious in playing his role; he and the squad returned to the barn after only a couple of hours. To their credit however, they slept out of sight in the loft for another couple of hours, and it was doubtful that anyone could even identify them as the men who had left with Hawk early that morning.

It was after the day was over that the duty of Ralph Armistead began. His job consisted of sleeping out on the open ground behind the farmhouse, between the trapdoor leading down to the cellar and the ventilation shaft of the impromptu bomb shelter. The shaft was merely a pipe sticking out of the ground, and he spent most of the night sitting up against it, sleepless. Such inconvenience would have been much easier to bear, had he not fully known its cause. Rudiger, Trudchen, and Ilse slept, comparatively comfortable, below him, in the tight quarters. Hawk was up at dawn and found the usually good-natured Armistead, still propped up stiffly against the shaft.

"Morning, Ralph," he greeted the corporal.

"How are you, James? Guess you can see how I am."

"You're looking mighty fit. See any Japs?"

Armistead grimaced, his face contorted as he prepared to deliver a tirade on the subject. Hawk raised his hand to silence him, then pointed down the ventilation shaft in explanation. He motioned for the corporal to follow him, after a quick wink. They proceeded toward the barn, passing between the smokehouse and plantation house and disturbing the knee-high ground fog.

"Look here James," Armistead shouted, when they were safely away from the cellar. "I ain't perchin' out there every night like a buzzard on a stick just because that crazy bastard thinks there's Japs out here. He ain't nearly as crazy as the bastard that told him there were Japs running loose around here. Now what are you gonna do about this? It's gonna take me all day to loosen my joints."

Hawk smiled and almost laughed. "I'll get him to let you sleep in the cellar with 'em tonight. How'll that be?"

"That ain't worth a shit. You tell him the truth. Or tell him you found a Jap and killed him. Do something."

"I'll try. This ain't gonna be easy to undo, though." That satisfied Armistead.

As they spoke, they could see the Van Speers

coming up out of the misty dawn fog. They went from the cellar, straight to the house. Hawk bid adieu to the corporal and rounded

the house, crossed the moat, and knocked on the front door. Ernst opened it. His left cheekbone was so swollen that the eye was forced shut. Hawk nodded politely to him, without speaking. Ernst waved him in; any expression caused by the sergeant's presence was indiscernible on his distorted countenance. The entire Dutch family and crew were present around the breakfast table. The bridge of Klaus's nose had tripled in size; he did not look at Hawk. Rudiger stood up at his entrance.

"Sergeant Hawk! Good Morning. Did you find anything yesterday?" Hawk smiled at Gretchen, who looked fearfully away, at the display of such boldness.

"No sir, not a damn thing out there. Probably just a rabbit, or a herd of rabbits. Maybe some of the guys were just making up stories. They been running out of things to do lately."

"Nonsense. You take the matter too lightly, sergeant. You are a soldier and this is your job, but we are civilians and are not so casual about it."

"Uh...yessir, but I really don't think there was anything. We didn't see no brush stomped down or anything like that."

"Nonetheless, my family and my workers are going to arm themselves, in the event of an attack. The Japanese who reach this end of the island will be quite desperate."

"Yessir." Hawk could not deny that. "I guess that's okay with me." Then, deciding that it was harmless enough: "We'll dig a couple more foxholes if you like. I guess you'd feel better if Corporal Armistead slept in the cellar with you?" Hawk could hardly keep a straight face when he thought of Armistead and what his reaction would have been had he heard this conversation. Hawk wanted Van Speer to forget about the Japanese scare, and to feel totally at ease again. He felt that a few nights cramped up with Ralph Armistead would make the Dutchman less allergic to Japanese and possibly drive him back to the comfort of his own bed in the farmhouse.

"No, Sergeant Hawk, I do not want one of your men down there with me."

"Now, I know you don't, but you'll feel a lot safer with him down there, till all this blows over. Then y'all can all come on back to the house where you belong." Hawk was quite pleased with his ingenious plan; it would hasten a termination to Rudiger's self-imposed exile and thereby end the scare. The Dutchman protested vehemently at the very idea of Armistead's presence in the shelter, but Hawk was unwavering. He left an irate and still fuming Van Speer, to find Armistead.

* * *

"WELL, Ralph, all your troubles are over. I fixed everything," Hawk told the glowering corporal, sitting against the side of the barn.

"Oh? How'd you do that?"

"I told him you wanted to sleep down in there with 'em."

"You what? I *don't* want to sleep down there with 'em. I'd rather stay awake sitting on top of 'em! Why in the goddam hell did you do that? You was supposed to straighten all this shit out!"

"I tried to, but that's how the old man wanted it. He's afraid of Japs now, and there ain't no reasoning with him. Besides, in a couple of days he'll be so sick of smellin' you, he'll go back to the house and forget all this shit. Don't go washin' out them duds now, I want this to be real rough on him." Armistead didn't answer. His rage knew no bounds. He could only turn away.

Hawk went down to one knee. "Come on, now Ralph, I'd do the same for you." The corporal turned toward him. Slowly a smile crept across his face. At least that much of what Hawk had said was true.

* * *

THE NEXT FEW days did not prove as dreadful as the corporal had anticipated. Reluctantly he would trudge over to his post at dusk and meet the Van Speers at the head of the ladder that led into the earth. They greeted him with the coolest of salutations at first, but gradually became used to his easygoing ways. Ilse grew especially fond of Armistead because he sat up nights showing her card tricks and telling her stories of his own invention. The quarters were quite cramped and, if Rudiger had hated the idea of the companionship of a marine before, he hated the reality even more. The stories drove him crazy, the cards drove him crazy, Ralph's unwashed, unshaven self drove him crazy. He adjusted the wine rack so as to make two rooms out of the eight-by-ten hole, but the resulting confinement only made him crankier. Trudchen didn't mind the corporal half as much, because he entertained Ilse, but she could have survived quite handily without him. The primary advantage of his absence would have been the end of Rudiger's complaints.

To make matters worse and increase Rudiger's rage, Ilse occasionally insisted that Rolf join them in the shelter. No matter how ridiculous the situation became, Rudiger never attacked his youngest daughter, the perpetrator of it all, but chose Hawk, Armistead, or even Trudchen as the target of his displeasure. Perhaps his blind spot as far as Ilse was concerned was the cause of all of his trouble, and would eventually prove his undoing.

Hawk and Gretchen were discreet during the next few days, meeting at the cove, at the chicken coop, and even in open view, in the garden, but only for a few minutes at a time. What romance would be complete without the giving of gifts? Hawk was no slacker in this regard. He surrendered his handmade treasures to Gretchen one day in the garden, after they had tired of throwing wildflowers at one another. One gift was a bracelet of Australian coins, the other a set of salt and pepper shakers made from .50-caliber machine-gun cartridges. Needless to say, the articles were priceless, at least to Gretchen—due more to their source than to their artistry.

Some of the men looked with envy upon their sergeant as the days dragged by, but most were glad just for the respite from the campaign. Brock had nearly killed Bertoni again, but the other outran him and hid in the jungle for an entire day; no one mentioned the incident to Hawk, for fear that he would administer severe discipline. The sergeant's punishments were known to increase in their austerity, and his last confrontation with Brock would be hard to top. Perhaps the men even feared Brock a little, or possibly even what he would do to Hawk. Brock was becoming more and more unmanageable, raging about like a maniac whenever he saw fit. He was far from completely mad, however; he still chose his victims carefully.

Gaedcke kept up his vigil on the radio, always sending and seldom receiving messages. Rudiger paid him occasional visits, asking if he had told his commanding officer about hearing the Japanese nearby. Gaedcke put him off, saying Hawk hadn't told him to send such a message. This seemed to be enough to satisfy the Dutchman, and he would walk off, only to return the next day and repeat the question. Hayes had got one message through, informing the squad that his forces had struck a stone wall and that the Japanese seemed to be reading his mind. There was nothing new, in other words, and no projected linkup date was given at all.

Fine sat off by himself, writing in his journal. Claiborne sat off by himself, sitting. Lundstedt, Ewell and Canlon played cards, horseshoes and checkers until their cash holdings changed hands several times. Ewell made fun of Canlon, who laughed as much as Lundstedt at his gibes. Lundstedt griped incessantly about the inactivity. Beckwith, Armistead, Gist and Quiroz hung together talking and occasionally exploring the forest. Hawk joined this last group when he was not with Gretchen. They gave him the idea of sending out one-man patrols to look for the enemy in the jungle, as a further means of easing Rudiger's tensions.

Mayeaux, Klazusky and Marks stayed together a lot and volunteered for most of the watches. No one took the watches very seriously; men often fell asleep in the foxholes. Hawk had ordered two more foxholes dug, closer to the house, on its right and left sides, so that now there were five in a jagged inverted v-shape in front of the Van Speer home. Neither the Bren nor Armistead's American machine gun were used to defend these holes, which demonstrated how frivolous Hawk considered the whole undertaking. But he had been off guard too long. He had forgotten the old days and some of the old ways.

7

THE NIGHT MURDERS

"HEY HAWK, YOU BETTER WAKE UP THERE. THEY KILLED that boy, Marks, last night." The cheerful voice of Gist caused Hawk to open his eyes slowly and sit up quickly upon his bed of hay in the corner of the barn.

"What? Who?"

"Hell, the Japs, I imagine. They're the only ones doing any killing on this rock, ain't they? It was them all right. He's cut to pieces." Hawk picked up his Thompson and he and Gist left the barn. The entire marine patrol was gathered around one of the newest foxholes. As Hawk got closer, they parted, and he saw Marks pitched forward on his face, his legs still in the foxhole. His back glistened with red in the morning's first light.

"Got him good," Beckwith observed when Hawk joined the group.

"Them son of a bitches," Hawk whispered as he looked upon the grisly sight. Reflexively he looked out at the jungle. "Which way'd they come from?"

"Can't tell," Beckwith said, mystified. "Looks like they dropped outa the sky and left the same way."

"Yeah, well they didn't. Fan out. Look for some bushes broke down. Japs don't sneak in unless there's a bunch of 'em. There's got to be signs." Hawk knelt down and turned the body over. "Poor kid," he shook his head. "How old was he, Mayeaux?"

"Said he was seventeen. Probably fifteen."

"Well." Hawk stood up and cleared his throat. Then he nodded. "We'll get 'em for this, you can goddam sure bet on that." There was no sound from the circle of men. They knew that he meant it.

"They're out there now and they mean business," said Beckwith finally. "Just sliced that boy to smithereens."

"Mighta done it with his own bayonet," observed Armistead. "It's gone. His rifle's gone."

"How in the hell could anybody get to this damn hole without the guy out front or the one in the back seeing him?" said Hawk. "He was between and behind two posts. It don't make sense to me. Who was out here last night?"

"Me," said Klazusky. "I was in the middle hole, out front."

"Which watch?" asked Hawk.

"The whole night. That's how we been doing it."

"Well goddam, you probably slept the whole shittin' night."

"I slept," Klazusky admitted. "We weren't expecting anything, Sergeant. We just figured we either sleep in the barn or sleep in the hole—we didn't know anything was gonna..." His voice trailed off. Hawk paced up and down angrily. He was a man of action, but the action was over. The lack of discipline was his fault; he had no one else to blame, nor did he. He found himself using Klazusky's words to excuse himself; he just didn't expect anything. He sat down in the hole beside the body, propping his head up in one hand. Quiroz, Lundstedt, Claiborne and Canlon came back from the jungle.

"Didn't find nothing, for sure," said Joe Canlon. "There's places trampled down, but we've done a lot of that ourselves." The other three nodded in agreement.

"Well, we been slacking off and we paid for it," said Hawk. "I guess the wrong one paid for it, but it's done. We know the son of a bitches will be back. I figure there's only a few of 'em. Otherwise they'd have come stampedin' in here and killed us all. Sounds like *one* of 'em coulda killed us all last night."

They buried Marks at the edge of the jungle. Everyone was somber. The impact of the death upon them was greater due to the almost civilian atmosphere that had prevailed over the previous few weeks. They would have numbly accepted dozens of deaths in a landing, but that was war. That wasn't here.

"So, Sergeant, the enemy is upon us?" Rudiger Van Speer stood upon his moat with Moritz as Hawk returned from the burial. His expression seemed to say, "I told you so."

"Yeah."

"They will be back. Are you prepared?"

"Yeah. We'll get 'em next time," said Hawk. His thoughts were elsewhere. "Probably some stragglers or deserters. We're still sendin' out our one-man patrols every few hours. They ain't gonna sneak up here again."

Gretchen came out of the front door.

"Father, I want Sergeant Hawk to stay in the house with Moritz and me," she said.

"Nonsense. Sergeant Hawk will be much too busy for that," answered Rudiger, shaking his head.

"I insist that he guard us, Father. You have an American guarding you and I want one guarding me."

"Oh, I guess I'd better stay out here and see if I can catch one of them little...guys," Hawk declined.

"James, I insist that you stay in the house with me," said Gretchen, almost as if they were alone. Hawk flushed.

"Well Gretchen, I got responsibilities. I just lost a man..."

"Your orders were to guard us, not your men. I want protection. I cannot protect myself. I should hope your men can protect themselves."

"Perhaps another soldier, one without as many responsibilities, such as Corporal Armistead?" Rudiger suggested.

"No, Father. He is watching Ilse and Ilse likes him. I want Sergeant Hawk. Sergeant Hawk?" Gretchen turned to him, eyes flashing. Hawk looked around. No marines were listening. Perhaps he should guard Gretchen. He was torn between new and older, ingrained obligations.

"I guess somebody should keep an eye on the house," he mumbled sheepishly, eyes aimed at the ground. "I can use it for a command post."

"You certainly can." Gretchen scolded. Rudiger groaned and dashed back into the house. Moritz smiled and followed him. Gretchen took a step toward Hawk. "What is wrong with you, James? I don't want you out here where people are getting killed."

"That's what I do, Gretchen. That's why I'm here. To

kill and take a chance of gettin' killed. I can't forget about it anymore. They just killed a half-grown boy. I'll stay there at night, though, to keep an eye on you. Those Japs are pretty tricky—they could probably get in the house."

"I'll see you this evening, then," she said, still simmering at the very suggestion of his remaining outside. She turned angrily and entered the house.

Hawk looked back at the jungle. He decided that his various duties overlapped sufficiently to be performed simultaneously. The watches were spread out so that almost everyone had at least one shift to perform every night. The men were especially alert that night. Hawk was confident that they were safe for the time being. He went to the house and silently slumped into an easy chair in the living room. Gretchen's ire had eased somewhat. She came in and sat in a chair across from him. Only Moritz and Rolf were still in the house. Ernst and Klaus had gone to their shack. Rudiger and the rest were in the cellar.

"Are you angry, James?" asked Gretchen.

"No."

"That is gracious of you, after someone tries to save your life." Hawk shifted uneasily. She was prepared to start again and he wasn't. His position was not as clear as hers yet, so he felt uncomfortable arguing.

"Those men are...like your family is to you. We've been through a lot together. I have to look out for them, that's all."

"You do look after them, quite well. Must you sleep out there with them, too? When you are killed, who will look after them?"

"I wouldn't get killed," said Hawk confidently.

Gretchen sighed impatiently and went into the other room to get two drinks. She returned, handed him one and sat on the arm of the chair.

"James...I am sorry that I am afraid...but I am. I need you in here. Let's not fight about it." It was phrased like a question. Finally he smiled up at her and nodded, but she knew he was still thinking of his men—of Marks. She had to change the subject.

"What did you do before the war? I can't picture you as a civilian. You must have had a job that you could be moody with or feel guilty about—you are so good at it now."

Hawk tried to smile. "I never did a whole lot of anything. Sharecropped, rode the rails, stole to eat, worked on government projects. Just barely got by, most of the time."

"Maybe that is why you are so infatuated with this Marine Corps. You haven't been exposed to...anything better. After the war, you must become a planter. There is plenty of room on the island and there is always a good market for rubber." Hawk was irritated by the first part of her statement, but he had recovered before she finished.

"Yeah, maybe."

"Oh, James!" She fell into his lap. "Don't be moody!"

"Okay," he laughed.

* * *

THE NEXT DAY brought a new mystery. Gaedcke searched the plantation before he discovered Hawk in the farmhouse. Hawk had neglected to let his whereabouts become common knowledge. He himself answered the pounding at the front door. The usually nervous Gaedcke was even more excited than normal.

"They got the radio, Sergeant Hawk. Chopped it up. It's finished." Hawk reacted with a curse.

"All right, I'll be down to look it over. All the guys okay?"

"Yeah, they're all right. But we're cut off for Mire now."

Hawk nodded, but he thought it no great loss—especially compared to the life of Marks. The only thing that bothered him was the ease with which the Japanese were entering the camp. He slowly closed the door and returned to the kitchen. He met Rudiger halfway there.

"Well, is Achilles still brooding in his tent?" Rudiger asked.

"What?" the distracted Hawk snapped.

"I hear there was more infiltration—while you were in here, last night."

"Yeah," Hawk answered rudely. He picked up his gun and helmet and left through the kitchen door. He had no desire to play word games with Rudiger. The radio shack was still intact but the equipment itself was a shambles. Most of the men were there, gaping at it. No one had any leads in the matter. Hawk sent out the usual one-man patrols in several directions with no positive results.

"They must of come up from the water," Hawk told Beckwith later in the day, as they sat in the loft of the barn, looking out at the jungle for a clue. "That would explain how they got the kid, too, without anybody seeing them. They came up from the water, sneaked around the house and got him from behind. We were all pointing toward the woods."

Hawk called the men together, behind the radio shack. He ordered a foxhole dug facing the path that led down to the cove, even though he found no evidence of the enemy down there.

"Okay, this is where they been coming from, I think. I need three of you to man this post at all times. Who wants to get killed?"

"I'll do it," Gist volunteered in his rough cowboy accent. Quiroz was the second to step forward.

"How about you, Brock?" Hawk asked, before another good man could endanger himself. Brock shrugged, shook his head and shrugged again.

"I don't care," he answered. Hawk nodded. Brock would be no great loss, and Gist and Quiroz were capable of keeping him in line. It was settled then. The house was surrounded with defenses.

The night passed, tensely but harmlessly. The men stayed awake virtually from sunset till sunrise, causing them to have to sleep for a while during the day. Gist, Quiroz and Brock had taken turns sleeping, but Quiroz awakened during Brock's watch and discovered that he had left Gist and himself sleeping there, and had walked off. Quiroz was not one to complain but he felt Hawk should know of this. It was dangerous practice to leave two buddies sleeping in the path of infiltrators.

Hawk and Beckwith were sitting up on some empty oil drums behind the smokehouse when Quiroz found them and related the story. Hawk ordered Brock brought to him. Quite some time later. Brock slinked up.

"I hear you was sleepwalking last night?" Hawk stared straight into Brock's clear, dazed-looking eyes. Brock shook his head in denial.

"Well Cal, I never beat the shit outa nobody without

tellin' 'em what for." Hawk leaned forward from his, seat on the oil drum. "Quiroz woke up and you weren't in the hole. Where were you?"

"Taking a shit, probably."

"Yeah? Well you never came back." Hawk slid down off of the drum, to stand toe to toe with the boy. "If that smart mouth don't start talkin' fast, I'm gonna slap it right off your silly lookin' face."

Brock cleared his throat and collected his thoughts for a moment. "I thought I heard something, down toward the water, so I walked down the path to have a look. I scouted around the beach and in the woods a little. I figured those two were all right with me between them and the beach." Brock looked away after he had spoken. Hawk made no response until the boy self-consciously glanced at him again.

"That's a crocka shit."

"I swear it ain't, Sergeant Hawk."

"Okay. I don't know what in the hell you'd be doin' at three in the morning, but if I ever see anybody prowling around at night, I'm gonna blow 'em in two. That's if I catch 'em. Now if I don't catch 'em, I'll just find you the next day and blow you in two. Do you read me, Brock?"

"Yes...sir." Hawk waved him away.

"I don't like that bastard," said Beckwith after Brock had left. "You know, I been hearing some rustling around out in the jungle. Hell, it might've been him." Beckwith adjusted his short, bulky frame on the drum.

"I don't know. I figure he's just being a shitass—you put him one place, he's gotta be in another. But he's gonna get himself shot, especially if he comes messin' around the house." Hawk jumped back up to his seat. "You know I been thinkin'," he said after a reflective pause. "Hayes said something about there being natives on the island, and he said they probably weren't too friendly, because of the way the Japs treated 'em. Maybe that's what you heard and maybe that's who has been causing us all this trouble. I imagine they're pretty sneaky and quiet, like Indians or something, you know?"

"I don't know, I ain't never heard of none of these natives bothering the marines. They're always on our side. Why don't you ask that old fart Van Speer if he's ever had any truck with the natives?'

Hawk considered that for a moment and resolved to ask Rudiger that very thing. That evening when he quizzed Rudiger on the subject, he received a very interesting response: there were no natives. It was an uninhabited island, except for the Europeans. He could not explain Hayes's mistaken information regarding the native population. Hawk could only deduce that some green pilot had mistaken loincloth-clad Japanese for natives. It was no wonder that they were reported to be hostile.

* * *

RUDIGER GAVE Gretchen his Webley revolver and Moritz an ancient twelve-gauge shotgun before retiring to his bomb shelter. He greatly feared for their safety here, above ground, which did not speak well of his confidence in Hawk.

After Rolf and Moritz retired, rather late in the evening, Gretchen and Hawk retreated to the privacy of the den. She embraced him and held him for a long time, before saying anything.

"I love you so, James. You are the finest man I have ever known." Being maladroit with words, he lowered his head and kissed her.

"James, I have been thinking. I have an idea that I want you to listen to. And think about it before you answer." Hawk could read expectation of disappointment in her words and in her expression. "Suppose we sailed over to the western end of the island and stayed there for a few weeks, together, until the Japanese and the Americans leave."

The shock that the suggestion gave him was not apparent upon his face. "But I *am* an American," he reminded her.

"You are an islander now. You are mine, you are not an American." How could he explain his loyalty to the fourteen filthy fleabags that were his charge, the loyalty he felt to the marines and the Corps, or even to his very own country? He could not. He felt it, but he could not express it convincingly in words, and he knew that she would never understand.

"They shoot deserters," he said simply.

"They will never find you. You will stay here. They will think that you have been killed."

"No, they'll take this island and they'll stay here a long time, probably even after the war's over."

"Maybe the Japanese will win," she suggested. He smiled.

"No, they won't. I couldn't..." He released her and struggled to find the words. "I just couldn't run out on everybody..."

"But you can run out on me?"

"No, I'm not running out on you. I'll be here a long

time and if I have to go, I'll come back as soon as possible."

Her angry face seemed to melt; tear after tear fell from her eyes. She threw her arms around him and held him tightly.

"Oh, James, you won't come back. I know you won't. They'll kill you. Please don't go." He put his arms around her. She felt their great strength and the inexplicable security that they could produce.

"Nobody's gonna kill me," he consoled her, in his ever-positive and confident tone.

"I knew that you didn't love me enough to do it, James, but I had to try. I had to try for us and for your sake."

"I love you enough..." He steered her to the leather couch and they sat down there. "It's just a bad situation, I guess, but it won't last forever. Believe me, things look bad but then they blow over before you know it." He knew her to be young and impatient but he dared not call that to her

attention. "Let's do everything right?" He pleaded. She could only acquiesce and dry her eyes, and lay her head on his shoulder.

* * *

AFTER TWO MORE UNEVENTFUL NIGHTS, the men developed a relaxed attitude again and, predictably again, tragedy struck. They found the body beside the barn. The throat was slashed and there were several deep stab wounds in the back. No one saw it happen, but when Fine was not relieved from his watch at the central foxhole on the apex of the v-shaped defenses, he became suspicious. It was about four in the morning when he and Mayeaux located the remains of Klazusky. There were few signs of a struggle, which was peculiar, because Klazusky was big, and a rough customer. He had evidently been waylaid on his trip out to the foxhole. Mayeaux thought it best to inform Hawk immediately, and he sent Fine to get him.

Wide-eyed and alert, carrying his gun, Hawk answered the front door and listened intently to Fine's story. He rammed his fist into the door when he was told of Klazusky's fate. An insane rage seized him. The deaths of comrades had always occurred on the front line, where he could easily vent his anger on the nearby enemy, but this maddened him. Slinging the strap of his gun over his shoulder, he stalked out to the scene of the murder with Fine.

"Did anybody see anything?" Hawk screamed at the men, who cringed at the outburst. No one spoke. "No, hell no, nobody saw anything—it was a ghost!" he answered for them, waving his arm.

"Did you see anything?" Lundstedt had the audacity to ask. Everyone gasped in horror at his words and waited for Hawk's reaction. To their amazement the ground did not open up and swallow Lundstedt. Hawk only turned his back to them and stared down at the slain man.

"I sent out some guys to look around," Beckwith interjected meekly in the pregnant pause. Hawk put his hands on his hips.

"One by one," he growled. "They think they're gonna get us all." Hawk turned back to the men. He spotted Gist. "Who was on watch over there behind the house?"

"Brock," Gist answered.

"Okay, what'd you see, Brock?" Hawk asked.

"Nothing. How could I see around the house and through the barn way over here?" Hawk brought a powerful uppercut to Brock's chin. The blow was so quick and the night so dark that no one, including its recipient, saw it. Brock's feet left the ground and he went hurtling backwards, to fall in a heap.

"Get up, Cal, you're a dead man," Hawk commanded in an unemotional tone.

Beckwith, somewhat reluctantly stepped between them.

"Wait, James, he's right. He couldn't see over here. He had that coming, but you can't beat him to death for being impolite." Beckwith was almost whining. Hawk looked back at Gist, his fiery eyes clearly visible in the darkness.

"Was he there all night?" Hawk asked Gist.

"I believe so, Sergeant. Me and Quiroz been watching him."

"Quiroz?" Hawk looked to him.

"I was asleep, Sergeant."

"Okay," Hawk said, regaining his composure with a deep breath. "Brock, you let somebody get by you, probably more than one. I ain't never seen any one Jap that could do this to Klazusky. I got a suspicion you weren't even in that hole and I, personally, want to kill you right here and now. But I'll wait for Hayes to take care of you."

"If I wasn't there, why didn't they kill Gist and Quiroz?" Brock asked from his supine position. Hawk took a step forward, to stomp Brock. Beckwith held

Hawk's arm lightly, more as a reminder than as a true restraint. Hawk demurred and began pacing angrily.

"I don't know...I don't know anymore... They must be comin' from the jungle. Get up, Brock, and watch your mouth, it's gonna get you hurt. I was just shittin' you about turning you in to Hayes, because you got a damn smart mouth."

Rudiger Van Speer and Ralph Armistead joined the chaotic scene. Hawk could feel the Dutchman's cold gaze upon his back, ever questioning his right to be in authority. Hawk was having second thoughts himself. He was adept at exposing himself to enemy fire, but he couldn't seem to muster the brains to cope with this. Perhaps being a platoon sergeant took more than raw courage.

"All right, let's get the man buried. Now all this stuff has got me a little shook up, so I ain't in no mood to play mama and daddy to you. Brock, you start acting like a man and like a marine, quicker because I'm damn sure gonna treat you like one from now on."

As the men shuffled about their fallen friend, Hawk turned with some reluctance to Rudiger. They glared at one another for a moment before the Dutchman spoke.

"Sergeant Hawk, you are a madman," Rudiger said icily. "You have placed my family in grave danger." With great difficulty, Hawk overcame his urge to strike the man. He thought it best to say nothing in reply.

"I demand that you and your band of hellions withdraw from my home immediately, before your madness and incompetency costs any more lives. You would have left long ago were you not so intent upon badgering my daughter with your rancid presence. Isn't it time you faced your responsibilities? You must answer for these blunders to your superiors, you realize." It was doubtful that Rudiger realized that his life was hanging in the balance while Hawk endeavored to restrain himself.

"We ain't leaving here, Van Speer, till that battalion of marines comes walking out of the jungle. If they don't ever come, we ain't ever leaving. So get that bee outa your bonnet."

Rudiger softened, and gestured appropriately. "Be reasonable, man. We are noncombatants. The Japanese will afford us courtesies due that status. With you here, they have no choice but to kill us all. If you had a larger force, perhaps you could defend us properly, but with things as they are you are a serious liability."

Hawk seriously considered the proposal. It almost made sense. They could beg the enemy for mercy; the marines could not. Would the enemy treat them as noncombatants? He didn't think so. There weren't enough of them; they would be too easy to annihilate. Hawk's conception of Japanese prisoners consisted of only entire towns of civilians, too numerous and expensive to kill. Even with this impression, he would have gladly left Rudiger there to plead his case with some fanatical Japanese officer. Hawk doubted that any officers or organized enemy forces were to blame for the recent killings. He suspected deserters and cowards were at work here, and that they would have no mercy —that was for certain. But he could not conceive of leaving Gretchen, or even Trudchen and Rolf. He would feel guilty about leaving Moritz—although he could recover from any pangs of guilt caused by leaving Ernst and Klaus.

"Well, you're a stupid old son of a bitch, but I'll leave you here, if you let me take the women, your boy and the old guy with us," Hawk finally said. His compromise was against orders, but in his best judgment. That was what the situation called for.

"You *are* a foolish swine, Hawk. Why would I want only to protect myself and those two dogs Ernst and Klaus? It's my family I want protected. Not to be somewhere out there with you, getting massacred. In fact, I fear you and your men more than the Japanese. You are a fool but I am not. They stay with me. You would be wise to leave and possibly save yourself before the Japanese come in full strength. And you would also grant us the favor of not being adjudged guilty by association with you, in the eyes of the Japanese."

Hawk was afraid of the kernel of common sense in the suggestion, but he was adamant. "No."

Rudiger stalked away.

"That guy's full of shit," said Armistead, who had been standing beside Van Speer. Hawk's mouth was open and his teeth clenched.

"I hope so," he answered. "He just doesn't understand Japs. They're gonna be desperate when they all get cornered on this end of the island. Why in hell should they take prisoners when the marines are gonna wipe 'em out?"

"Hostages?" Armistead replied. The answer didn't add to Hawk's peace of mind. He only gave Armistead a whose-side-are-you-on look. There were several theories and possibilities regarding a course of action to take. Each had its good and bad points; no *one* was the correct choice. But Hawk had to choose one and live with it. He had chosen to stay.

Klazusky was buried before dawn, beside Marks. Hawk was now convinced that the infiltrators were somehow using the vast jungle as the base of their attacks, rather than the sea. He surmised that they killed by night and ran as deep into the tropical rain forest as they could get by day. Thus they were eluding the range of the systematic one-man patrols being sent out after them. He decided that in order to remedy this, he himself would prowl the jungle, for as many days as necessary until he should find signs of the enemy. He told Gretchen of his plan first, and she put up no small show of resistance. She was angry and stubborn but when she saw that he was determined to go, she made up and bade him a tearful goodbye, knowing that she might never see him again. All in all, it was not as big a scene as Hawk had feared. He was expecting the full gamut of tantrums and threats, rather than merely a reluctant concession.

* * *

ABOUT AN HOUR AFTER DAWN, Hawk had the men assembled at the edge of the forest near the point where they had first come upon the house. He was helmeted, his gun slung over his shoulder, with two grenades looped over the back of his belt.

"Okay, I'm gonna see if I can put a stop to this horse-shit. I'm leaving Sergeant Beckwith in charge and then... uh, Mayeaux, and if anything happens, then Armistead. I'll probably be gone two days; I'm going as deep as they could run overnight, anyway. While I'm gone, the Dutchman's gonna give y'all a buncha shit about leaving here, for the safety of...all concerned. My order is: stay till battalion links up with you. That's the order Hayes gave, and kept giving me, till they got the radio. Of course now, if I ain't here and something new develops, it's up to Sergeant Beckwith to decide what's best. For right now, Hayes, and me, think it's best to stay put. Well, I guess that's about it. Adios." And then he was gone. The jungle swallowed him up and it was almost as if there had never been a Sergeant Hawk.

The miserable half-trail that the men had beaten on their way to the plantation had become overgrown again, but Hawk was able to make fairly good time. He was a hard-boned, hard-muscled outdoorsman whose only thought was putting one foot in front of the other. He watched the trees and brush for snipers, but not carefully. He was a speck in an ocean of green and he knew that he would have no chance against an observant sniper. His plan was to surprise the enemy with his passage. He came to the narrow, black bayou that had been his avenue of approach to the northwestern corner of the island. With the day only half spent, he unhesitatingly plunged into its stagnant, slimy waters. Waist-deep in the scum, he slowly pulled one foot over the other on the swirling, silt-covered bottom. Disturbed waterfowl, reptiles and amphibians splashed and screamed at his passage. The unending, living jungle was a huge intimidating creature of mystery and death, even from the safety of the plantation. Here he faced it alone, unfaltering, going deeper and deeper into its unsavory recesses, daring its infinite power, begging it to challenge him. He was carrying his Thompson now, partly to use on overzealous snakes and partly to balance himself in the thick waters. As he waded, he used it like a tightrope walker uses his bar, shifting it with his weight.

The afternoon was waning when he took his first pause, there in the bayou, beneath the overhanging canopy of trees and shrubs. He removed his helmet and let it float against the muddy bank. Sweat and condensation from the surface of the ditch had bathed his face in moisture. He unfastened his canteen and took a drink. There was nothing in sight, and he had seen nothing all day. Nothing. He leaned against a large branch that grew out over the water. Somewhat dejected, but even more determined, he replaced his helmet and slogged on—on into the hideous night like some mindless, blood-seeking monster.

The cries of the jungle in the almost total darkness were paralyzing in their stark tones of terror. But all was wasted on James Hawk, for as terrible as nature is, man, the killer, is more so. It was midnight or after before he stopped. He disgustedly jabbed a thick snake off a tree limb and propped himself up on it, inches above the bayou. He slept there, soundly and comfortably, just as he had during countless artillery barrages. He had become Hawk, the animal, the unfeeling, uncaring right hand of Satan, once again.

8

THE KILLINGS BY BROCK
AND HAWK

BECKWITH CONTINUED THE POLICY OF SENDING OUT periodic, one-man patrols. He was surveying a group of idle men for a likely candidate for one of these sorties, the third and last of the day, when he spotted Bertoni. It occurred to him that he had never seen the man returning from the jungle, and he realized that he had evidently been overlooked with regard to this unwelcome duty. Bertoni was summoned to Beckwith's base of operations, the empty oil drums stacked beside the smokehouse.

"Bertoni, ain't it your turn to do some scoutin'?" Beckwith asked, rising from a prone position.

"No, sergeant, I don't believe so."

"How many of these patrols have you been on?"

"None, but neither have a lot of other guys."

"I don't know about that. I can't think of nobody that ain't been out there at least once, and most of 'em been out there a half dozen times. You make the rounds this time." Bertoni stood there without answering or carrying out the order.

"What's wrong?" Beckwith asked.'

"Well Sergeant, when those other guys went on patrol, there hadn't been two men killed. It seems pretty risky now."

"You ain't afraid now, are you?"

"A little. I sure am. Seems like I ought to at least have another man go with me. That only seems fair."

"Nobody else had any company," Beckwith sneered.

"Well, it just seems fair that now, things being the way they are and all..." Bertoni mumbled and kicked at the ground. Beckwith had no intention of letting Bertoni weasel out of his duty, but the man was so hesitant to go on patrol that he wasn't sure that he could force him to either.

So, in keeping with Marine Corps policy, Beckwith resolved to make the assignment even more distasteful, while on the surface making it appear to conform with Bertoni's specifications.

"Okay, Bertoni, you got it—a two-man patrol." Beckwith smiled and then raised his voice. "Brock! Get your sorry ass over here!" Brock shuffled over, as slowly as humanly possible and quite obvious about it. "Brock, Bertoni wants a buddy on his patrol. You're it." Brock looked Bertoni up and down with a blank expression.

"Wait a minute, Sergeant Beckwith. You can't do that," Bertoni complained. Since Hawk's departure, he had spent the whole day trying to stay out of Brock's sight, and now Beckwith was purposely trying to get him maimed. "He's as crazy as a loon." Brock stared at the side of Bertoni's head.

"That he is, but you wanted a buddy. Brock, you leave your rifle here. Bertoni will take care of you."

Brock snorted and shook his head affirmatively. "All right, get movin', you two."

Armistead walked up and saw the pair retreating to the jungle, Brock lagging far behind, eyes aimed at the ground. "Bertoni is a dumb ass," Beckwith told Armistead. "He could have went out there a few feet and took a nap and came back. Now he's gotta keep an eye on Brock."

"I don't know if that was such a good idea," Armistead observed, rubbing his beard.

"He asked for it, dodging duty like that. It's time he got some guts." Beckwith had to defend his decision. It was a bad decision. It put Bertoni on a terrible spot.

* * *

BERTONI KEPT FAR AHEAD of Brock, who only stumbled after him with his hands in his pockets. As much as Bertoni feared the jungle, he feared Brock more, and Brock knew it. The boy kept a weird half smile upon his mirthless lips and every time Bertoni looked over his shoulder, the smile was aimed at his back.

The congested, trackless vegetation shuddered at the disturbance of some ground birds. Bertoni halted in mid-step. There was quite some distance between the two men and the plantation. Brock caught up with him, for the first time.

"What's wrong?" Brock muttered. His voice was nasal and inarticulate but Bertoni never had any trouble understanding him.

"I thought I saw something. Something scared those birds," Bertoni whispered. Brock smiled to himself, never taking his eyes off of the other man. Bertoni was frightened and had momentarily forgotten about his deadly enemy.

"What's that?" Brock pointed at the ground in front of them. "It looks like a Jap shoe print, don't it?" Brock's sense of humor was stimulated by the suggestion. It was difficult for him to restrain a guffaw as he spoke and even more difficult when Bertoni knelt over the point at which he had been indicating. Bertoni strained his eyes at the ground, leaning on the only rifle the two men had between them.

"No, that's not a track," Bertoni answered. "The ground's just soft. Looks like quicksand right here." Brock reached down and seized the barrel of the M-1. It was an easy matter to rip the rifle from Bertoni's awkward grip. Bertoni fell off balance and was left sitting on the ground, looking up at the muzzle. Brock pulled his lips back over his teeth in psychotic glee as he aimed straight down at the other marine.

"I must of been mistaken, dago," he said in mock apology. He pulled the trigger at point blank range, blowing Bertoni's face off. Seizing the seat of the dead man's trousers, he dragged the bloody remains into the quicksand and let them disappear below the mire. Brock aimed the rifle skyward and squeezed off the entire clip and then tossed it after its erstwhile owner. Unable to control himself any longer, he threw back his head and laughed.

* * *

HAWK WAS up at dawn and on the trail again. On the spur of the moment, he decided to climb a tall tree and have a look around. Removing his helmet but retaining his weapons, he clambered up some forty feet into the tortuous limbs of a forest giant. His efforts were immediately rewarded. In the distance, rising just above the canopy of green, was smoke. It was, he believed, the spiraling evidence of breakfast cookfires. He ran his sleeve across his brow and leaned back against the thick tree trunk to rest. Beneath his breath he swore an obscene oath. Today he would get them.

He left the comparative comfort of the bayou and wound through the relentless underbrush. His pace was not hurried, for he thought that his prey was a stationary force, probably encamped. The terrain became hilly and the density of the undergrowth diminished into pliable stalks of high grass. At the summit of one of these small hills, he sighted his goal. There, in the hollow below him, was a single Japanese soldier, perched on his haunches, apparently field-stripping his flimsy rifle. He was shirtless but wore uniform pants, and a helmet lay nearby. Hawk positioned his Thompson carefully and began walking cautiously toward the man. An extinguished fire was nearby; the marine suspected other enemy soldiers were in the vicinity.

Hawk was down the hillside and almost upon the man before he turned his shadowed eyes in that direction. The alarmed soldier jerked his head in several directions, looking either for a place to run or for other Americans. Hawk held his left hand out in front of himself with the palm down, signaling the man to be still. The submachine gun was cushioned between his right elbow and body. The disheveled apparition continued to approach and the captured man backed away from it. His nerves finally shattered and he broke and ran. A faint smile touched Hawk's lips. He squeezed the trigger and the breechblock shuddered frantically. A jagged flash leapt from the muzzle and the .45-caliber barrage dragged down the fleeing man.

The little warrior wailed and writhed in agony, clutching at his back. Hawk walked toward him, his expression unchanging, his eyes shifting to the left and right. When the range was certain, he ended the man's death throes with another burst. Coldly, Hawk studied his handiwork, then turned and ran back up the hillside, flattening himself in the tall grass. For an hour he lay there, watching the draw below.

No other soldiers appeared. He sat up and bit off a plug of chewing tobacco. After another hour, there had still been no sign of activity. Slowly, he went back down the hill, in a crouch, his eyes always on the surrounding grass and hilltops.

Near the fire was a sack of rice that he ripped open with his hunting knife. He spilled the contents out onto the ground and crawled over to the dead man. Taking another cautious look around, he inserted the blade into the dead man's throat and severed his head. Lifting the grisly thing up by its hair, he deposited it in the sack and tied in onto his belt. Then, like a cat, crouching and running, he proceeded up and over the hill to retrace his route and return to the plantation.

Brock came running out of the woods at breakneck speed, sans rifle, helmet or Bertoni. The marines saw his speedy approach and watched him intently. Halfway across the cleared field between the farmhouse and the jungle, he screamed.

"Japs! Japs! They got Bertoni!" Beckwith jumped down from the oil drums he so frequently occupied.

"Get in them holes!" the sergeant ordered, and men scattered in four directions. Brock dived in the foxhole on the extreme left flank, occupied by Beckwith.

"They're out there, Sergeant. We walked right into 'em." Brock was gasping. His chest heaved from exertion.

"What the hell happened?" Beckwith asked, watching the forest, prepared for the worst.

"We was walking along and bang, we didn't even see him. He got Bertoni through the head and kept shooting at me, but he missed and I took off running. He was up in a tree so he couldn't chase me. If I'da had my rifle I coulda got him right off."

"One? Just one?" Beckwith asked indignantly.

"One with a gun," Brock replied just as indignantly. "And one of us dead because of it." Beckwith helped himself to his feet by leaning on his BAR.

"All right," Beckwith shouted. "It was only one Nip. Canlon, Gist, Quiroz, go get him and watch yourself. We'll watch the place here." With surprising alacrity the designated men plunged into the forbidding wood. Brock stood beside Beckwith and drew a deep breath.

"That was close. He like to got me, Beckwith." Brock choked, still breathless. "You shouldn't of sent me out there without a gun or nothing."

"I guess, I guess," Beckwith answered distractedly. "Goddam, Hawk's gone one day and I lose a man. He's gonna be one mad son of a bitch."

"Hawk? Shit on Hawk. What about Bertoni? What about me?" Brock asked self-righteously. Beckwith shook his head guiltily.

"We heard the shootin', too," Beckwith moaned. "I thought y'all were shittin' around."

Brock snorted in disgust. By this time, he believed his story himself and was no longer merely performing a role. He threw himself down in the foxhole and kept shaking his head and mumbling about "poor Bertoni." It sufficiently convinced Beckwith of Brock's sincerity. In fact, he never doubted it.

The patrol that Beckwith had sent out returned with nothing to report. They could not even find Bertoni's body. Beckwith decided to try again the next day, with Brock as a guide. But again there were no results.

* * *

Two tense and sleepless nights passed before Hawk returned from the bush. Before anyone had discovered him, he cut a bamboo-like pole from the edge of the forest and propped his ghastly prize up on it, its mournful face grinning at the jungle. Gist saw the obscene little ceremony from the central foxhole and walked out to the sergeant to see what in the hell was going on.

"Kinda pretty, don't you think?" Hawk smiled, sliding a cigar between his cracked lips.

"Yeah, real cute," Gist answered, spitting tobacco juice in disgust.

"That's my new welcome mat, for out little buddies."

Gist spat again and nodded. Then he told Hawk: "They got Bertoni."

Hawk cursed, removed his helmet and cursed again. When he was told of the circumstances, however, he immediately became suspicious. He had only the facts to go on, not benefiting from Brock's histrionics. Hawk asked Gist if he had heard the shots and the other answered affirmatively. Hawk asked what they sounded like.

"Loud and heavy," Gist spat. He looked straight ahead. "

"Twenty-five calibers are light and snappy," Hawk noted. Gist never faced him.

"Yeah, I know, I've heard 'em," said Gist sagely.

"Did Brock kill him?"

"That ain't for me to say. There's Japs out there. You found one. I don't much care one way or the other." Gist turned completely away to spit this time. "If I was you though, I'd be careful. You ain't exactly that kid's favorite."

Hawk snorted in reply.

Never one to let sleeping dogs lie, Hawk went straight to the heart of the matter. He stalked across the open field to the foxhole containing Brock and Beckwith. The two men squinted up at his towering figure from the floor of their entrenchment.

"Morning, Brock. Did you kill Bertoni?" Hawk chewed disinterestedly on his cigar.

"No sir," said Brock, flabbergasted. "A Jap got him and almost got me, too." Hawk only nodded with an unbelieving scowl on his face. Brock sensed a serious beating forthcoming, so he augmented his reply. "I probably would have got the Jap, but Sergeant Beckwith made me leave my rifle behind. That's why I almost got killed. I probably coulda got that Jap."

Hawk nodded. "I think you killed him," he said, without emotion. He left them there without another word and knocked on the door of the plantation house.

Gretchen opened the door and threw herself into Hawk's arms. Rudiger appeared in the door behind her, enraged. But he said nothing. Hawk took Gretchen's hand and led her away from him. The two men traded dark looks of hate. Gretchen and Hawk crossed the moat and stood in the front yard.

"James, I've been so worried about you," said Gretchen with tears in her eyes. The brimming tears disappeared when she laid her head against his chest. They were replaced by a broad smile.

"Aw, I'm all right," he answered. But he looked different: cold and hard with a two-day growth of beard. Secretly she wished that he were clean-shaven again, but her eyes only radiated the love that she felt for him.

"Hey, come see," he chuckled proudly. "See what I brought back." That was of course, an ill-advised move.

"What is it?" Gretchen smiled, trying to focus her eyes upon the-head jammed up on the stick. Hawk gave another self-satisfied chuckle.

"Can't you tell?" he asked. "That'll keep 'em away."

"But what is..." Then her eyes picked up the clear image of the severed head. "Oh, oh..." She gasped, turning away. "Oh my God, did you do that?" She held her stomach and forehead and turned her back.

"Uh...yeah," said Hawk, his smile fading.

"How could anyone do that to another human being?" she cried in unrestrained anguish.

"It ain't a human... You didn't get close enough. It's a Jap. Come see, it's just a Jap." She ran away from him and into the plantation house.

Hawk took a half-burned cigar from his pocket. "Well, I'm a son of a bitch," he soliloquized in amazement at the reaction. He lit the cigar. With a shrug he joined his men; she would get over it. Perhaps he would stay away from the house for a couple of days and let her cool down. He didn't see how anyone could stay angry over something that foolish. Besides, it was a useful and necessary talisman, to discourage the wanton murdering of the Americans.

In spite of her anger, or revulsion, Gretchen had no intention of letting Hawk sleep outside. She sent Rolf to get him when the night came. She made no appearance that evening but did check with Rolf to make sure that he had performed his duty. Hawk spent the night in a large easy chair, on the veranda that opened off of the den.

He sat up most of the night, taking his liberties with Rudiger's gin supply and watching the apricot glow of a tropical crescent moon rise over the treetops. The beautiful scene belied the danger that lay out there. Hawk sighed deeply and was about to permit himself to drop off to sleep when he heard footsteps near the house.

From his vantage point on the screened and shuttered porch, he could see Brock, oblivious of being watched. The boy sneaked up to the moat, crossed it and then tried to peer into the front window. Reflexively, but groggily, Hawk reached to his side for his submachine gun.

It wasn't there; he had left it in another room for once. If it had been, he would have killed Brock. Instead he slumped back in the chair and just watched until Brock recrossed the moat and disappeared around the corner of the house. Hawk gave another drunken sigh. It looked innocuous enough, but he would make a point of letting Brock know that he had been the victim of an omniscient observer. Hawk dropped off into a fitful few hours' sleep. The incident was mixed and forgotten with his drunken dreams.

The next morning, the entire Dutch party was gathered around the breakfast table and nearly finished with the meal before Hawk shuffled wearily into the room. Rudiger could not restrain a sneer. Moritz could barely restrain a laugh. It was obvious that the sergeant had not completely slept off the effects of his hard night's drinking. Gretchen felt sorry for him, but she had not forgiven him as of yet for his rank sadism.

"Are you feeling well, Sergeant Hawk," Trudchen asked solicitously.

"Oh, good enough." The answer came back from deep within his throat.

"Perhaps protecting the house has become too onerous a duty for you," postulated Rudiger. "Perhaps you should remain in the barn where you belong from now on." Rudiger took full advantage of Gretchen's temporary disinterest in the man. Hawk only stared at him, studying him in such a way that made even Rudiger uneasy. Van Speer had heaped more abuse upon Hawk than any man and lived to tell of it. But at last, Hawk's patience was wearing thin. He slowly raised his hand and pointed his index finger at Rudiger's broad face. Moritz set down his fork and slid out his chair slightly.

"You know..." Hawk jammed his finger closer to the man's face and tried to collect his thoughts, but Gretchen intervened.

"James, I would like a word with you, outside." Hawk looked up at her and nodded weakly. He followed her out the back kitchen door.

"And keep the dog out there," Rudiger called after them.

They walked, virtually in total silence, down to the

cove where the sailboats were moored. Gretchen stepped aboard her boat and he followed. She sat on one side of it and he sat across from her. She looked out toward the reef for a long while. He stared at the deck mutely.

"I'm...uh, sorry about yesterday," he finally said, the deep voice cutting through the windy gale that blew along the beach. "I didn't know that...I mean, I guess I should have known..." He made a confused gesture and fell silent again.

"It's all right. It's war and you were doing...what you do, I suppose. I'll be glad when it's over, that's all."

"Yeah, it oughta be winding down here pretty quick. I don't know what the holdup is." He jumped at the chance to change the subject.

"Do you like the war, the fighting?"

"No, of course not. But I'm good at it." He spoke matter-of-factly. "If they want killin', they're messin' with the right outfit. I was pretty mad about those three boys I lost. I don't like that sneaky business."

"Oh, it's all so disgusting." She folded her arms around her knees and let her head fall back lightly against the gunwale. "I'm afraid for you and for my family. I'm afraid for myself, too; I feel so powerless, in the middle of all of this brutality. I've been spoiled, I suppose. I've always been given my way. I fight with a sharp tongue." She laughed and he smiled, his warm, deceptively tender smile. "Yes, this.is real fighting, that I can neither take part in nor run away from." Her voice was far away.

"Well, it's no place for you. But I won't go talking against your...father. You know how we don't get along. I'd like to take you some place safer, before things get really rough. He doesn't understand how bad it can get. He's gonna think hell opened up and fell on him if those Japs hit the plantation."

"Yes, I suppose we are in a precarious position," she said, in an uninterested tone. "But you will take care of us, won't you?" For the first time she looked at him and smiled.

"Goddam right," he answered with only half a smile.

"Then what have we to fear? No one in the world could take better care of us." She smiled again. He nodded his head in immodest agreement. He didn't know for certain if her words were entirely correct but he knew that he would entrust her care to no one but himself. If he were not the most capable, he was close enough to it—a head taller than the other men in his world, as Rudiger had phrased it.

Gretchen stood quickly and bounced lithely up onto the gunwale, stretching her youthful form.

"Do you want to go sailing to the western shore?" she asked, her face bright with exuberance. Hawk hesitated before he answered. He knew that he shouldn't.

"Just say when."

"Now. I'll run and get a lunch and some blankets."

"Okay," he answered slowly, and she was off like some bounding veldt doe. "Hey, bring my gun, would-ja?" he called after her. She turned and made an unresponsive grimace and was off again. His head fell back against the gunwales with a hard thud. Though the day was warm, the wind was cool on his fevered face. He sighed deeply.

Love and war could not be mixed, he thought. His alcohol-addled brain hovered lazily around that thought. War was a savage and rampant monster that could not be corralled, not even by James Hawk, not even for love. He closed his eyes. Beckwith could handle the men for another day. He dozed off.

The deck of the boat shifted as Gretchen boarded it. She had planned on startling him, but one of his eyes opened as she crawled across the deck. They gazed at each other for a moment and then burst out laughing.

He reached out and pulled her over to him. She put her arms around his neck. He stopped her laughing with a kiss.

"Well," she whispered when it over, "I suppose we should be setting sail."

"I suppose," he answered, imitating her accent. She laughed again and jumped to her feet. She reached down and tried to pull him up also, but that was no easy matter. It was another hour before they were sailing the winding course to the western shore.

The wind made delicate ripples on the still water between the reef and the shore. The emerald tree line and flower-strewn white sands rocked gently with the intermittent gusts. After dark, there beside the waterfall, at the mouth of the lagoon, the first stars became visible. The sky was still blue, though a dark blue, and the celestial display was dazzling. Never had Hawk seen larger or brighter stars, not even in the pristine piney woods of Mississippi. The alien southern sky with its new constellations made him feel as if he had left the earth and was viewing the universe from a different perspective.

They remained there until the golden quarter-moon set, huge and luminous on the horizon, paving a gilded pathway over the waves. The outline of the unlighted portion of the lunar sphere was visible, glowing faintly against the dark blue background of the sky. The night was melting gradually into a hazy dawn when they again set sail and departed from the western shore. Mooring the boat in the cove, they ascended the rocky path to the plantation.

"I think I might stay away from Mr. Van Speer for a day or so," said Hawk, stopping at the back kitchen door.

"I think that's a good idea," Gretchen answered with a smile. "I wish that I could do the same." He winked at her and turned away, walking toward the barn. She stood watching him until he disappeared inside it.

9

THE SIEGE

"Where in the hell you been?" Joe Canlon called down to Hawk from the loft.

"None of your goddam business. Anything going on around this dump?"

"Well, nobody got killed last night. I guess that's something new," Canlon informed him. "Things been real quiet." Ewell and Lundstedt came in and threw themselves down.

"Hey, Sarge, when are we pullin' outa here?" Lundstedt demanded curtly. Hawk flung himself down beside them.

"Hell, I don't know. You think they forgot about us?" Hawk fired up a torn cigar butt.

"Shit, I believe so," Lundstedt said. "We oughta do something, head back or something."

"We can't do that with Japs picking off people right and left," said Hawk. "We gotta stay here till they come and get us. I just wish they'd do it before there's any more trouble."

But as the men spoke, trouble was walking out of

the dense tropical rain forest. The tall, lean figure strolled at a leisurely pace, up to the central foxhole. There he asked for his platoon sergeant's whereabouts, then turned his unhurried footsteps toward the barn. Everyone looked up when Pogue Gist stepped through the wide door. He nodded a greeting and sat down beside Hawk.

"Well, they're comin'," Gist drawled.

"Well, goddam, it's about time!" Ewell cheered. But Hawk was watching the scout's hard-boned face.

"How many?" Hawk asked.

"I don't know exactly. They're in different bunches. Quite a few, though. You got an hour if they're headin' this way on purpose, but I ain't really sure of that either. They're just kinda wandering around."

"Don't they have the shittin' map?" Ewell asked.

"Japs, Ewell—he's talking about Japs," Lundstedt explained.

"Oh shit!" Ewell exclaimed in alarm.

"Yeah, and they're gonna give us hell," Gist predicted.

Hawk stood up and paced slowly back and forth for a few seconds while the men continued talking.

"Well there ain't no sense in trying to hold them foxholes," he finally said, overriding the chattering of Ewell. The other three looked up at him. Canlon joined them, standing beside Hawk.

"What *are* we gonna hold?" Ewell asked.

"The house. We can shore it up, make a fort out of it." Then turning to Gist, Hawk asked, "How were they equipped?"

"Aw, not too good. Most of 'em was wearing them diapers they wear. No machine guns or mortars. They was just leftovers, I guess. They had rifles and grenades, though, that's for damn sure." Gist spat tobacco onto the earthen floor. "They're gonna give us hell," he repeated and shook his head to emphasize it.

"Did they see you?" Canlon asked in his dumb voice.

"Naw. Almost did, though. There's different bunches of 'em roamin' around, joining together. Everywhere I went I'd run into a new pack of the son of a bitches. Good thing they're deaf and blind."

"All right, Ewell," ordered Hawk. "Get some guys and take some of them empty drums and fill 'em up with rock and coral—like the Nips do. They'll make good cover. I don't think we oughta hold those foxholes, do y'all?" Hawk was not above seeking other opinions, even when convinced that he was right.

"No, they'll grenade us too easy in them bastards," Gist said.

"No," Canlon added. "From the house we got all that open ground between us and the jungle. We can cut down a whole shit load of 'em crossing that stretch. We're too goddam close to 'em in those holes."

"We can't just all get in the house, either, though," said Lundstedt.

"Yeah, yeah, I know," said Hawk impatiently. "Let's push down that radio shack so the foxhole back there has a clear shot at the back of the house. That's where we need some good cover fire. We'll get that thirty-caliber machine gun back there with Armistead, and Gist can cover him. Mayeaux and Beckwith can cover the sides. I'll cover the front."

"We probably need that machine gun up front, don't you think?" Canlon suggested.

"Yeah, I guess, till we see what's going on. Get that

English machine gun in the back then. We don't have much ammo for it but we may not need any back there. You can have that Sten gun if you want, Joe, but there ain't many shells for it either." Quiroz was sent out into the forest to watch for the approaching enemy.

Rudiger was outraged at the herd of marines trooping through his home, throwing valuable antiques here and there, piling them up to hide behind. They did afford him the courtesy of removing his bamboo screens, rather than ripping them down. The final act that totally unglued him, however, was the rolling of ponderous oil drums, filled with rock, across his expensively carpeted and finished floors. They were arranged in front of the windows and a few were scattered in front of the moat as a first line of defense. The moat itself, a product of old Dutch custom, was a formidable defense, being ten feet across and about four feet deep.

When the clouds of dust had settled, both inside and outside of the house, the forest was just as quiet as ever it had been. The marines stood expectantly at their posts. Their adversaries made no appearance. Quiroz had not returned from his lookout post by dusk, and by then the flow of adrenalin had subsided. Just at dark, the lone, slight figure walked out of the forest.

"Quiroz?" Hawk shouted, training his weapon upon the silhouette.

"Yes, Sergeant Hawk, it's me. I didn't see anything."

When Van Speer heard this, he became a bit unmanageable, and Hawk had Armistead escort him to the cellar. His wife and two daughters were also sent down with him. Ernst, Klaus, Rolf and Moritz went with Gaedcke over to the quarters of the hired hands. They reinforced this little two-room barrack, and the Dutch were given Enfield rifles. These quarters were a little behind the farmhouse and off to one side, so if the Dutch proved to be less than proficient fighters, the rear machine gun and the plantation house could cover them. Gaedcke was put in charge of them, but in this position he felt more like a noncombatant than a commander. The entire makeshift defenses would have to fall before the Japanese could get at him or his contingent. They were instructed to stay put, no matter what happened. Rudiger was given the same order, for the Bren machine gun had to fire directly over the cellar.

Hawk and Canlon went out to the veranda and leaned over the oil drum defenses that had been erected there. Joe rubbed his nose vigorously.

"Looks like all this might put a crimp in your social life," Joe said after a while.

"Damn sure might," said Hawk, his eyes roving back and forth across the wall of motionless vegetation.

"Things with you and the girl went pretty good, didn't they?"

"Yeah. It surprised the hell out of me. Nothing like that has ever gone right for me before. I must be getting ready to get blown to hell."

"I don't think your in-laws are gonna be too crazy about you, though." Joe gave a short laugh. "You talked about getting married to her yet?"

"Not in so many words; you know how it is. The old man hates my guts all right. I ain't fond of him, but shit, I don't hate him as much as he hates me."

"I wouldn't pay that son of bitch any mind," said Joe. "He'll get used to the idea. They always do." Hawk nodded, somewhat unsure of that assessment.

The men slept at their posts that night. Hawk did not see Gretchen again until the next morning and then only for a few minutes. She looked worried and he tried to console her. The poorly equipped Japanese and the well-fortified farmhouse were consoling factors to a marine veteran but of little solace to Gretchen Van Speer. There would be shooting and killing; no one denied it and everyone was resigned to it.

The morning was unusually cloudy, the ground fog lingering until almost midday. It seemed that there was to be a bit of rain, but it never developed. The black clouds and hovering mist distorted the rays of the sun, softening them against the background of the forest and creating an eerie jade lighting. The earth was awaiting a storm, just as the men within the house awaited a life-and-death struggle; but neither came. The day dragged on interminably, into a pitch-dark night. Hawk saw Gretchen again, briefly after the sun had set. She was quite distraught about the situation, it seemed, though she never complained in any specific words.

The pending battle did not unnerve Hawk as much as did seeing Gretchen this way. He could deal efficiently with the enemy, but fear was something with which he coped poorly. It was an impossible factor in his life. He denied its existence within himself, refusing to indulge the emotion. In direct contradiction to his inner conviction. He openly admitted to being afraid under harrowing circumstances. This was due to his dislike of false bravado. In the back of his mind he knew that he wasn't afraid, no matter how often he might confess to being scared. He was not above being extremely cautious, but he was above being afraid. Perhaps he overtly acknowledged his fear, while secretly denying it, in order to lessen the dependence and the expectations of his comrades.

The Marine Corps mystique made it easy to deal with fear among the men. They either denied its existence or staunchly purported to be able to handle it. They overcame it and fought anyway. They expected as much from their fellow men at arms.

But with Gretchen, fear was permissible. She did not have to deny it, nor did she have to invent convolutions of reason and emotion to deal with it. She unabashedly felt it. For Hawk, this was an alien and difficult-to-handle position. He could not tell her to act like a marine. This admission of fear made him uneasy, though he tried to be comforting. He may well have thought fear a contagious thing, and that was what made him uneasy. He didn't want to think about it, he wanted to deal with situations, not with thoughts. Concrete reality was much less intimidating.

And yet he was forced to think about it. He wanted to say or do something that would make her unafraid, but he could not. He could not discover what it was within himself that gave him courage, he could not pass it on. He only hoped that it, too, was contagious. All that he could do would be to rely upon his unexplained resources of bravery, and ask her to do the same.

* * *

"HERE THEY COME!"

Hawk's head jerked in sudden surprise. He had not realized that he had been asleep, that his rambling thoughts had merged into fitful dreams. His hand was asleep and stinging, entangled in the trigger guard of his submachine gun. He heard Canlon's deep-throated warning but it took a moment for him to focus his eyes upon the distant forest. He was weary; he knew that he needed more sleep. Adrenalin would have to serve as a substitute.

Crouching, almost squatting in a cautiously slow advance were half a dozen, nearly fourteen naked Japanese warriors. The farm may have looked deserted to them in the early morning light. For a moment the men felt the thrill of excitement that always followed the sighting of your enemy: alien men in an approaching group, bent on killing you. Civilization, human reason, these were dead commodities now, as two packs of vicious animals faced each other. Hawk opened his mouth to speak, but no words came out. It seemed that his voice was still asleep. Angrily he cleared his throat.

"Hold your fire!" he ordered. His jaw muscles twitched in anticipation. Another handful of the enemy came crouching out of the protective forest. Two skirmish lines were approaching the house, one behind the other. Hawk hoped that Armistead and Gaedcke were awake, but he made no move to awaken them: the first shots would take care of that. The misty morning, a duplicate of the previous morning, was pierced only by the shrill calls of exuberant birds arising after a good night's sleep: Those calls would end soon, and the callers would retreat deep into the jungle before speaking again, or partaking in gay acrobatics.

"Okay," said Hawk calmly. "Left to right, get your man." Still the enemy proceeded forward, unaware that their observers were each picking one of them out for slaughter.

"Nothing over here," Mayeaux called out from the far side of the house.

"Then get that M-3 in here," Hawk said. "Ewell, get over on that side and let us know when it gets too hot to handle." There was no emotion in Hawk's voice, nor in his expression, but large drops of perspiration tumbled from beneath his helmet and ran down to the tip of his straight, narrow nose.

"Eleven of 'em," Canlon mumbled. The Japanese were half way across the open field and Hawk still gave no order to fire.

"Yeah but the woods are full of 'em. Or at least they will be," Hawk answered. "They oughta see us by now," he added.

"They're all blind," Canlon whispered, his voice almost completely choked with emotion.

From their position on the veranda, Hawk and Canlon were thrust out a bit from the rest of the house, so that they could see the other men in profile. They were also unprotected by the moat, because the porch extended out over it. The front of the house only contained two rooms, three if one were to include the partitioned-off dining room as a separate entity from the living room: the den, from which the veranda extended; the living room, containing one window and the front door; and the dining room, which had a double window. Quiroz guarded the living room window, Mayeaux and Lundstedt were at the door and Brock and Gist were together at the double windows. Beyond the moat and behind several barrels, Fine was in front of Quiroz. Claiborne was in front of Brock, behind identical fortifications. Find had been stretched out sleeping on the ground behind his barrels, and his awakening started the fireworks. It was best that it did, for it appeared that Hawk intended to let the enemy walk right into the house.

"Stay down!" Canlon called to Fine when the other sat up and stretched. But his warning had been a bit too loud.

The Japanese ceased their stiff-legged advance. They froze in unison. Hawk would not give them a chance to gather their wits.

"Fire!" It was a loud, raucous scream that was almost as terrifying as the barrage that followed the command. The range was quite deadly for the marine sharp-shooters and several of the half-naked forms dropped beside their comrades in the deafening roar of gunfire. Hawk had held his fire, in order to clear up the leftovers that the first volley might miss. It hadn't missed much, however; the selective process of fate had preserved only five of the enemy. Four of these turned and ran unashamedly for the forest. One raised his rifle to fire at the front door. Hawk fired at him, but so did half a dozen other marines. His riddled body hit the ground and continued to shudder under the impact of each additional unnecessary shot that it absorbed. One of the men sprinting for the jungle made it. Hawk fiercely poured a stream of bullets at the others but the range was against his Thompson. Gist brought down one more, just at the forest's edge. The other two made it to the forest in a hail of lead. The scene fell quiet.

"That was damn good," Canlon observed.

"Ah shit, we shoulda got 'em all," Hawk replied in disgust. "We didn't let 'em get close enough."

"They were close enough to suit my ass," Canlon

said, rocking back his helmet and wiping his brow. He stood up straight.

"You're making a pretty good target there, Joe," Hawk reminded him. Then raising his voice: "Keep down! They can pick you off from here, you know." Mayeaux and Lundstedt closed their door until just a crack of light showed through it. In contrast to such caution, Brock sat up on the window sill, in full view. With great delight he surveyed the dead Japanese. He would have liked to have got a better view of them.

"Not a bad job, don't you think?" Gist asked Hawk when the latter sauntered into the dining room.

"We got about one apiece—that ain't good for havin' the drop on 'em," judged Hawk. "I don't think I even got one. The one I know I hit, everybody else hit, too." Hawk laughed shortly. Brock laughed with him. Hawk knew that he must be laughing at the wrong thing if Brock found it humorous.

"I believe I got a couple of 'em," said Gist.

"Yeah, we'll do better next time," Hawk speculated. "We'll have to. They'll come from all sides. They're out there cookin' up all kinds of shit to pull on us." Hawk stuck his head out of the window. "How'd it go out there?" Claiborne only shrugged.

"It's a little dangerous out here," Fine answered.

"Y'all wanta come inside?" Hawk asked. Again Claiborne shrugged.

"We'll try it a little longer," Fine said. "I hope they don't get that close next time." There was a sharp crack that sounded at the edge of the jungle. A second later there was an explosion on the white wall of the house, about a foot from Hawk's helmet. A little round, black hole was left in the adobe by the shot. Hawk snapped his head back inside.

"Son of a bitch!" he exclaimed.

"They don't go for all that jawin'." Gist smiled and spat a. stream of tobacco juice through the window. Hawk smiled, too,· and returned to his post. He sent Canlon to check on Gaedcke and Armistead. Both were doing well; neither had fired a shot yet. Hawk put the thirty-caliber machine gun at the window held by Quiroz, letting Quiroz and Lundstedt worry about who was to operate it. During the next hour, less than a dozen shots peppered the exterior of the house, usually near the windows.

Once satisfied that that was all that the Japanese intended to do for the present, Hawk ran and crawled out to the cellar. He pounded on the door, waving at Armistead while he awaited its opening. Trudchen opened the door and Hawk climbed down into the damp, cramped hole. All eyes were upon him.

"Perhaps you should surrender, James," Gretchen suggested.

"They'd mow us down quicker'n shit," he said, shaking his head. "They don't take prisoners. These are a crazy-lookin' bunch, anyway. They probably been blasted all the way across the island and are feelin' pretty mean."

"I should like to take my family and surrender," Rudiger said, in his most obnoxious tone.

"Can't let you do that," said Hawk, staring at the floor.

"I will do it anyway," said Van Speer, defiantly. Hawk looked up at him and a dark cloud came across his brow.

"I'll knock you on your fat ass, too," he replied.

"I won't leave here, Father," Gretchen jumped in. Rudiger turned toward the wall, exasperated. Had he been given to profanity, he might well have indulged himself. Hawk had wanted to speak with Gretchen for a few minutes, but after the confrontation with Rudiger, he only wanted to beat a swift retreat. He climbed back up the ladder to the door. He looked down at Rudiger before crawling out on the ground.

"If you stick your ass out this hatch, I'll blow your guts out, Van Speer." Rudiger turned away. Gretchen glared at Hawk. She didn't appreciate the remark very much. Hawk only shrugged and shut the door. As he knelt there, he heard a crack from the jungle. Before he could react, a spout of dust erupted from the earth, inches from his knee.

"Goddam," he cursed, then spun around and ran for the kitchen door. He heard another shot, but he never knew where it landed. Ewell was answering the fire from the jungle when Hawk entered the house.

"They plan on just sniping us, I guess," Hawk told him.

"Looks that way for now," Ewell replied, drawing a bead at a spot where he had seen a muzzle flash. He squeezed the trigger of his M-l. The shot seemed to have hit a tree. Hawk slapped his back and returned to the veranda. Canlon was also sighting in the distant jungle.

"They keep that shit up long enough, I'm going to nail me one," Joe muttered. He squeezed the trigger and his rifle recoiled. Hawk's keen ears could hear the shot slashing through the trees.

"Save your ammo," Hawk snorted. "You'll need it tonight. They go for that night-attack dogshit."

But they didn't have to wait quite that long. The apparently random sniping was really a well-calculated attempt to estimate the number of defenders within the house, and to pinpoint their approximate locations. The attackers knew that the front was strongly manned—the evidence of that fact lay sprawled in the open field. They knew that Ewell was on one of the narrow sides and that he was watching them fairly close. They knew that Beckwith was on the other narrow side with a powerful and accurate BAR. Ewell was in the kitchen and Beckwith was stationed in Rudiger's bedroom behind the den. But the attackers had seen no sign of life from the rear. Armistead had not wasted any of his precious Bren machine-gun rounds playing tag with snipers. Consequently, they didn't even know that he was back there. They chose the rear for their next assault.

Armistead, fortunately, heard the bare feet pounding on the sand of the path that led down to the cove. His machine gun was aimed at the rear of the house, so he picked it up and moved it to the opposite side of his foxhole. It was a light weapon, with a curved banana clip jutting from its topside; it rested on a bipod. He wanted to benefit from the element of surprise, but he wanted help, too. He could not have both.

"Japs in the back! Japs in the back!" he screamed. He knew that his clip could not withstand a prolonged attack and he also feared getting a grenade tossed on him from the side. Ewell first appeared at the back kitchen door. Eyes and mouth wide open, he thought he saw movement down by the path.

"Cover me!" he called to Armistead, who sat up, ready to riddle the first man who appeared. Ewell drove off the back steps, ran madly to the foxhole and straight into it without even trying to cushion his fall. Hawk appeared at the back door a second later.

"Stay down. I'll tell you when," he called to the two men. "Brock, get back here." Brock went into Gretchen's bedroom and knocked down the shutters. The noise blocked out the sound of a small object whirling through the air, but Hawk saw the grenade thud onto the ground between the foxhole and the house.

"Duck!" He stepped back inside the door and saw the shower of black and white dust and smoke through a crack. Gravel and shrapnel splattered violently on the other side of the door, but almost as soon as it did, Hawk flung the door open and held back the trigger of his submachine gun. He fired blindly into the cloud, expecting an attack on the heels of the grenade explosion. As the opaque fogbank became translucent, it was obvious that no attack had followed. The Bren fired a short burst, Brock fired two rounds, but Hawk could distinguish no targets amidst the flowery vegetation where the path met the cleared ground that surrounded the house.

Then, with astonishing swiftness, the enemy struck. The choking vegetation disgorged what looked like a ubiquitous horde of madmen, running bandy-legged and howling like banshees. Some wore uniforms, some wore loincloths that nearly dragged the ground. The sudden appearance and clamorous outburst came close to paralyzing the four observers. What looked, and more importantly, what felt like a full division of attackers was perhaps a dozen and a half at most.

Hawk's reflexes were the first to react. A handful of the enemy had carried their stiff-jointed dash to within thirty feet of Armistead, but he and Ewell only seemed to be sitting there, enchanted by the oncoming spectacle. The lethal staccato report of the Thompson sent a fiery chain over the heads of the two marines and crashing into the charging front line of their foes. One flew backwards, tripping the men behind him and splattering them with flesh and blood torn from his body by the rending .45 slugs. The legs of a second man flew limply from beneath him, causing him to fall forward onto the hard earth.

The check of the onslaught galvanized Armistead into action. He maneuvered the conical muzzle back and forth at the charging line, never stopping to check any specific target. Ewell squeezed off an entire clip and was replacing it with a new one. Brock's rifle was sending round after round into the decimated ranks. A grenade bounded off of the house near Brock's window and plunked into the moat. It discharged a moment later, temporarily deafening Brock and covering Hawk with mud. Hawk had stepped out onto the kitchen steps, in full view and whirled his machine pistol wherever it was needed, as a fireman wields his hose. He could hear the rifle bullets spewing off of the adobe wall behind him. He knew that more of the enemy were therefore probably covering the charge from the jungle. He brazenly remained there, intentionally drawing their fire to himself while the others picked them off.

The ground was strewn with the writhing Japanese. Many were within inches of the foxhole occupied by Armistead and Ewell. The mad rush had been halted from around the foxhole and from the corner of the house occupied by Hawk. But down the moat, Hawk saw three or four of the enemy wading across the little ditch, headed for a window situated in the opposite rear corner of the house. The room was occupied by Beckwith, but it appeared as if he was not looking out on the back. Hawk did not know, nor could he ascertain in the pandemonium, whether the house was under a full attack. He had to assume that it was. He ran back inside and down the hall between the bedrooms of Gretchen and Moritz, into Rudiger's bedroom. Beckwith was standing at a side window, watching the jungle.

"Get outa here," Hawk ordered. A second later, they heard the thump of a heavy metal object upon the floor. It was probably a pipe bomb, for when it went off, the wall cracked and the entire door jamb was blown out. Hawk could see the three Japanese clambering up the blown-away portion of the wall, where the window had been. The swirling dust and the dark interior hid him from their myopic view. As they pulled themselves up into the house, he rolled a primed grenade across the floor at them. The blast knocked all three back out into the moat, only shredded remnants of human beings.

"Thanks," Beckwith gasped. "That was close."

"We're gonna have to do something about this," said Hawk, surveying the gutted room. Only a jagged knee-high wall was left of what had been the outer wall. The joists and studs were severed, causing the roof to dangle precariously over the room. The inner walls were still intact, but the door jamb was gone, and there were several deep splits in the adobe.

The attack was over, its fury spent. The wounded Japanese moaned and twisted all across the open space between the forest and the foxhole. A soldier dashed from the jungle, latched on to a wounded man and dragged him back under cover. Hawk watched coldly, lifting a cigar up to his mouth. He made no attempt to kill the rescuer. Possibly he thought that the range was too great for his weapon.

No other attacks followed that day. The wailing and groaning of the wounded increased as the day wore on. Hawk ordered Gist and Brock to put the wounded out of their misery, and they did so with a passion. After each slug rammed into a disabled man's body, loud jeers went up from the jungle, followed by shrill, maniacal screams. Hawk watched the drama from the kitchen door. Canlon came up behind him. He watched for a moment as Brock picked off another wounded man from his post at the window. The top of his head was blown asunder and the men in the jungle set up a horrid din.

"I don't think we're makin' too many friends that way," Canlon said nervously.

"Who gives a goddam," Hawk growled.

"If I had a girl out there, between me and that foxhole, I'd care. If I was sittin' out in that hole with Armistead and Ewell, I'd care. There ain't no guarantee we're gonna win this one, you know." Canlon was quite agitated.

"Forget it," Hawk said grimly. "They're gonna treat us the way they always do, regardless of what we do. My advice is make sure we win this one."

"That yellin' sure makes a man want to win. I bet they'd eat us alive." Canlon exhaled harshly.

"Yeah." Hawk gave a short laugh and turned back to watch the forest.

"You're a mean son of a bitch, Hawk," said Canlon. "This time you might have to pay for it."

"Maybe," Hawk answered simply. Canlon turned to walk away.

"Joe." Hawk stopped him. "Listen, I don't like this either. It's just the way things are. You know that. They're too damn sneaky to even let 'em haul off the wounded."

Canlon was not swayed. "Yeah, maybe," he said, and returned to his post on the veranda. Hawk shrugged and turned back to the forest.

"You'll learn, Joe," he whispered. Brock's rifle snapped. He heard Gist and the boy chuckle. "Gist, Brock," Hawk called; his weary voice was cracked. "Cut that shit out." Gist lowered his rifle and leaned on it, but Brock continued to aim.

"Brock, knock it off," Hawk said, a little more sternly. Brock lowered his rifle.

"What's the matter, gettin' soft?" Gist asked. Hawk didn't answer at first.

"Maybe," he finally said. "Maybe I am."

Hawk anticipated a night attack. He was now uneasy about having Gretchen out in the cellar, between him and the Japanese. He called Beckwith and Mayeaux together to discuss the matter. Mayeaux thought it would be best to bring them into the house.

"I don't know. Did you see what that bangalore torpedo did to the back room?" Beckwith asked Mayeaux. The other nodded pensively.

"If they'd just lay off the back it'd be all right out there," said Hawk. "It's safe from grenades and all that shit."

"Face it," said Mayeaux. "Nothing around here is safe. We're surrounded by Japs. I think it's safer in the house. If they get Armistead, that cellar is in Jap territory."

That comment sounded ominous to Hawk. He realized that it was true. That situation must be remedied, he thought. We must make it our territory.

After dark, a blue and white flash exploded in front of the foxhole containing Ewell and Armistead. Hawk and Brock saw their silhouettes flinch and submerge into the trench. Hawk fired a burst into the forest to let the enemy know that the grenade had not gone unanswered. He needed flares, but he had none. If the Japanese could get a few more feet on their throwing range, Armistead and Ewell were dead men.

Hawk paced up and down the dark kitchen. The Van Speers had to come out of that shelter, and the two marines had to come out of that hole.

A piercing scream came from the jungle. "Marine—you die!"

Hawk walked back to the kitchen door. We'll see who dies, he thought.

"Roosevelt is sonny bitch!"

"Must be Republicans." The voice belonged to Canlon. He had come up behind Hawk. Hawk removed his helmet and laid his head back on the bullet pocked door jamb.

"What am I gonna do, Joe?" Hawk breathed. "I don't know what to do. If I could just get everybody outa here, I'd be glad to stay by myself. There ain't no neat way to do this. A bunch of us are gonna get killed." He replaced his helmet. "Everywhere I go, a bunch of us get killed." Another blue and white flash ripped the night, fortunately even farther off target. That did not console the leader of the marine contingent.

"Hell," I don't know," Canlon answered. "I'm...sorry about....gettin' on you, you know, about shootin' them Japs. I guess you was right. All their carrying on scares me, though. I don't want them bastards gettin' ahold of me."

"Ah, they're full of shit," Hawk sneered. "I might do a little infiltratin' myself. I'd kinda like to discourage 'em from hittin' this back side again. Since they done blew the shit outa one room, they might be planning on hitting it again."

"You'd have to be fallin' down crazy to go out there, Hawk," Joe said with surprise. "No telling where they are or what they're doing out there. Don't do that."

"Shit on 'em," said Hawk, as if that settled the matter. He went to the back room and rubbed ashes on his hands and then on his face. He took two grenades from Beckwith and returned to the kitchen, where Canlon still stood.

"If you get killed, that gets you off the hook," said Canlon. "Just remember, we're still stuck here and so is the girl. You'd come in handy when the shootin' starts, a lot more handy than committing suicide out in the dark for no reason."

"Ain't nobody gonna kill me," Hawk answered, and stepped out onto the back steps. He paused there for a moment and then strode out toward the barn, as if he were out for his Sunday constitutional.

Hawk knew that the area behind the house had few trees, and that the few that did grow there would not support a man. All of the enemy soldiers that the thicket concealed had to be on the ground. Hawk remained out there all night, crawling upon his face and belly, one inch at a time. His body was so tense that it barely touched the ground, and he moved so slowly that it seemed that he was in truth a part of the forest. If he found more than a single soldier hiding in the bush, he would give them a wide berth. At the darkest point in the night, just before dawn, he returned to the house.

Canlon jumped back in shocked horror when the specter of the destroying angel appeared at his elbow. Joe dropped his rifle and fell back through the kitchen door. Hawk stepped into the house and picked the rifle up for him.

"Good thing I ain't a Jap," Hawk told him. Joe was at a loss for words. Hawk's clothes were covered with dirt, his hands and arms with blood. "Go get Gist, Brock, Mayeaux and Beckwith," Hawk ordered. Canlon returned with the men shortly. Hawk lit a cigar before he spoke.

"I killed a bunch of 'em. There's still, a bunch out there, though. Most are gathered around in a camp about thirty yards down the path, right in the middle of it. They were scattered all the way down to the cove and all along the edge of the weeds facing the house. If we hit that camp now, I think that'll clean out the back. There's not enough trees for snipers, so they may stay away from out there if we give 'em a good beating. I got a few minutes here before daylight. I'm gonna put a grenade right in the middle of that camp. When y'all hear it, come running straight down the path. There won't be nothing in your way. By then it'll be getting light and we can beat the bushes for any that get away. If any of you don't want to go, say so." No one demurred. Hawk nodded and snuffed out his cigar. He turned and slipped out the back door.

The five men clustered around the back door,

waiting for the sound of the grenade. Half an hour went by and dawn began firming up the hazy outlines of the forest.

Hawk dragged himself by his fingertips along the floor of the thicket, in the direction of the jabbering men encamped in the pathway. He passed two corpses that he had left there earlier and then stopped a few feet from the camp. There were two roughly shaped circles of half-clothed men. Slowly his hand went down for a grenade. He slid out the pin and let the safety lever spring free. He held it and the forest seemed to hold its breath. He raised himself up on one arm and threw it among the men. It bounced off of the back of one of them and onto the ground.

The sharp blast was heard at the house and out galloped the marines with reckless abandon. They heard the stuttering of Hawk's submachine gun as they ran down the path. Beckwith was in the lead and he ran headlong into a fleeing Japanese soldier. The smaller man fell down and Beckwith sprayed him mercilessly with his BAR. The bushes were alive with the sound of thrashing, terrified Japanese. Brock saw a shadow in the tangled vines and creepers and burst into the trackless vegetation to chase it. His rifle snapped repeatedly and he continued to bulldoze his way through the brush.

Another grenade exploded, only a few feet ahead of the men on the trail. Gist took the lead and charged at the sound.

He was the first to see the remains of the camp. A dozen maimed men were crawling about, groaning and squealing. Three or four corpses lay about like rag dolls. Hawk was standing in the weeds on one side of the path, changing a clip. He pointed across the path, urgently.

"Look out, Gist!" he yelled. Instinctively Gist ducked and faced that direction. He saw three enraged warriors swivel their muzzles from Hawk to him. One barked and then another. Gist threw himself into the thorny verdure in a desperate effort to preserve his life. He heard another shot explode right over his head, and then came the rabid coughing of Mayeaux's M-3. Beckwith ran up behind Mayeaux and between the two of them, they cut down the three Japanese. Brock ran past them and down toward the cove. Beckwith and Mayeaux looked frantically to the right and left. Seeing no enemy soldiers that were not sufficiently disabled, they followed Brock. Hawk stepped over a Japanese crawling blindly upon his hands and knees. He gave Gist his hand and helped him to his feet.

"Thanks, Pogue. If you'd come any later, I'd be dead meat."

"If I'd come any sooner, I'd be dead meat," Gist answered, looking himself over in disbelief, for he was unscathed. He kicked a crawling Japanese in the face. The blow silenced the wounded man's plaintive wails. Hawk turned to the horrid scene and began dispatching the enemy with methodical efficiency. Before he completed the labor, Gist had regained enough composure to help him in the task. The gunfire from the three marines who had gone down toward the cove had never ceased. Hawk and Gist turned their sites in that direction.

Cautiously they proceeded down the path. When it broke through the vegetation, they saw the other three marines. They were chasing what appeared to be unarmed men, hither and yon, up and down the beach, executing them like mad dogs. A sound behind them made Gist and Hawk split up, to hide upon either side of the trail. Canlon, Ewell and Armistead strolled into view. Hawk stood up, startling Canlon.

"Go down there and tell them jokers to get back to the house," Hawk told Canlon. Joe scampered down the rocky trail, hailing the three men. Their task seemed to be complete and they started up the trail. Hawk noted that two sailboats had been sunk, but that Gretchen's had survived.

"That oughta hold them son of a bitches for a while," said Gist angrily.

"Yeah, it was a good job," said Hawk, almost on the verge of a smile. The dawn was breaking into a beautiful day. The men carefully retraced their steps to the farmhouse.

Hawk's first stop was the cellar. He called to Gretchen and told her to bring up Ilse. The other marines formed a semicircle around the door to the shelter. When Ilse and Gretchen were out, Hawk ran with them to the kitchen door.

Before they got there, a cacophony of shots erupted from the jungle behind the barn. The bullets whined and whistled through the marines standing guard over the cellar. Rudiger's head popped up in spite of the shots. He crawled out onto the ground and ran for the house. Gaedcke and the Dutchmen opened up on the forest. Trudchen came out of the shelter and the men covered her retreat. The entire party reached the safety of the kitchen unharmed.

All day, shots popped off the walls of the house. The men constructed barriers to cover the windows after a few of these shots came dancing through the interior. Hawk was quite pleased with his counterattack and remained at the back of the house most of the day, looking for any signs of Japanese attempts at recapturing the area that had been cleared out. He saw none, and after dark embarked upon another brazen sojourn into the rear area. He found the region deserted by the living. So confident was he of its vacancy that he walked boldly up the path and back to the house. Evidently, the enemy had not considered the territory defensible.

All night, shots and taunting screams were hurled from the distant jungle. The other three sides of the forest were not so close to the house as was the rear, however. Thus it was that the inhabitants of the makeshift fort felt comparatively safe as they grabbed a few hours of well-needed sleep.

Ilse cried most of the night. Rudiger walked her and carried her throughout the house, trying to calm her, but he could not. He finally gave up and turned her over to Gretchen, that she might try her hand at it. Ilse sensed that the grownups were afraid and had no control over their present predicament. She knew that her world was in turmoil and that anything could happen at any moment. Gretchen could not quiet her; only a return to normal life could accomplish that—or some sense of stability. Gretchen turned to Hawk.

He was seated in Rudiger's plushest easy chair, his feet propped up on an ottoman that was worth a small fortune, or at least had been. His arm was draped over a dusty end table as he looked out from the veranda toward the gloomy forest. Ilse fell silent when she entered the room with her sister. It was strangely placid in the room. Hawk was sprawled like some king in his parlor. His demeanor was relaxed, almost drowsy. The tension and panic that seized the rest of the world was not present here. Hawk's teeth shined in the dark at their entry.

"Ilse's not feeling well," Gretchen announced.

"Is that right? Well, we'll take care of that. Let old Doc Hawk have a look." He leaned forward. Ilse dropped Gretchen's hand of her own accord and walked to him. He lifted her up on his lap, pretending that she was heavy. "What hurts?" he asked. There was no response. "Does your head hurt? Does your stomach hurt?" The little girl shook her head crankily at both inquiries. "It can't be both, now. Which is it?" She shrugged. "I bet it's your nose, isn't it?" She agreed again. He reached up and pulled it. "Now, you don't have one. It stopped hurting, didn't it?" Ilse laughed and shook her head no. "Now don't lie to the Doc. He knows when you're lying." Hawk adjusted her in his lap, so that she could see the end table. He drew faces in the dust, telling her that the one without a nose was her. She laughed again. He looked at Gretchen. Gretchen looked desperately at the ceiling and started to back out of the room.

"I'll bet you haven't talked to Ralph in a while, have you?" Hawk asked Ilse.

"Ralph?" Ilse looked up expectantly. She liked Armistead. Hawk knew that the corporal's powers of entertainment far exceeded his own. "Where is Ralph?" Ilse asked.

"He's on his. way here, right now," said Hawk, aiming his voice at Gretchen, who was watching from the darkness in the living room. She disappeared to get Armistead.

A shot whined off of the wall of the veranda. Instead of flinching or screaming like the others, Sergeant Hawk laughed.

"That was close, wasn't it?" he said.

Ilse laughed. "That *was* close," she said.

"Can you draw, Ilse?" The girl said that she could. "Here, draw me a picture." She put her miniature finger into the dust.

"What will I draw?"

"Something easy," Hawk answered. Armistead entered the room. Hawk looked up at him and smiled. When he looked back down at the table, a swastika was drawn there.

"Isn't that pretty?" said Hawk. "What is it?"

"Hitler's sign," Ilse answered.

"Hitler is a bad man, isn't he?" Hawk asked.

"Mother said to never talk about him," Ilse answered.

"She sure told you right," said Hawk, casting a pleading glance at Armistead. The corporal laughed aloud and Ilse noticed him for the first time. Hawk helped her down and she ran to him.

At that moment, Rudiger appeared in the doorway.

"What are you thugs doing with my daughter?" he asked.

Lest the fragile mood of Ilse be broken, Hawk leapt to his feet and seized Rudiger's arm.

"You talk to Ralph, honey, and I'm gonna talk to Daddy," Hawk said with a smile. He roughly shoved Van Speer out of the room. "Shut up, you ignorant son of a bitch," Hawk told him, when they were safely out of the room. "We got the kid quiet now."

"I wish that I could see the attraction that you filthy

swine have for my family," Rudiger snapped, wrenching his arm free of the sergeant's grasp.

Hawk only gave him a blank look.

"Beat it," he ordered. Rudiger complied without further comment.

* * *

THE NEXT FEW days went by peacefully enough. It appeared that the Japanese were intent upon starving out their besieged foes. There was scant possibility of that. The Van Speers were well stocked with every sort of supply that a resourceful pioneer family might need —more than a squad of marines might need. The attackers never again tried to garrison the strip of jungle behind the farmhouse, and Hawk began thinking that he might use a similar strategy on the other three sides. The tall, thick trees, a favorite of snipers, discouraged him. They could see him crawling about from their vantage points above the ground. He became content with staying indoors and awaiting relief from the battalion. The constant sniper fire never let up, and occasionally a soldier could be seen in the forest. The marines' sole pastime was studying the forest and doing a bit of sniping of their own. Hawk, however, did not participate in this because his weapon could not reach the forest with any degree of accuracy and he did not want to waste ammunition during the indeterminate period of his stay. No one did very well at the sniping, although Gist was probably the best at it. It was difficult to tell for certain whether your shot was a hit or miss from the covered windows.

Because he spent the most time concentrating upon

the edge of the forest, Gist was the first to notice a change that had occurred there. A week had gone by since the rout at the rear of the house. It was around noon on a Sunday, and no shots had been fired at the marines since the morning of the day before. When Gist called this to Hawk's attention, Hawk authorized him and two others to go out and look around. Quiroz, Brock and Gist ran a zigzag course to the foxholes and from there right into the forest.

An hour later the men walked back, unhurried, and announced that the siege had ended.

There was little reaction to the announcement until the next day when the beleaguered Dutch and marines again began to journey out of doors. Then only did they appreciate their newly found freedom. Everyone was naturally leery of the forest and kept close to the house. The Dutch made no attempt to resume normal work operations. But even so, it was a marked improvement over the listening to pounding sniper fire from the darkened interior of the house.

The men propped up the roof of Rudiger's bedroom, but made few attempts at conscientious repairs to the quarters. This was probably more due to a general dislike for Rudiger than because of any indolence. Hawk did set them to work, digging a trench from the kitchen door to the cellar, so that they might have cover during any excursions in that direction. He felt that it was best for Ilse, Rudiger and Trudchen to remain in the shelter once again. The next Japanese attack might be preceded by a mortar shell through the roof of the Van Speer house. This very real possibility was most unsettling to the men who had to sleep in it, and Armistead made no protests this time about having to sleep in the cellar. Rolf also found room there for a comfortable night's sleep.

Hawk had more barrels deployed in front of the moat that surrounded the house, allowing the men to sleep behind them upon the ground if they so desired. Most did so, preferring the open air to the thought of being skewered by a mortar shell in the dead of night. Hawk and Brock remained in the house. Gretchen and Moritz moved to the quarters the hired hands. Gaedcke was relieved of his duty as overseer of the Dutchmen and took up residence behind a barrel stronghold along a narrow side of the house. He was still able to keep an eye upon the civilians from this point.

10

DEATH OF THE VAN SPEERS

THE SENSE OF SECURITY THAT PREVAILED ONCE MORE proved false. Three days after the Japanese were purported to have pulled out, another marine was killed. His body was face down between the forest and the quarters of the hired hands, his own bayonet protruding from the small of his back. It was only a few minutes after first light when the entire population of the plantation, excepting the women, gathered around the body.

"We couldn't see over here from the house. Did you see or hear anything?" Hawk asked Moritz. The body was lying fifty feet from the window under which Moritz slept.

"No, Sergeant," he answered, staring down at Gaedcke's narrow form. "I want you to move Gretchen from our quarters, though. A hand grenade might have killed us all."

"Yeah, goddam it. I thought that place would be safe. The little son of a bitches couldn't whip us fightin', so they went back to this shit. He was a nice kid, too."

Hawk's usually blank expression seemed distracted and disturbed.

"Yes, he was," said Moritz, continuing to stare at the remains. "We came to know him quite well, while we were all trapped in there." Hawk was too heartsick to even curse. He turned his back to Gaedcke. Gaedcke had always been nervous and afraid, but he had never shirked his duty nor performed any less valiantly than any other man. Hawk would have liked to have been there. He would have liked to have saved the marine.

"Well," he exhaled at last. "Let's get him buried then." But he took no part in the preparations. He only returned to the house.

Gretchen followed him inside and into the den. He fell into what was now his chair and tossed his helmet to the floor. She sat down on the ottoman at his feet.

"You liked this one. Very much," Gretchen stated.

"He was a good kid. Yeah, I liked him."

"I'm sorry. For him...and for you."

"Don't be sorry for me. I ain't dead," said Hawk, his rage barely concealed now. "A kid like that gets cut down and a sorry bastard like me just keeps on going. Why Gaedcke? Why not me or Brock or Gist, we've been asking for it. No, they gotta sneak up on some scared kid." Hawk lowered his forehead to his hand. He had been around these men too long; he knew them too well. They were friends, they were family; but more than that, they were fellow men at arms. "I couldn't kill enough Japs to make up for this. Not even if they dropped me into downtown Tokyo."

"Remember what you said," Gretchen begged. "This is temporary. This will end. Don't let it destroy you." Hawk didn't answer. This didn't seem temporary. For

Gaedcke it was forever. He had been wrong. War was not temporary. It was permanent.

Gretchen reached for his hand and squeezed it. Then she stood up and left the room.

Remorse and regret were new to Hawk's young life. The slaughter that he had inflicted upon the enemy had seemed ' temporary, for when he killed one nameless man, another replaced him. The men that he had killed had names and faces, just as did Gaedcke. Hawk considered that thought for a moment, but with great difficulty he drove it from his mind. His habits were too well formed. He must not go soft now, when the enemy deserved the most severe retaliation. Keep going, keep killing Japs. That is what he had told' countless marines as he looked coldly into their dazed faces. That was the answer

* * *

THE MOOD of the men was somber after Gaedcke's burial. The quiet, brooding figure of Hawk epitomized their feelings. No one stayed around the sergeant for very long, including Gretchen. His baleful demeanor drove away anyone who might try to intrude on his solitary cogitations. He tended to his duties in the most perfunctory manner possible, continuing to stay rooted to his chair in the den. The now-familiar pall, accented by the strange, reseda light, fell over the landscape. It seemed most appropriate for the situation and for the humor of the people involved in the prolonged tragedy.

Before dark, Armistead came into the den and began rummaging through an overturned desk. Hawk watched him silently for a full two minutes before his curiosity got the best of him.

"What the hell are you doing?" asked Hawk impatiently.

"Looking for a tablet and a pencil. Me and the kid are drawin' pictures tonight. I need something to keep her busy. Can't find none nowhere, though. You seen any?"

"Yeah, Fine's got some. He's always writing. Ask him for a piece of paper." Hawk's omniscience was not even bounded by such trivial matters.

"Hey, right," said Armistead. Then he paused by the door. "That was an awful thing about Gaedcke," he said at last.

"Yeah." Hawk forced the single word out. "I'm gonna do something about that," he added, clearing his throat.

"What?" Armistead asked. But Hawk only shook his head. He was so accustomed to speaking confidently and positively that he had done so now without the slightest idea of what he meant. He only knew that he would do something. Armistead knew it too.

"Watch yourself, Hawk. You're a good man. I wouldn't wanta lose you, podnuh." Armistead smiled his frequent smile. Hawk looked up.

"I will." Armistead waved and left.

* * *

HAWK BELIEVED that he had fallen asleep, but he heard the muffled explosion. It was probable that the unexpected sound awakened him. He sat up, picked up his gun and helmet and ran to the rear of the house. Rolf was in the kitchen, on his knees, sobbing. Canlon had a hand on his arm, preventing him from falling to the floor.

"What was that?" Hawk breathlessly questioned Canlon.

"Grenade. Japs dumped one down the ventilation shaft of the cellar. Better not go out there." Hawk stared incredulously at Joe and then stepped to the back door. He could see the deadly column of smoke winding out of the hatch that led down to the cellar. It was a sickly, flowing ghost light against the background of a dark night.

"God Almighty," gasped Hawk. He had let himself become so preoccupied during the day that he was not sure who all lay inside the shelter. He dropped his gun and stumbled out the door toward the swirling smoke.

"Hawk, get back here!" Canlon called. But Hawk never slowed until he had climbed down the ladder and lit a shattered lantern that hung at its base. The horror of what he saw stripped the veneer from his jaded sensibilities. Ilse was mutilated beyond recognition. The fronts of both Armistead and Rudiger were ripped off, the blood still draining from their bodies. Trudchen was thrown against the wall with half a dozen neat puncture wounds in her head and neck. Hawk's experienced eye knew at a glance that all but one were already dead, and that the last one would soon be dead. He knelt and gathered the corporal into his arms. Ralph's eyes were open; he seemed to be looking far into the distance with a pleading expression melting across his features.

"Daddy! I think they got me there, Daddy!" Ralph cried, tears distorting the words. "Don't tell mama now," he wailed. His head twitched spasmodically.

"Ralph," Hawk whispered. "Ralph, don't die. Please. Please, Ralph. I want to talk to you, Ralph."

The head twitched again. The eyes never closed, but Hawk felt sure that Armistead was dead. Virtually every drop of blood in his body ran across the floor or soaked into Hawk's clothes. Then, with terrifying suddenness the head jerked up. The mouth opened.

"Don't tell her now!" Ralph screamed madly. Then he retched and retched again, and became still. Canlon reached the foot of the ladder. Hawk looked up at him. Canlon could see no emotion in Hawk's rugged features.

"They got him, Joe. They got my boy Ralph." Hawk spoke evenly, setting the body down. He stood up. Tensely he gripped his hands together, cracking his joints. "They got my boy," he repeated. Canlon watched Hawk, averting his eyes from the carnage that surrounded him. Before either man knew or could prevent it, Gretchen was standing beside them.

She broke into shattering screams and sobs, throwing herself first upon her mother and then upon Ilse. Dazed, Canlon and Hawk only stood there watching her anguish. She dragged finally through the ankle-deep blood to Rudiger and fell exhausted upon him.

"Y'all better get on up outa there," came Gist's gruff Texas accent from above. "They're probably gonna hit us."

Hawk was relieved that Gretchen had not been in the cellar, but he could not feel any elation in the present circumstances. The loss of Armistead came like a physical blow, right between his eyes. He found it difficult to adjust his thoughts. But he did. He reached down and seized Gretchen by the arm. In spite of her fierce struggles he lifted her to her feet. She continued to sob.

"Come on, Gretchen. We better go now," Hawk said. His words sounded far off to his own ears. It was as if his soul had fled such untold horror and left his body there to deal with it.

"Let go of me, you animal! You filthy murderer! I'll kill you for this!" She tore free of his grasp and struck him in the chest with her fist. Hawk stood there, staring mutely once again. "All you care about is this swine!" She screamed into his face and kicked at Ralph's dead body.

Hawk winced. For the first time in his life he winced in revulsion. Involuntarily his hand came up and dealt Gretchen a sharp slap. She was knocked, still sobbing, back into the pile of corpses.

"Get her in the house," Hawk told Canlon, and turning his back on the nightmare, pulled his leaden limbs up and out into the clean night ail. Gist helped him to his feet.

"We're sittin' ducks, Sergeant Hawk," said Gist, spitting a stream of tobacco. He looked out into the darkness.

"It's all right, Gist. We're all right," Hawk said weakly.

"They got Ralph?" Gist asked. Hawk squinted painfully and nodded his head. He called down to Joe to hurry up. Joe was cursing and struggling. Hawk put a hand on Gist's shoulder.

"Cover him for me, Pogue. I'm going back to the house. Okay?" Gist looked at him. Hawk, visibly shaken, was an unnerving sight.

"Sure. Go on," answered Gist. Hawk stumbled back

down the trench and into the house. Reflexively, he picked up his Thompson from where he had dropped it. He studied it for a moment, and then, as if reconsidering, he set it back down. He slumped against the wall at Ewell's feet.

"You okay, Hawk?" Ewell asked, quite concerned.

"Yeah, Ewell. I'm okay. There ain't no time to not be okay. Every time you worry about somebody gettin' killed, they get somebody else. I guess you just can't care about nothing, if you want to keep everybody alive."

* * *

HAWK PULLED the stub of a cigar from his shirt pocket. He lit it and stared at the walls of the kitchen. When he had finished it, he got up and blackened his face with ashes. The men did not see him again until morning. They heard no sound of his activities in the forest.

He swaggered out of the early morning fog, from the jungle that was located upon the opposite side of the house, away from the portion of the forest that he had entered the night before.

"Nothing," he said to fine and Claiborne as he crossed the moat and entered the front door. He had found no signs of life in the forest. The Japanese killers were very adroit. He imagined that a Japanese Sergeant Hawk was at work, hell-bent upon murdering the entire population of the. Van Speer farm. As frightful a thought as that was, Hawk swore to be avenged, to catch the beast red-handed.

He stayed awake for the next two days, staring hollow-eyed from each window and prowling the jungle like some nocturnal predator. Still, there was no sign of the Japanese demons. The more elusive they seemed, the more obsessed he became with capturing and destroying them.

He did not see Gretchen for these two days. She remained in the separate quarters, presumably being comforted by Moritz. It was probably better that way, he reasoned, for the comfort that he could give was only of the roughest sort. Kill Japs—that was his answer. Of what solace was that to the bereaved girl? Hawk knew that he was of little value to a civilized person. He only dreaded admitting that he was becoming of little worth to his men, and to his mission. The family he had been charged with protecting was nearly wiped out, along with a substantial number of his men, his friends.

Depressed about his men and depressed about Gretchen, Hawk returned to the bombed-out shelter to think. The dead had been removed from the cubicle, but the evidence of their passing could never be erased. He sat down on the shattered wine rack. His fatigued muscles made him move slowly, like an old man; at least that was what he attributed his lack of agility to. Actually, his muscles had been far more exhausted than this on previous occasions, with little outward effects. This time his fatigue was of the spirit.

His eyes narrowed as they surveyed the dried brown splotches on the walls and the floor. He cringed when he again looked at the spot where Ilse had lay slain. The senseless violence that he had always taken as a matter of course took on a new perspective. Perhaps he had enjoyed it all, just a little. Men fighting men, men killing men, men taking care of themselves or paying the supreme sacrifice. Fighting was part of being a young man; that was one way to view it. But when a family became involved, the true degradation of humanity was starkly evident. The marines and the Japanese had sunk below the most craven of the lower orders, feeding on bloodlust: He wondered if the fighting in Europe had sunk to such depths.

And then, Rudiger had wanted to surrender. Hawk would not hear of it. The thought nagged and ate at his innards. Would the Van Speers still be alive? They would certainly have had better luck pleading their case with an enemy soldier than they had had pleading it with a tiny sphere full of gunpowder and metal. Hawk tried not to admit it, but he believed that they would be alive. They might well have been tethered in a pig pen, eating dirt and being constantly beaten, but they would have been alive.

And Ralph would be alive. Ralph Armistead, his friend, who had never had an enemy in his life, who hated no one and left everyone laughing with his pleasant ways. A hand grenade cared little for charm. Hawk stooped to pick up a crust-coated piece of metal. It was the safety lever from a hand grenade. He slipped it into his pocket.

Hawk took a ragged breath. He was, for once at least, a pitiable specimen, slumped there in the morbid sepulcher. Gretchen hated him, and rightly so. The first and only woman ever to acknowledge his existence now acknowledged it only as an object of loathing. Who can better take care of us, she had asked him. No one, he had boastfully thought. He stood, and laboriously ascended the ladder. As he raised his eyes from the ground, he saw Gretchen step out of the hired hands' quarters.

He hoped against hope that she would come his

way, even if only to berate him again, to inject him with all of the venom that he so richly deserved. Her delicate little frame swayed rhythmically as she walked across the long open space. She deliberately averted her eyes from him, but she was walking in his direction. A sad, almost invisible smile touched the corner of his mouth for a brief moment. He loved her. In the midst of his irreversible sorrow, that somehow consoled him. Though it was all over now, it gave him the vestiges of joy. He looked up at her from the trench. The Viking princess. Her beautiful features were trying to look hard but such a thing was impossible.

"I would like to speak to you," she said flatly.

"Shoot," Hawk replied, his outward demeanor as tough as ever.

"Not out here. In the house, if you would."

"Okay," he answered. Without another word they proceeded to the kitchen door and she led the way into the den. Hawk's mind was a blank as he followed her, he could not imagine what she wanted to talk to him about. She seated herself on the ottoman there and gestured for him to take his accustomed place in the plush easy chair. Canlon, who had been on the veranda, nodded politely and left the room quickly when no one nodded back.

Gretchen silently hung her head. Her narrow shoulders were drooped. Her grief had not marked her young features but her soft expression was even softer now, as if a summer breeze would be more than her heart could withstand. Hawk wanted to reach out and touch her, to hold and protect her. But he sat there, perfectly still, the most terrible engine of destruction that the human race had ever produced, at the mercy of a fragile little girl.

As he waited for her to speak, his mind vividly snapped back to their last confrontation in the cellar. The smoky reflections from a flickering lantern were indelibly impressed upon his mind.

"I'm sorry I slapped you," he rasped. "I don't know what came over me."

"That wasn't your fault. I want you to know that none of...what happened was your fault. If anyone is to blame, it is me. I knew that at the time. I was just upset. Please forgive me."

"Well, there's nothing to forgive," said Hawk, taken aback by his sudden role as the one granting absolution.

"You are very kind," said Gretchen, but the stilted words made Hawk more uneasy than a curse. "I must talk to you about us and what has happened to us, now." She looked up at him. He gestured for her to continue. "I suppose, it's like Father was always saying, you and I are worlds apart, from two different cultures." Hawk could not be still any longer. He feared her prefatory comment.

"I know I'm kinda...rough and all, but Gretchen, I'm in the middle of the war. If you were in Holland right now, you'd see your own people looking and acting just like I look and act." Hawk failed to disguise his desperate tone. She shook her head.

"I know, James. But if there were no war, I think we would still be too far apart. Perhaps it was, after all, just physical attraction. You're a man who hasn't been home in years, who has only been around other men. I would be a poor excuse for a woman if you didn't show me some attention."

"Hey, listen..." Hawk began, but she stopped him.

"And I was lonely, and you were so handsome. You

strutted around with your gun like the bravest man in the world." She smiled. "I couldn't resist you. You are a real man, James. I don't think that I was meant for a real man, though. I want someone who can be kind and gentle all the time, who doesn't have to force himself. You can't go against your own nature just to keep me happy."

"I can keep you happy. I can be gentle. Gretchen, how can I be gentle here?" She didn't answer, she only smiled softly. She was not really up to debate at the present. She couldn't realize that the words she spoke came from the mouth of her dead father, not from her own heart. Hawk could not argue with a dead man.

"We're just too different. We really don't even know one another or if we even have anything in common. We're from two different cultures." She spoke with a shrug. Deep within her subconscious, she hoped that Rudiger was satisfied.

Hawk leaned back in his chair. An emotional appeal would do no good. Calmly, he spoke.

"Gretchen, are any two people meant for each other? How can you ever know that, when you don't even know yourself, much less someone else. People are always changing. They change with their place, with their age —I can't even remember what kind of person I was three years ago. I thought different, I acted different. I don't even know me, so how can I know you—and how can you know me? You have to have some kind of faith in a person, just trust him, that's all. You don't have to know him. I have faith in you because I love you and that's all I ask in return."

Hawk slid a cigar from his shirt pocket and lit it. He stared at the floor a moment and spoke again.

"Don't think about this...now. Too much has happened. There's too much bad tangled up with the good. Let yourself settle down a little before you worry about...us. I ain't going nowhere and if I do, I'll be back —no matter what you decide, I'll be back." Hawk leaned forward again. "You gave me the happiest time of my life. I knew it while it was happening. I wanted it to last forever, but you can't stop time. The things that have happened to us are not normal. If there were no war, we would be happy again. We can't be happy with all of this going on."

"No, we can't," she answered sadly. "You and the war, James, are one and the same. That's why I fell in love with you. You were danger, you were manhood, you were violence and nothing could hurt you. But you were just a dream. I don't love the war anymore. I see it for what it is, and—" she whispered—"you."

Hawk couldn't answer that assessment of himself. For the very same thing had been recently dawning upon his own dim self-conceptions.

"The war isn't a dream, and even if you can't be hurt, others can be. You're not a dream either, James, you're just a man. Luckier, and more cruel than the rest, maybe, but just a man."

"That's right, Gretchen. Please think of me as a man and not as some knight on horseback. I don't stack up as a knight, but I might as a man."

"It can't work. Those two people who sailed to the western shore just don't exist anymore," she explained.

"Give it a chance?" he asked hoarsely. But she stood.

"I want to, but I just can't." And she left.

Hawk raised his hand to his chin. He heard her footsteps retreat through the living room.

"We'll see about that," he said aloud. As he settled back into the chair, Canlon reentered the room.

"I kinda overheard," said Joe sheepishly. Hawk made no reply. "I told you not to get too mixed up with her," Canlon reminded him. Joe walked out onto the veranda and jumped up on the barrels.

"That you did. Maybe you were right." Hawk dragged thoughtfully on his cigar.

"That kinda stuff could happen a hundred times before you find the right woman. Don't let it bother you," Joe advised.

"I ain't bothered."

"Shit you ain't. This ain't nothing to let yourself get all down about. It ain't worth getting killed over." Joe expected the worst from the volatile and violent Hawk.

"What the hell are you talking about? Why don't you mind your own goddam business?'

"Okay," said Joe, sliding back down off the barrel. "I will. Don't be stupid, though." He left the room.

"Says the stupidest son of a bitch that ever walked the face of the earth," Hawk called after him. Hawk sat there motionless for perhaps another hour before Rolf became the next person to disturb his solitude. He brought a bowl of *erwtensoep*. The old man did not speak until spoken to.

"Where were you, when Ilse and Mrs. Van Speer were killed?" Hawk asked, recalling Rolf sobbing on the kitchen floor on that fateful night.

"When the hand grenade hit the floor, I had just climbed the ladder and was standing outside," Rolf answered.

"Shit. That's pretty close." Rolf bobbed his head glumly. "You musta heard the Japs runnin' away?"

"I neither saw nor heard anything," Rolf replied. Hawk banged his fist on the dusty end table. The blow distorted the faces that he had drawn there for Ilse.

"Goddam it!" he barked. "What's going on around here? How can them little son of a bitches get in and out so goddam easy?" Rolf shrugged and sat down in front of Hawk. He seemed to be thinking of an answer to the riddle.

"The corporal was drawing a picture for Ilse. Mr. and Mrs. Van Speer were talking. I had been sent for a bottle of spirits. And then...it happened. One minute they were alive and the next, all dead."

"Yeah. Well, listen Rolf, we might need that goddam hole again, if things get hot. I saw some hardware cloth in the smokehouse one day. Why don't you stuff some of that shit up the vent pipe for me. Them people would still be alive if there'd been a dirt screen in that shaft."

"Very well, Sergeant. Mr. Van Speer recently replaced that pipe. The old one that had rusted, had such a screen."

"Ain't that the shits?"

"Yes sir," Rolf answered sadly. Hawk looked down at him and considered a facile way to change the subject.

"Rolf, you been around Gretchen the last couple days. How's she been acting? Has she mentioned me?"

"She has not. She is distraught over her family. They are the only matter that concerns her for the present. She spends a great deal of time talking with Moritz. Perhaps they have discussed you, I don't know. I wouldn't worry about anything she says at the present. Her world has just fallen apart. It will take much rebuilding."

"Yeah, I guess. Thanks." Hawk smiled. Rolf returned

the smile and gestured to the bowl of soup before making his exit. But Hawk wasn't interested in soup.

He put on his helmet and picked up his Thompson. He heard a great deal of commotion in the dining room. When he entered, the crowd of marines fell silent. They faced him with questioning looks.

"What the hell's going on?" he asked impatiently.

"They're back," said Lundstedt. "Gist saw them prowling around out there."

"Of course they're back," said Hawk. "Ask Gaedcke or Armistead or the Van Speers if they're back."

"Well, we see 'em this time and they don't care if we do; there's even more this time." Hawk walked to the window. He saw no signs of life out in the jungle.

"Well, dogshit," he growled. "Where is that shittin' Hayes? You guys better get the hell outa here before they drop a knee mortar on the house."

The men looked about nervously and began to file back out to their respective barrels that stood before the moat. Gist, Brock and Hawk stood staring out of the window, after

the house had been evacuated.

"What do you figure they're up to?" Brock asked.

"I figure they're gonna wipe us out if something don't happen quick," Gist speculated.

"The stupid bastards would be better off killing us at night, one by one," said Hawk. "We're gonna blow the shit out of 'em if they try for the house again. Why waste the men when you can do as good a job as they been doing?"

"Shit, Hawk, a Jap ain't got no brain," Gist spat. That answer had to suffice for the moment.

"Where'd you see them?" Hawk asked. Gist aimed

his rifle barrel in a westerly direction. He couldn't speak until he spat again.

"Crawlin' around about twenty yards back. They see us but they ain't shootin' yet, so I ain't either. I ain't gonna let 'em know I see 'em just yet."

Hawk sighed deeply and turned away from the window. "Let's get 'em good this time," he exhorted. "Mow the sorry bastards down. I wish there was a way to blow up the whole island with them on it."

Brock smiled. "Don't worry, they're gonna wonder what happened when we start droppin' 'em," said the boy. He was joyfully anticipating the attack. Hawk smiled at his comment.

"This is one time I'm glad I got a crazy son of a bitch in my outfit," Hawk told him. What he didn't say was that Brock was no great loss to the human race and that he would at least take a few of the enemy with him. "Pogue, make sure all the Dutch are in the workers' house over there and tell Ralph..." Hawk paused. His voice grew weaker. "And you watch the back, in case we need the Bren or the thirty-caliber out there."

Rolf walked into the room.

"The vent pipe is fixed, Sergeant Hawk," he said.

"Good deal. Where's Gretchen?"

"In the quarters of Ernst and Klaus. All of us are staying there."

"Good. Maybe I oughta move the girl into the shelter."

"Because her parents died there, I do not believe that she will go back to the cellar, Sergeant. Perhaps it is better for her to take her chances with us."

"Yeah...shit, I guess," said the confused Hawk. Gist's rifle barked and Rolf jumped in alarm.

"Got one!" Brock laughed. A body lay sprawled twenty feet from the workers' quarters. Hawk surveyed it with some consternation.

"Goddam, he got close!" Hawk exclaimed, pointing his weapon through the window.

"Aw shit, I seen him," said Gist. "I was just shittin' around, lettin' him think he was goin' somewhere."

"The girl's in that building. We best get them people outa there," said Hawk, ignoring Gist's odd method of reassurance. Gist and Hawk, half crouching and half running, charged over to the building housing the Dutch.

"Y'all get the hell outa here," was Gist's friendly greeting. All of them but Gretchen dashed from the house, watching the forest warily. Hawk peered out of the window at the fallen man.

"Hey, Pogue, check this," said Hawk. Gist walked over.

"What the hell is that? It ain't no Jap," Gist said. The corpse had ebony skin and tight hair.

"It's one of them natives that don't live here," Hawk answered. "Rudiger told me that no natives lived here." He turned to Gretchen. She shrugged.

"Maybe he came with the Japanese," she said. Gist knitted his brow and studied her intently. She turned nervously away from his gaze, as almost any sane person would do. Hawk cleared his throat.

"Yeah, well. I don't know about that," said Hawk, still looking out the window. "But we better get the hell outa here." With his eyes shifting rapidly back and forth, scanning the dark forest, Hawk led the way out. He kept himself between Gretchen and the forest. Gist attempted to shield her with his body also. They made it without incident to the cellar. Hawk let the girl hold onto his arm and leap into the pit, without the benefit of the ladder. Gently, he eased her to the floor.

"They must not be ready yet," said Gist, still watching the jungle as Hawk lowered her. Hawk grunted, and clutched his gun tightly in his free hand.

"I don't want to stay here," Gretchen called up in a wavering voice. "I want to stay with my brother."

"I'll be back for you later, honey," Hawk replied. "It's too goddam risky in the house."

"I don't care, James. I don't want to stay here alone."

"That's the best way," Hawk apologized and shut the trapdoor.

Gist and Hawk backed down the trench that led to the kitchen door. Both sighed with relief once they were inside. The two men watched out the door for a moment, but nothing stirred.

"They saw it was a girl. Maybe they'll leave her alone," Gist said,

"Maybe. Who knows what them bastards will do," Hawk answered. "You know, that native guy is mighty suspicious. Reckon he's a Jap scout that's been knockin' off our guys?"

"That sounds about like them Japs," said Gist. "His knockin' days are over now, though—I drilled his ass good."

"Yeah, but if they brought one of them suckers here, they're bound to have brought two," Hawk thought aloud.

"Probably," Gist acceded. "Like snakes, they come in twos."

"And Gretchen's out there by herself," Hawk continued. "And she wanted to come in." Three minutes later he had brought Gretchen back into the house. He and Gist constructed a shelter out of the heavy wooden tables that had belonged to Rudiger, edging them into the narrow and well-supported hallway. It wouldn't protect her from a mortar round, but it could certainly withstand flying shrapnel or a poorly placed grenade.

Night fell and the Japanese had not made their move. They were apparently awaiting some sort of buildup prior to making any further attacks. They knew that the Americans were few in numbers and poorly equipped, but that their fortifications were fairly well constructed and their fighting spirit knew no bounds. The Dutch asked permission after dark to return to their quarters and retrieve a few belongings left there. Once he was sure that they were well armed, Hawk acceded to their request, except that he insisted upon Gretchen's remaining in the house. The four men dashed out under the cover of darkness, and were virtually on their own, for the night was so dark that no one could see the Dutch quarters from the house. Hawk only shrugged to himself as he listened to their retreating footsteps. He hated to see Rolf and Moritz get killed. He didn't see how a few measly personal articles were worth a trip out into the harrowing darkness, but. they were grown men and they knew what had been going on. It was their choice.

Hawk thought of the dark-skinned native. He would be virtually invisible in the night. The natives of these islands were Stone Age wildmen. Some were still cannibals. The Japanese might have a whole platoon of them crawling around in the night, cutting throats. But they may have watched him on his excursions into the night and watched him slay the Japanese, for he could not conceive of a native being truly loyal to what he considered the cruel imperial soldiers.

Claiborne heard footsteps in the darkness, proceeding straight for him at a bold pace. He leveled his M-l at where he thought them to be. Many times he had thought that he heard things in the night, many times he had been so frightened that he thought that his heart would stop beating and never start again. But this time, it was not an overactive imagination: real and loud sounds came for him. He was about to call out, but it sounded like a single man, so he prepared to fire into him, surprising him. As he held his breath and his finger tightened on the trigger, a voice slashed through the darkness.

"American! American! It is I, Ernst! American!" Claiborne exhaled in relief.

"What are you doing out there, Ernst?" Claiborne called back, the fear still trembling in his voice.

"We need help carrying our trunk, and we think we hear movement in the forest. Will you help us?"

"Yeah. Let me tell Sergeant Hawk."

"Please don't bother the sergeant. He will think that we are foolish old women, afraid of the dark. He told us we could go over there if we could handle it on our own," said Ernst, coming up to Claiborne's barrel and leaning on it. The marine couldn't see the Dutchman's eyes because of the jutting shadow caused by his prominent cheekbones.

"Well, all right."

"Good, good. And what is your name?"

"Claiborne," he answered, rounding the barrel and following Ernst into the opaque obscurity. As they neared the quarters, Claiborne saw a faint glow coming from the far wall, a glow that a lantern might produce. Ernst led him around the corner along the outside of the building to the lantern. Klaus was leaning against the wall; the lantern was on the ground at his feet. The lantern couldn't be seen from the house.

"Hey are you crazy?" Claiborne exclaimed. "We're gonna get picked off with that light shining like that—the jungle's right there."

"Don't worry," Ernst reassured him. "The Japanese won't attack tonight."

"They don't have to attack to blow our brains out. They can see that light for miles." Claiborne's boyish face was animated by innocent amazement.

"Very well, we must not hurry then. Do you need something to pry that lock with, Klaus?" ask Ernst. The other man nodded slowly with a smile. "Claiborne, may I borrow your bayonet for a moment?" Claiborne looked nervously out at the invisible jungle. He knew that he was standing on a bull's eye. He could feel a hundred rifles aimed at his head. Another man would have kicked the lantern over and cursed Ernst for his stupidity; another might have even reasoned with him. But Claiborne was neither the garrulous nor the impetuous type. He only wanted the mad Dutchmen to get on with their moving procedures. Quickly he slipped his knife from his boot and handed its blunt end to Klaus.

"Now, hurry it up," Claiborne advised Klaus. While the marine was turned, giving the warning, Ernst snatched the rifle from his light grasp. Ernst expected that his maneuver would cause Claiborne to turn his attention toward the stolen rifle, enabling Klaus to stab easily. But Klaus had moved prematurely, allowing the marine to size up the situation and deftly parry the bayonet thrust toward his chest. Ernst swung the rifle butt at his head but Claiborne blocked it with his shoulder. Again Klaus lunged at him and again he avoided him as might the most poised matador. Ernst drew back to swing at him again, but Claiborne dropped back a few paces and then ran around him, and ran around the corner of the building, back in the direction of the farmhouse and safety. He was abruptly halted.

Rolf stepped from the doorway of the hired hands' quarters; in his hand was a Webley revolver.

"Stop, American!" It was a loud whisper. Claiborne stopped, but his eyes searched for a direction in which to flee. He didn't know why, but he knew what the Dutch had planned.

"Rolf! What..." Claiborne fell quiet as Ernst rounded the corner. "Sarge..." he cried, but the scream never left his throat.

"Did you hear something?" Hawk asked Ewell.

"Naw."

"I did. One of them Dutch guys musta stubbed his toe. Or else a Jap did."

"I hear so much and think I hear so much that I can't be sure when I'm hearing something and when I ain't," Ewell said.

"I'd go see how they're doing, but I don't owe them nothing," Hawk grumbled as he dropped a spent cigar. Then he raised his head. Someone was coming. He aimed his gun at the approaching figure, but it was Moritz who stepped up to the deadly muzzle.

"How's it going, Moritz?" Hawk greeted him. "Where's your buddies?"

"Oh, they're so slow. I think they're moving the entire building over here, Sergeant Hawk."

Hawk nodded. "They better get their ass back here if they know what's good for 'em."

"Yes, I told them as much."

But it was quite some time before the remaining Dutch returned. Hawk positioned Ernst and Klaus at Beckwith's post in Rudiger's bombed-out bedroom. He figured he would need three men there because the room was open, with nothing but a two- to three-foot wall around it, and because the enemy had hit it once before. He put Moritz with Brock at the front dining room window, knowing that the Japanese would have to deal with Brock before getting the boy. He didn't assign Rolf to any particular spot, but only advised him to watch himself and help out where he could.

It was still dark, in the early morning. The night was hushed and quiet. No one had heard any sound of the Japanese.

A roseate blast shattered the night with an ear-splitting roar. Hawk's eyelids jerked open and he saw Fine's silhouette against the explosion. It had hit near his barrel and given him a jolt that rolled him into the moat. He came back out of the water, however, dragging like a stomped insect.

"What was it?" Hawk asked Canlon, as he peered out from the veranda.

"Mortar. Had to be a mortar. We better get outa here." Hawk, Canlon, Brock, Beckwith and the Dutch were the only ones still in the house.

"Wait. I wanta see another one." Hawk held him. Hawk could identify any blast that the Japanese or American armed forces could produce. He had been asleep, but even so, he felt that the explosion was only that of a grenade. The intensity of a mortar was lacking.

Hawk heard alien voices. "Japs! Japs are in the foxholes, Joe," he rasped. "Get some guys in the house, get Quiroz on that thirty-caliber, hurry. It was just a grenade." Joe ran out for the back door and began ordering the men into the house, where they took up their former positions. Quiroz poured tracers into the former marine trenches. The Americans studied the bombardment silently.

A flash came from the farthest, central foxhole. Then half a dozen more. Hawk opened fire on the position, Quiroz did the same and Lundstedt fired a short burst with the Bren. Hawk ordered Beckwith into the front with his BAR, replacing him with Mayeaux to guard the bombed-out room.

Strongly resembling a fireworks display, the forest lit up with blazing gun muzzles. The fire was not ordinary sniper work; it appeared that there was a plan in operation. The men could see the huddled forms of enemy soldiers crawling to the next foxhole. Quiroz splattered the ground and men with the raking incendiary bullets. Still, they persisted, crawling over and through the dead until they were fairly streaming into the closer foxhole. On the opposite side of the V-shaped network of holes, Japanese were similarly advancing. Beckwith and Hawk were carefully picking their shots on this side before spraying the creeping invasion. Consequently, here the advance was more rapid and unfaltering.

Canlon, Lundstedt and Brock were firing at the central foxhole which was the apex of the V, nearest to the forest and therefore literally teeming with enemy soldiers. Every shot found a target, but another target quickly replaced it. The men continued to struggle, never noticing the quiet growth of the dawn and daylight. Gist came stalking onto the veranda and interrupted Hawk's attempt at slowing the rising tide. The enemy now held three of the five foxholes.

"I'm gonna get in the hole closest to us and put a grenade in on 'em," Gist told Hawk, in reference to the unoccupied hole on his flank.

"No, they'll put one in on you," Hawk answered.

"I don't give a shit," Gist snapped angrily. Hawk turned to face him.

"Okay, go ahead. Watch yourself," Hawk said reluctantly. Then to Canlon: "We were stupid not to fill them shittin' holes in."

The two men on the veranda watched tensely as Gist threaded through a storm of lead and dived into the nearest hole. Bullets kicked up dust on all sides of the trench, but a few moments after he had reached it, his arm came flying up and a black explosion rocked the Japanese in the next hole. The burst tossed out a half dozen of them onto the ground and they flailed about, much like beached fish. Without waiting to see the results, Gist had leaped out of his foxhole and returned to the house. The Japanese were too shaken to fire at his retreat.

"Damn, that was good!" Hawk exclaimed.

"Yeah," said Canlon, his nerves too shattered to be elated over anything. Hawk jumped up on the barrels and before Joe knew it, had let himself over them and was charging the nearest foxhole on his side of the V. He obviously intended to duplicate Gist's accomplishment on this flank. Novel deeds are novel only once, however, and every Japanese rifle was trained on Hawk.

He disappeared in a cloud of dust caused by the roaring barrage. When it cleared he was seen crawling on his belly, and at last he rolled over into the hole. His arm flew up, and almost simultaneously the Japanese popped out of their hole and ran for the central foxhole, closest to the forest. The grenade hit their erstwhile position, the shrapnel slinging into one fleeing man. Quiroz turned his machine gun on the others, slashing them down into the earth and raking them over again for good measure. Imitating Gist, Hawk came running back on the heels of the grenade explosion. The Japanese had learned also, and chased him with a few close shots. Miraculously he leaped over the barrels and back onto the veranda, once again unscathed.

"You got more lives than a bucket of cats, Hawk," said Canlon, breathless. Hawk didn't answer; he leaned against the barrels, wheezing, trying to recapture his wind.

"That oughta hold 'em," he finally gasped. Canlon fired a shot.

"Yeah, look, they're pulling outa that last hole," he observed. Hawk jumped up to have a look. He cursed them resoundingly.

"Nail 'em!" he screamed. "Don't let 'em get away!" And the marines didn't. Not a single enemy warrior lived to reenter the forest.

Hawk looked out over the smoking battlefield, surveying the night's work.

"Must be a hundred of 'em layin' out there," he judged.

"Yeah, they are the craziest bastards I ever heard of," said Canlon, his voice still weak with emotion. "Why don't they leave us alone? I bet there's a thousand of 'em out there."

"The battalion's got to be close. They must be drivin' 'em down on us," Hawk said, offering Canlon a plug of chewing tobacco. But Joe refused it. Chewing tobacco was only an experiment for him. He lit a cigarette.

"Banzai!" The cry went up from the forest and then, shoulder to shoulder, the enemy charged out of the forest. They blanketed the entire front portion of the field in front of the house. Ignoring the foxholes this time, the running phalanx bore madly down upon the house.

"Mother...of God!" Quiroz gasped and jerked the machine gun trigger. But it was jammed. He banged on it with the heel of his hand. Lundstedt opened up with the Bren and a jagged hole was cut out of the charging men. They never slowed, however. They stampeded the wounded and dying, intent upon overrunning the house.

Hawk clenched his teeth and held his fire. Huge beads of perspiration fell down from his forehead and into his whiskers.

"This is it, Hawk. They got us!" Canlon whined.

"Stay cool," said Hawk in a low voice. "Get as many as you can." He reached over and gave Joe a reassuring slap on the back.

Suddenly Quiroz's gun opened up, with devastating range and accuracy. As if that were the signal, Hawk and the other marines opened fire. The rage of the enemy seemed to be checked. Their dash hesitated. Men dropped wherever the flying lead from the farmhouse met them. The machine gun spat shivering slivers of lightning into the indecisive ranks.

Though they might have overpowered the marines, their casualties would have been atrocious. They backed away firing, probably losing as many men in the retreat as they would have if they had pursued their original plan. The barrel of Hawk's Thompson was hot enough to melt, and he painfully dropped the over-heated weapon when it touched his skin. Canlon threw off his helmet and sat on the floor to take advantage of whatever respite the enemy deigned to give him. The Japanese were crowded around the edge of the forest, tangled up with one another as they sought cover. The marines who were able continued to fire into them.

"I tell you, Hawk, I ain't never seen so many of 'em before," said Joe, shaking all over.

"The battalion'll be here any second," said Hawk, spitting out tobacco juice. "Don't worry." Hawk knew he was lying, but it was the only encouragement he could give.

Quiroz stuck his head through the, portal to the veranda. "Sergeant Hawk, we're out of ammo for the machine gun," he said.

"Shit," Hawk growled. That was the end of it, and he had to admit it. By the most optimistic estimate, he was outnumbered thirty to one, and this was no time to be optimistic.

"Okay, Quiroz," he finally said. "You did a good job. See what you can do with that old rifle of yours now."

Quiroz smiled. He also knew that it was over, for it was only with great difficulty that the machine gun had staved off the Japanese victory. He pulled his head back.

"I'm scared, Hawk. Scared shitless." Joe shuddered.

"Stay down a while," Hawk advised him. "Catch your breath. You can get back in the doorway there, so you can pick 'em off when they come over the barrels." The words only made his trembling intensify. Hawk heard the crackle of a loudspeaker and he looked back out at the forest and the milling enemy soldiers.

"Marine! We kill all!" a deep, angry voice raged. "March out marine. We kill all! March now!"

"Oh God." Canlon buried his face. Hawk spat contemptuously over the barrels. Loudspeakers made him angry. The voice continued to babble in annoying electronic mutations. Hawk walked into the living room and everyone gathered around the various doors leading into it, to see what he would do.

"Sergeant Hawk next?" Klaus whispered to Ernst.

"Too dangerous," the other snapped.

"Who, then?" Ernst shifted his eyes toward Mayeaux, the only marine that was stationed in the same room with them.

"Okay, looks like they got us," said Hawk, slinging the strap of his Thompson over his shoulder so that the muzzle aimed at the ground.

"We gonna surrender, Sergeant?" Ewell asked fearfully.

"I ain't. They want us to march out there so they can cut us down. If anybody wants to surrender, I'll let you, but you'd be crazy. These Japs are cornered by the whole Marine Corps. They're all gonna be wiped out pretty soon themselves. There ain't no way they're gonna take prisoners."

Lundstedt spoke up. "Maybe they done whipped the marines. Maybe they're just moppin' us up." Hawk glared at him.

"Nobody whips the marines," he replied, "but you can go if you want to." Lundstedt could still hear the voice over the loudspeaker. He could hear the snorting and dripping of saliva in its guttural tirade.

"I reckon I'll be stayin'," he mumbled. Hawk nodded his satisfaction. That was the only sane thing to do, as he saw it.

No other marine mentioned surrender.

"Sergeant Hawk, my sister and I would like to surrender," said Moritz. Hawk tightened his lips as a fog of indecision clouded his besieged mind.

"After...they...take care of us, y'all can surrender," he said at last. "Not until." Moritz looked displeased.

"Hey, this son of a bitch is givin' us till noon to come out," said Gist, looking out the front window, in the direction of the bullhorn. Noon was a long way off.

"That don't sound like a bunch of cornered Japs to me," said Lundstedt. "I bet they done took the whole island. I bet we're the only marines left on it, and they can take their own sweet time about dealing with us."

Hawk shook his head negatively. He would not even consider such a ridiculous suggestion. "If you want to leave, let me know and then take off. But let me know first. I want to see your guts blown all over the ground out there." His words were rendered even more frightening because of the guts already lying blown out on the ground. The words were not idle verbiage but horrifying reality. Lundstedt hung his head.

"I ain't afraid or nothing," he mumbled, "but we ain't got a chance."

"That's right," said Hawk. "If you ain't afraid, you're the only one here that ain't. It's just a bad situation, I guess, but we're in it. Get to your posts—them bastards won't be waitin' til noon."

Hawk walked slowly to the hall. "Hey, Gretchen,

come outa there," he said to the pile of tables that formed her shelter. She crawled out, her eyes wide with fear and her lips trembling. Hawk smiled and winked. He put one arm around her and steered her into "the kitchen.

"What's going to happen, James?" She could barely be heard.

"Ah, nothing. A little fightin', I guess."

"They're going to kill you all, aren't they?"

"Ah, shit on 'em," he snorted. They reached the back door and he paused there and looked out. The rear forest appeared to be unoccupied. He rocked back his helmet and she watched every movement in his face.

* * *

"Sergeant Mayeaux," said Ernst casually, "would you mind terribly, placing your bayonet out here where it is convenient."

"Oh, sure," said Mayeaux. Klaus, Ernst and Mayeaux were lying behind the knee-high wall in the bombed-out bedroom. The sound of sniper fire and return fire could be heard throughout the house. The noon dead-line was apparently not a moratorium on all fighting— just on an assault.

"Guess we'll be gettin' in some close action," Mayeaux said seriously as he rammed the point of the blade into the floor, Klaus crawled to the remains of the doorway that led to the hall, inconspicuously blocking any retreat from the room.

"A fine weapon," said Ernst, pulling the knife from the floor with some difficulty. Mayeaux nodded disinter-ested agreement and looked back out at his quiet sector of the forest. Ernst thrust the weapon viciously at his ribs. To his embarrassment, however, the sergeant had his shirt open, and the blade only penetrated and ripped it, completely missing the American's compact body.

"What the goddam hell..." Mayeaux jerked away and dropped his M-3. Ernst kicked it across the room. Risking a sniper's bullet, Mayeaux stood and ran for the door, but Klaus stood also and blocked his path. The Dutchman held his rifle across his chest and Mayeaux simply drew back his fist and flattened him. Ernst suddenly regretted his choice for a victim but he nevertheless lunged at the sergeant's unprotected back. Mayeaux wheeled to face him and caught his wrist. They struggled across the room and Ernst was finally out-muscled. The knife bounced off the floor and Mayeaux forcefully shoved the Dutchman into a dislocated beam, knocking the wind from him. His back was to the door when Moritz stepped over the fallen Klaus. Moritz raised his short-barreled shotgun and blew a hole the size of a basketball through Mayeaux. Klaus struggled to his feet and dragged the nearly severed torso and legs to the wall. Awkwardly, he pushed the bloody corpse into the moat. Moritz turned and left the room. Canlon could see his exit from the veranda.

"I can't hit a thing at this range," Moritz called to him, holding up the shotgun. Canlon nodded; he had heard the shot. He was not very interested at the present, however, in the range of shotguns.

Sergeant Hawk was, after all, a primitive sort of man, a man who lived by nerve and instinct. His intellect was not especially dull, but unfortunately, it was untrained. In his breast was the instinct of first man to protect the female, for the survival of the species. The male, including himself, was expendable. Even if he had not loved Gretchen as he did, he would have tried to save her. But he did love her, deeply.

"Gretchen, I think we can make it on down to the boat," he said. "Ain't nothing stirring in the back right now."

"James, you will leave here?'

Hawk looked away and nodded. "Yeah, ain't much chance here."

"I will get Moritz," she said, a spark of hope returning to her face. But Hawk restrained her lightly.

"He...uh, wants to surrender to the Japs."

"Oh," she said simply, and then, to his amazement: "Let's go then."

"Okay, I want to go tell Beckwith, something," he said. He left the room to tell the other sergeant that he would return from the cove in thirty minutes. In the interim, Gretchen had spoken with Moritz. To Hawk's continuing amazement, her brother made no proposal to accompany them.

"Stay low," he said, stepping out onto the kitchen steps and down into the trench that led to the cellar. No sniper fire vexed them; the rear of the house was still deserted. Brock sauntered up to the back door and watched their flight—from the trench, over the cellar, to Armistead's foxhole and from thence to the path that led to the cove. His eyes narrowed and his widely spaced teeth appeared from beneath his thin lips.

Holding his Thompson in his right band, Hawk tugged Gretchen along the path with his left. The ever-cool sergeant was now tense with anxiety as he filed down the treacherous leafy corridor. They stepped over the rotting corpses of the dead Japanese and raced down the cove to the only boat that remained afloat. Hawk helped her aboard and turned to watch the rocky coast and forest above them. There was no sign of the enemy. He turned and stepped aboard nimbly. Setting down the gun, he set the sails as deftly as might the most experienced of sailors. Then he tossed the strap of his gun over his shoulder and vaulted from the deck onto the shore. He gave the boat a push and waded knee deep into the lagoon. Then he backed up and waved. "Take care of yourself, kid," he smiled.

"James, what are you doing? I knew you were lying."

"Yeah, I'm just a character, I guess." Gretchen grabbed the tow line and dived into the waist-deep water, she slipped the loop over the piling that stood there.

"Hey," said Hawk, angrily. "You gotta get the hell outa here."

"Oh, James." She threw her arms around him and he clutched her tightly. "I do love you. I shouldn't, but I do. Please come with me, James. I can't stand any more of this. Please come with me." Tears poured from her sad and beautiful blue eyes. He put his rough cheek next to her delicate face.

"I can't," he whispered.

"Why?" Her fingers bit into his hard arms.

"I...just can't."

"James, I have so much to tell you. I have so many things to explain to you. Please don't go back." She sobbed.

"You don't have to explain anything to me. I love you. I'll always love you."

"But you don't understand." She choked on her

tears. "You can't go away without knowing...how much I need you. Father stood between us, James. I loved you so much, but Father..."

"I know. I know." He brushed the tears from her eyes and gently pushed her face against his shoulder. "Don't worry about all that. I know. You have to get away from all this. You belong in Europe with all those barons and counts. You'll knock 'em dead over there. You're gonna end up a princess or something, I'll be damned if you don't."

"I don't want to go to Europe. I want to go with you, James. I've lost everything, I've lost everyone. Oh, God, James, please come with me!" She buried her face in his chest and tried to shake his unshakable frame. Hawk took her face in his hands.

"No, you were right, baby. We are from two different worlds. This is mine. I'm just plain backwoods trash that found something he was good at. You'd hate me in the real world. I'm a nothing—I never will be anything. But you, now you're a real lady, quality all the way. Go on, now, please?"

"No, James." She fell exhausted to her knees. "They'll shoot you down like a dog," she screamed. "Why, why would you let them shoot you for no reason?" He knelt on the sand beside her and replaced his arms around her. Tenderly he caressed her yellow hair. After a moment of silence, her hysterical crying stopped, easing into occasional painful sobs.

The gunfire back at the farmhouse increased. Hawk raised his head over hers, like the wolf listening to the call of his pack.

"I better go now."

She looked into his eyes, those flashing blue eyes

that burned with the fires of war. Her lips parted and she kissed him.

"Someday I'll have you, James. I don't care what you are or what I am. Someday you'll be mine." Hawk smiled, for he had once made that same vow. He helped her to her feet. They waded out to the boat and he lifted her aboard effortlessly.

"Nice day for sailing," he laughed. His hand reached for hers.

"Someday, James. Somewhere..." she gasped weakly. Their hands met.

"Yeah. How about the western shore?" Their hands slipped apart.

"Yes, the western shore." The boat slid away with alarming rapidity. The sergeant watched it for a moment and then turned back up the cove. But Gretchen watched him until he was only a shadow in the leafy jungle path. Then the shadow disappeared.

"Goodbye James," she whispered. Her drained spirit slowed her considerably, but the girl managed to lower the sails. The residue of the waves that spilled over the reef gradually pushed her back to shore. Wearily she jumped into the water and moored her little sloop. She stood there in the surf for a moment, looking at the path that led to the plantation house, where Armageddon awaited.

11

THE PLOT

Hawk entered the kitchen where Brock, Fine and Ewell were seated on the floor. Fine was writing.

"Anything happening?" Hawk asked.

"Not yet," Ewell answered. Ewell gestured toward Fine and Hawk smiled at the madly gyrating pencil.

"Hey, Fine, you got me in your book?" Hawk asked, going down to one knee. He didn't really know Fine; this would be his last opportunity to do something about that.

"I sure do, Sergeant Hawk. Quite a bit about you."

"About how I'm a lowlife murderin' son of a bitch?"

"No. About how you have adapted so well. About how a man can adapt to anything. That is what raises man above the animals, don't you think?"

"Yeah, I guess it does," said Hawk thoughtfully. "I never been raised that high before," he added, winking at Ewell.

Hawk returned to the veranda and Joe Canlon.

"Well, I put her on her boat, Joe. I think she'll be all

right till the marines get here." He fell into his easy chair. Joe had regained his composure somewhat, enough to take a proffered plug of tobacco.

"Pretty rough...on her and on you, huh?"

"Yep." Hawk took a deep breath. "It never would have worked out. Can you see her living in a shack back in Mississippi with me?"

"I don't know. It's been done, I guess."

"It don't seem right that your life should all fit together real neat for once and, bang, it's over."

"Don't seem right, but it seems like it always happens that way. Now you take my old lady... Are you in the mood for a story?" Hawk smiled. He wasn't really, but he nodded affirmatively.

"Well, she raised kids for forty years, by herself. My old man left her when I was a baby, they say. She never had a goddam nickel of her own and neither did we. When I left home, she marries this old wino, you see, and goddamned if she don't have to support him for another two years. And then you know that happened?' Hawk shrugged. "Well, I'll tell you. She dies. A week later her sister dies and leaves her eighty thousand bucks. Who gets it? The wino. That's the way life is, Hawk."

Under normal circumstances, Hawk might have laughed at such an absurd story, but today he was moved. He shook his head.

"Well, at least we ain't got to raise kids for forty years —right, Joe?" Hawk tried to smile.

"Yeah, we're a couple of lucky son of a bitches, Hawk." Hawk reached into his pocket for a cigar. Instead his fingers pulled out the safety lever of a hand grenade. The grenade that had killed Ralph Armistead. Hawk looked at it. "Yeah, I just hate losing all these men and that kid's family. And then like a jerk, I get her to love me and go get myself killed."

"That was some kinda shit, losing all those guys like that," said Canlon. "Them natives are pretty sneaky."

Hawk continued to study the lever. It was from an American grenade. A scowl crossed his face and he fell back in his chair. At his elbow lay the swastika that Ilse had drawn in the dust. His brooding face stared at the table, his eyes flashed lightning bolts.

"Jesus Christ!" he gasped. "Joe, who's in the back room?"

"Mayeaux and them two foreigners."

"That's all?"

"Oh, I seen the girl's brother go back there once." Hawk jumped to his feet and crossed the hall. He looked in on Ernst and Klaus.

The floor was dark and wet, but the spots had been scuffed with dust in an attempt to hide the blood. "How are y'all doin'?" Hawk asked. "Seen Mayeaux?"

"We are as well as could be expected," Ernst smiled. "He left us quite some time ago." I bet he did, Hawk thought. Hawk walked through the house, looking in every room.

"Where's Claiborne?" he asked Ewell.

"You know, I ain't seen him since last night," Ewell replied.

"Well, shit on me," said Hawk, kicking the wall. Ewell scampered out of the way. Hawk retraced his steps to the den and picked up his Thompson. He took a step toward the room with Ernst and Klaus, then halted abruptly. He turned and stalked into the dining room.

He gestured for Brock to get away from the window. With a sigh of restrained rage, Hawk leaned over the barrels that guarded the dining room window. Beside him, Moritz leaned over them also, looking out toward the forest. Hawk held his submachine gun in his right hand and casually inserted the muzzle under his left arm, inches from Moritz's chest.

"Well, Moritz, it looks like the end of the line, don't it?" Hawk growled. Moritz smiled innocently.

"I'm afraid so, Sergeant Hawk. I suppose the end had to come."

"Yeah, ain't it the truth?"

"But I am strangely calm now, Sergeant Hawk."

"Is that a fact?"

"Yes, I know that I die for the cause that is right, and I am unafraid," said Moritz, turning his handsome smile to within a foot of Hawk's face.

"Well, you know Moritz, I wouldn't be afraid if I was you either," said Hawk, his chest heaving. "Because you're a backstabbin' Nazi son of a bitch."

The smile of Moritz faded. His eyes grew wide with terror. The room was empty, save for the two of them. But he realized that he was in a cage with the Devil himself. Hawk sneered as he stared into the boy's eyes. He enjoyed terrifying him.

Moritz lifted his shotgun barrel from the window sill and swung it toward Hawk. His movement was awkward; he was nearly paralyzed with fear. Hawk let the giant mouth of the shotgun level right on himself before he squeezed the trigger of the Thompson. Moritz was knocked across the room and into the wall. He twisted and squealed in pain. The breechblock of the Thompson had become entangled in Hawk's shirt sleeve, so he ripped the sleeve off and stood over Moritz.

"You're gonna be strangely calm for a long time, punk," he said, firing another burst into the dying boy.

Brock stepped into the room.

"Don't let them Dutch bastards get away," Hawk snapped. Brock reached into the kitchen and pulled Rolf in by the collar. He slung him to the floor.

"Here's one, Sergeant," Brock said.

"They're Germans, Brock. They were Germans," said Hawk with an insane glimmer in his fiery eyes. "They killed all my men, one by one, Brock." Rolf knelt on the floor and covered his head.

"Don't kill me!" begged Rolf. "Please don't kill me!"

"Are you Dutch, Rolf?" Hawk spat the words in his thick delta accent. "Tell me now that you're Dutch, Rolf!" Hawk kicked him. "Tell me, old man!"

"I am German, Sergeant Hawk. Please don't kill me!"

"Please don't kill me," mocked Hawk, pointing down at Rolf as he looked at Brock.

"You want me to do it?" Brock asked.

"Naw, wait," said Hawk, regaining some semblance of composure. "Hold him in the kitchen for a second. I gotta look in on my buddies in the back room."

Brock lifted Rolf by the collar and threw him onto the kitchen floor.

"What's going on?" Fine asked,

"This here's a German, Fine. Been killing us off at night, one by one. You missed your big chance, Rolf. Old Fine there's a Jew," Brock laughed. Rolf and Fine looked at one another for a moment without speaking. Brock aimed his rifle down at Rolf and backed toward the kitchen door. Out of habit he eyed the rear forest. At that instant Gretchen ran from the path out of the forest and scampered down the ladder of the cellar.

"My, my," Brock said to himself, when he spied the girl. Then he raised his voice. "Yeah, they been havin' a field day with us, Fine, but they missed the biggest prize of all...the old Jewboy himself."

Hawk stepped into the back bedroom, both hands tightly wound around his Thompson. Ernst turned around and smiled at him. Klaus cast a glance at him; his usual sneering expression was upon his face. Ernst was the first to read Hawk's eyes. His first impulse was to beg for mercy, but he knew Hawk too well for that. The crude American had no conception of the word mercy. Realizing that it was futile, but that it was his only alternative, Ernst jerked his rifle around toward Hawk. Klaus was a bit late in recognizing the gravity of the situation.

Back and forth, back and forth, Hawk steered the jolting muzzle, filling the room with the blinding blasts of fire and smoke. The two motionless bodies lay across one another, savagely riddled. Such was the verdict on a charge of treachery, delivered by the most callous of the hanging judges.

Hawk returned to the kitchen, his blood still raging through his veins. Rolf was on his knees his head bent down to the floor. Hawk leaned against the wall and pointed his gun down at him.

"Look at me, Rolf," he ordered. Rolf fearfully did so, raising his violently trembling head. "I got a few minutes here, Rolf, before the Japs blow my goddam brains out! I'm kinda in the mood for a little conversation. Guys get kind of talkative when they're fixin' to get killed, I guess. Just so I got somebody to talk to, I'll let you know something: you're fixin' to get killed before I do."

Hawk took a deep breath. "Marks, Klazusky, Mayeaux, Claiborne, Gaedcke." Then Hawk looked at Brock. "Bertoni and Ralph Armistead. What happened to Ralph? What happened to Van Speer?" Rolf sniffed and began crying, but he knew that he had better speak.

"Yes, we are all Germans. This island has been German for fifty years. We sold our rubber to the Japanese long before the war. Ernst and Klaus were SS officers sent here after the war started. We had a powerful radio and used it to relay messages to the Japanese."

The marines crowded around to hear the story.

"A white man, radioing to the Japs?" Gist gasped.

"Our countries are at war, God forgive me. The Japanese are my country's ally. When the Canadians came, Rudiger told them that we were Dutch, that his name was Van Speer, instead of Speer. That is how your intelligence heard of us and why they thought we were Dutch. The Canadians believed him. We knew that your patrol was coming. The Japanese tried to intercept you but they couldn't find you in the jungle. When you arrived, we were afraid of you. We couldn't speak Dutch but then when we discovered how..." Rolf started to say stupid..."innocent you were of us, we became less afraid. We only wanted you to leave so that we could evacuate with the Japanese. We received messages from the Japanese fleet and relayed them to the Japanese army by means of native runners, natives who had worked the Speer plantation. But when you began using the radio, we had to destroy it. Ernst spoke Japanese, he was our radio operator. We..." Rolf stammered, but

Hawk nudged him with his boot. This only frightened the old man more, causing him to freeze.

"Keep talking, jerk!" Hawk ordered.

"We killed Marks," Rolf cried, "to scare you off. To make you withdraw. We killed the second man for the same reason, so that you would think that the situation was hopeless and let us surrender to the Japanese. Rudiger killed him partly to get you to leave the house, to make you sleep outside with your men." Rolf cleared his throat. "The others we killed when we saw how proficient your defense was going to be. We were trying to weaken you, to hasten the Japanese victory."

"A white man on the Japs' side." Gist gasped again in disbelief.

"Gretchen was in on all this?" asked Hawk, his voice barely audible.

"She had a terrible time with her father. Yes, she knew; but she protected you. She kept you in the house away from the sabotage. The Speer family lived in fear of you and of attack by the Japanese. They feared the Japanese would mistake them for Americans, because of the racial similarities, so they remained in the cellar. Once the Japanese had killed you, they were relying upon Ernst to explain their position. Rudiger would have fled, but Gretchen wouldn't leave you and he wouldn't leave her, so he waited and hoped for the Japanese to kill you. We were all in on it though. We were all German, all Nazis."

"How could she know all along?" Hawk paced up and down now, shocked and dismayed. "What happened to Ralph?" He finally snapped.

"It was sad and uncalled for. The corporal was watching Ilse draw pictures, when she drew a swastika.

Before anyone could stop her, she was telling Corporal Armistead about Hitler..."

Hawk winced. She had done the same thing to him, but he had been too dense to recognize it. Ralph was still alive then; he might still be alive, along with Claiborne and Mayeaux, if Hawk had figured it out. But he had let himself become despondent and dull-witted.

"Corporal Armistead understood immediately," Rolf continued. "He was going to tell you our secret when Rudiger took a hand grenade from his belt and pulled the pin. He told the corporal that he would kill us all. I don't think he meant it, but the corporal struggled with him...and it went off. I ran when I saw them struggling. Gretchen blamed you for it at first, and then herself. She was in a terrible position, Sergeant Hawk."

"Yeah. She knew all along, goddam *knew.* She was part of it!" Hawk exclaimed. "How could she do that?"

"It was a war, Sergeant Hawk. She protected you as best she could. It was a relief for her when you went into the forest, because she knew that the real danger lay here. War is war, Sergeant Hawk. You Americans are so childish. She knew that you wouldn't understand."

"Childish? You Germans are crazy! Why in the goddam hell didn't you say you were German? We'd have let you go to the shittin' Japs. We didn't give a goddam. We came here to protect you, you sorry sacka shit. Those men you killed came here to stop the Japs from gettin' you—to die for you! You didn't have to be afraid of us—we'd have let you go!" Hawk hung his head. "You're the reason we're here," he moaned.

"Yeah, we're white people, too," Gist shouted angrily.

"Communications break down in a war," said Rolf. "There is no such thing as trust, that is why I said that you Americans are childish—you are too trusting. It is endearing, but Sergeant Hawk, our armies are at war!"

"All right, Rolf. You best get out there with your army, then," groaned Hawk.

"You gonna let that murderin' snake in the grass go?" Gist asked.

"Yeah, his army is waitin' on him. Get your ass movin', Rolf."

Rolf crawled slowly to his feet, incredulous. The brutal Sergeant Hawk was permitting his escape.

"You know, I thought you was a pretty nice old buzzard," said Hawk, helmet in hand.

"I liked you, too, Sergeant Hawk. You are a fine soldier. You would have made Gretchen a fine husband." Hawk walked through the dining room and into the living room, followed by Rolf. He swung open the front door.

"Adios, old man," said Hawk.

"Goodbye, Sergeant. Thank you for sparing my life. I shall never forget you." Hawk closed the door.

"You ain't gonna have to remember for long," said Hawk to the wooden door. When Rolf was halfway across the front field, a spate of shots poured from the jungle. He was killed instantly. "I'd rather be childish than crazy," said Hawk to the door. He returned to the kitchen.

"Well, they're all dead," said Lundstedt to him.

"Yeah, all but one," Hawk growled, tightening his lips. Brock watched his sergeant intently, casually he peeped out the back door at the cellar.

Hawk put on his helmet. Too much had happened and too much was happening for him to pause and reflect upon it all. He dropped back into his automatic, habitual thinking. Kill Japs, that was the answer. And soon he would have all of the Japs that his black heart desired. He scratched his thumbnail over the head of a match and it cast a flickering golden shadow beneath his helmet. Deliberately, almost frigidly, he lit his last stub of a cigar.

12

THE FINAL ASSAULT

THE SHOUTS WENT UP FROM THE EDGE OF THE FOREST. Hundreds of feet raced across the scraggly, corpse strewn grass. The marines fired gamely into the unstoppable horde, but they seemed to sense the absence of the machine gun. The Bren gun, the Sten gun, Beckwith's BAR and Gist with the M-3 managed to exact a high price for the enemy's passage across the open field. Joe, with the Sten gun, and Hawk with his Thompson, showered the oncoming men who chose the veranda for their goal. It was an accessible target because the moat did not protect it, but the blistering automatic fire held the enemy at bay. Bodies stacked up on the other side of the moat. The attackers climbed over their dead and splashed into the moat. They jumped at the windows and hung onto the sills in twos and threes, forcing the marines to step back from the crowded openings and fire into the faces of the enemy troops. Soon the moat had filled with bodies and the attackers tried to run straight into the windows.

Grenades rattled off the adobe walls and fell back

among the men who had thrown them. The grenades that went through the windows kept the marines hopping, in order to avoid or expel them. Brock and Gist retreated from the dining room as a trio of grenades bounced on the hardwood floor. The enemy flooded through the window, only to be annihilated by their own explosions. The dining room wall cracked and split open, changing the dining room window into a gaping, notched arch. Gist flattened down on the kitchen floor and continued to fire into this newest breach. Another grenade hit the outside and the dining room wall fell inward in a cloud of dust and shrapnel.

The pressing throng, a mass of blazing muzzles, pushed Hawk and Canlon from the veranda. Hawk let the little porch fill with the enemy before rolling a grenade into them. After a deafening roar, the sergeant was again the master of the room.

The Japanese fell back to catch their breath, but this time they did not return to the forest. They backed halfway across the clearing and persisted in drilling the house with rifle fire. Stronger arms pelted the house with grenades, causing sporadic black explosions all along the front wall.

"I think I'm gonna have a heart attack before the sorry bastards nail me," choked Joe Canlon as he changed his clip. Hawk peered over the barrels and fired single shots into the unprotected concourse that was arrayed before him. Burning shrapnel cinders dotted his fatigues.

Gist sat on the dining room floor, bracing his elbows on his knees and firing into the screaming mob. This would not have been unusual, except that there was no dining room wall and he might just as well have been sitting out on the open ground. A well-placed grenade finally chased him from the position and scattered the living room wall where he had been sitting. The roof came crashing down on the spot. The rubble would make his flank very difficult to defend. Gist and Brock crawled choking into the kitchen. They could hardly see one another for the dust and smoke.

"Hey, Gist. I got something to do, before they get me," Brock gagged. The demolition of the house continued on all sides.

"What's that?" asked Gist, wiping his watery eyes.

"That German girl came back. She's in the cellar." Brock crawled out the kitchen door and into the trench that led to the makeshift bomb shelter. He rapped angrily on the trapdoor and it swung open. Brock lowered himself rapidly down the ladder.

"Hi, little German girl." Brock smiled. "Heil Hitler! You know, there ain't many marines that get to plug a German. That's quite a prize." Gretchen backed away, but the room did not allow her to back very far.

Brock remained on the ladder, leveling his M-l at her with one hand.

"How...did you know?" she whimpered.

"That's something you'll never know, sugar plum. Know why? I'm gonna splatter you all over this shittin' hole, that's why." Brock threw back his head and roared with laughter.

"Please, American, please don't..." she begged, squirming in terror against the wall. Brock only laughed louder.

"Yep, that's what I'm gonna do. It's open season on Germans and damned if you ain't the only one left. You know, I ain't never killed a girl either. I'm going to hell today, but I'm gonna die happy." The laugh and his smile faded as quickly as they had appeared and were replaced by a snarl.

"No!" she screamed and hid her face. The tiny room was filled with reverberating shots. Her ears rang and she dropped to her knees. But when she looked up, Brock was hanging from the ladder, upside down by one leg. Hawk stepped onto the first rung of the ladder.

"Hey, Brock, tell me something. Did you kill Bertoni?" Hawk asked flatly. Blood gushed from the boy's throat and he groaned weakly.

"Japs..." Brock gurgled. "Japs did it." Then his body fell limp against the ladder. Hawk looked at Gretchen. The dark leathery trails under his eyes disappeared as he squinted down on her. He said nothing, but frowned darkly. She could not find her voice, and only continued to whimper. She dropped her head, either in shame or nervous exhaustion. When she looked up, Hawk was gone and the door was shut again.

As Hawk ran back along the trench, he saw a half dozen grenade-bearing, loincloth-clad soldiers round the corner of the house and step right up to the back door. He opened fire. They turned and fired on him. Gist fired into their backs from the kitchen. They were all disabled, but Hawk's helmet had been knocked from his head and blood gushed from his temple. He rocked back a step, the cigar falling from his lips.

"Goddam it," he cursed as he let the blood stream over his filthy palm. "Shot through the goddam head." He stooped to pick up his helmet and his eyes went out of focus. The earth and the sky seemed to change places and shift about at odd angles. He dropped the headgear down heavily upon his brow and stumbled over his vanquished assailants, into the kitchen.

"You're hit, Hawk," Gist exclaimed, as if such a thing were not possible.

"Yeah, it's a bitch, too."

"Lay down." An alarming deluge of brightly colored blood splashed down the Hawk's neck. He shook his head and squinted at Gist.

"No, it don't matter, we're through," he answered unemotionally.

As if to prove the statement true, the kitchen wall came cascading down and over them. Buzzing and whining steel licked at their ears. They were forced to their knees by the ponderous weight, but came rising up and out of the smoldering debris. Too evil to die, they returned from the grave prepared for them. Hawk's wound was invisible now, covered with a layer of grime. He staggered back weakly into a jumbled pile of rock. He saw a tidal wave of strong and enthusiastic Japanese hurdle what had once been the front wall. Beckwith and Fine stood directly in their path and fired, but the horde ran them down. He could see the two Americans in their midst, swinging madly at the Japanese with their emptied guns. One of the enemy placed a small muzzle to Fine's head and the sharp blast knocked him into the pile of bodies that filled the moat. Beckwith was clubbed to the floor. When the close-quartered struggle ceased, Hawk opened fire on the crowd of soldiers and without flinching they reciprocated. A bullet slammed into his right arm, he felt the heavy impact and a dull paralyzing numbness, but no pain. In the background, screams of agony and panic mixed with raging rifle fire impinged upon his euphoric senses.

"Get as many as you can," Hawk rasped. Gist was busy spraying the men that Hawk had stirred up. Hawk feebly managed to stand, and braced himself on two fallen crossed beams. By the time he got to his feet, Gist had somehow managed to clear the dining room area of the persistent foe.

The shattered rafter beams were draped with bodies eternally frozen in macabre poses.

The half of the house that contained the kitchen and dining room was a heap of smoking rubble. But for Gist and Hawk, it was now deserted by the living. The other marines were separated from them by a wall of screaming Japanese. They were holed up in the hallway and in Gretchen's bedroom, clubbing the enemy with their empty guns and batting away a torrent of hand grenades. The enraged attackers ignored Hawk and Gist, climbing over one another in an attempt to vault the hallway defenses. Suddenly, Gist spun around and fell sprawled in the wreckage. A stray piece of shrapnel had caught him in the ribs.

"You okay?' Hawk asked, ripping the bloody sleeve from his own loosely dangling right arm. Gist sat up slowly. Excruciating pain softened his hard features.

"Shit yeah, I'm okay."

"Good, let's get 'em then," said Hawk. Like an animal he fought; once he had tasted blood, the fight must be to the death—even if it were his own blood and his own death. A crimson haze hung over the roofless hall; it was time to pay the prince of darkness his due. With fire and brimstone fresh upon their nostrils, the two savage Americans stepped over the dead, stopping within inches of the attackers, who still were not cognizant of them. The floury white adobe dust powdered their fatigues; they moved drunkenly in the chalky-tasting cloud.

Gist and Hawk each had less than a clip left but they fired stubbornly into the backs of the men besieging the hallway. The Japanese turned on them, but they too were out of ammunition. The sound of the last shot died away, and the crowd of attackers paused for an instant to survey their opponents. Two bloody, half-dead but remorseless monsters stood before them, ready for the final hand-to-hand confrontation. It seemed to Hawk as if he had only blinked, and then they were upon him with lightning swiftness. A sword slipped through Gist's shoulder and he went down screaming in uncontrolled pain. Hawk stood over him, swinging his Thompson with his left hand at the surrounding warriors, until the stock was nothing but a fistful of splinters.

By sheer weight of numbers they tackled and dragged him down. He felt his exhausted body being kicked and pummeled, but presently he saw daylight amongst the flailing arms and legs. With the instinct of a mad dog and the tenacity of a headless snake, he struggled to his feet again. Joe Canlon stood beside him. Poised and ready, Hawk faced right and then left, searching for his next attacker. Rivers of red spilled down his face in a horrid labyrinth.

"Settle down, Hawk, that's it," Canlon said. He put a hand on Hawk's shoulder, in an effort to calm the indomitable beast.

"That's what?" Hawk asked, his breath gone.

"All of 'em, we cleaned 'em out. The stupid bastards just kept on comin' and we wiped 'em out."

Hawk sat down heavily, he tried to clear the scarlet flood that obscured his vision.

"Hey, Joe," he finally managed to say.

"Yeah?"

"Shoot the wounded," he gasped, and fell back on a pile of rock, his chest frantically rising and falling.

"Hey, get me outa here, you crazy bastards," Gist called from beneath the heap of dead and unconscious Japanese. Canlon dug him out. A samurai sword protruded from his shoulder and Joe grimaced.

"Don't that hurt?" Joe asked as Gist got to his feet.

"Goddam right it hurts, Canlon," Gist bellowed. There was no blood flowing from around the sword, but the big man had a bad wound in his side.

"Hey, Joe," Hawk wheezed. "Kill the wounded, quick."

"Aw, shit, Hawk, I ain't much on that kinda shit."

"There's enough wounded here to start a regiment —you better do it," Gist moaned.

"Get Brock to do it," said Canlon.

"Brock's dead," Hawk informed him.

"Oh? Yeah, Quiroz is dead. He jumped on a grenade and saved us all. I think Fine got killed and Beckwith was with him."

"Yeah, yeah. Just tell me who's alive," said Hawk impatiently.

"Ewell, Lundstedt is...I guess that's it," said Joe thoughtfully. "They was with me. That head wound ain't too bad, your arm caught a good one, though," Canlon said as he looked Hawk over.

Hawk flexed his injured arm. "Shit on it," he growled.

The men sat there, too dazed to speak any more.

Lundstedt began executing the writhing Japanese with a sword. He found Beckwith alive, with a giant knot on his head. The marines were tending to him when a blast shook the forest. A fountain of black blocked the sky and a tree toppled at the forest's edge.

"For shit sakes," Canlon said, falling to one knee. "What now?"

"It's a seventy-five," said Hawk. "There's your goddam battalion, right on time, after everybody's dead." Canlon sighed wearily. "Ain't that the way life is, though?" he mused.

13

CONCLUSION

A TANK CAME CRUNCHING OUT OF THE JUNGLE. IT WAS followed by a half dozen more. The infantry flocked after the metal monsters, excitedly surveying the carnage and rubble left by the squad of Sergeant Hawk.

"Ewell, go get Gretchen out of the cellar," Hawk ordered. Drops of blood fell from his face as he hung his head. He noticed a charred ream of paper beneath the heel of his boot. It was burned through and through, but the top half of the first sheet was still a legible, unbroken ash. It read:

War makes man into an enigma; fighting for what he trusts to be right, he becomes a terrible conduit for evil.

"Joe, what kind of a man is an enigma?" Hawk asked.

"Don't ask me. I can't even tell Dutch from German."

Hawk looked at Joe, silently studying him. "We whipped 'em, didn't we Joe? We whipped all of 'em." His voice was still full of anger. Joe nodded. Hawk dropped the paper and crushed it with his boot. Poor Fine, he thought, crazy kid.

"Sergeant Hawk? I'm Major Breeding, this is Captain Fankhauser."

Hawk squinted across the moat at the two officers. He nodded to Fankhauser. The captain barely recognized this creature as the once-confident Sergeant Hawk. The sergeant remained seated, covered with blood, grime and gore, very much disinterested in military courtesy. He could see Colonel Hayes in the distance, pointing in several directions in rapid succession. He cut an immaculate and distinguished figure.

"Lord, Hawk! Where's your patrol?" Fankhauser asked.

"This is it, cap'n."

"Where's the Dutch family?"

"Dead. This pile of rocks was their house."

"Dead?" Fankhauser repeated in disbelief. He and the major looked at one another.

"We got quite a story to tell, Captain," Canlon began.

"Shut up," Hawk snapped. Colonel Hayes walked up behind the two officers.

"We'll see if you're a platoon sergeant after this, Hawk," Major Breeding said. Hawk only stared back at him. Hayes smiled and saluted Hawk. He told the two officers to carry on.

"Looks like a hell of a battle here, Jim," Hayes said.

"Yessir, worst I ever been in."

"Don't pay any attention to Breeding. I'll get you a squad, at least. I know what kind of fight you put up. If you were as good at leading as you are at fighting, they'd put you over the Pacific Theatre."

"A squad? Thanks, Colonel." Hawk's tone was dazed and empty.

"But that's a terrible thing about that family of inno- cent civilians," Hayes sighed, looking out over the mire of flesh and blood.

"Damn shame," Hawk agreed, but he didn't seem sincere to the Colonel. Hayes smiled.

"You're quite a man, Jim. You'll have another platoon in no time."

"Yeah, I hope so," Hawk mumbled as a team of corpsmen worked over him and Gist.

"Well," Hayes stepped back and drew himself up to his full height, "I'm going to have a look around. I'll talk to you later." Hayes saluted Hawk and turned around. Hawk felt like crying but no tears could be dragged from his dead soul. There were tears in his voice, even if they could not run from his eyes.

"Colonel Hayes?"

"Yes, Jim?" Hawk swallowed hard, his lips trembled.

"I lost a lot of boys, Colonel Hayes," he managed to say.

"I know you did, Jim. So did I," Hayes said, staring back at him. Then he turned and left. A strong wind whipped through Hawk's disheveled hair; it whistled in his ears.

"A lot of boys," he repeated.

The last of the corpsmen left in order to bring back stretchers. Ewell returned. The men knelt in a circle around their two badly wounded saviors.

"Sergeant Hawk, you know who killed Brock?" Ewell asked, wide eyed with the information. "That German girl got him."

"Ewell, you're so goddam stupid," said Hawk

rubbing his stinging arm. "I killed the son of a bitch." Ewell looked at Hawk for a moment and then shrugged. He stood and turned to walk away.

"Uh...Ewell," Hawk called him back. "You did a good job here, you're a good marine." Ewell smiled broadly; it was perhaps the first vocal praise that Hawk had ever given him. Lundstedt smiled at Ewell.

"And, uh...I'd rather not tell the Colonel about...the girl being German. Maybe we'll just say Ernst and his buddy were." Hawk looked around the circle of marines that made up what was left of his patrol.

"It's okay with me," said Lundstedt. "They wouldn't do nothing to a goddam woman anyway."

"I know," said Hawk, growing weaker. "But she might have go to an internment camp or go through a buncha shit. I figure she's gone through enough."

"If that's the way you want it, it don't matter to me," said Beckwith. "It don't exactly set well with me though...that she knew about all that was going on. I could have been one of the guys they knocked off..."

"Y'all can do what you want about it," said Hawk. "I would have given my life for any one of those boys, you all know that. I'm just telling you what I'd rather you did."

Beckwith felt a little ashamed. "Whatever you want, Hawk, I was just thinking out loud." The men's respect for Hawk assured the acceptance of his wishes.

"What about her papers? They'll figure her out," Canlon said.

"Figure her out?" Hawk laughed, very low and weak. "What papers? She'll get by if she plays her cards right. She's pretty good at that," he said bitterly.

A Seabee bulldozer was hard at work upon funeral

arrangements for the fallen Japanese soldiers. Hawk was taken to a mobile hospital unit where he received an operation for the removal of a bullet, a transfusion and several stitches. Gist had to be taken back to the other side of the island and from there to the fleet. He required serious major surgery for the removal of the sword, but afterwards he was very proud of the souvenir. A camp was set up on the cleared field in front of the farmhouse and patrols continued to scour the jungle with search-and-destroy missions. The island was secured, for whatever it was worth. Fruitless battles undergo little scrutiny when they are successful.

Gretchen was treated royally by Colonel Hayes. She was given an officer's tent and her very own aide. Arrangements were being made to sail and fly her down to Australia, and from there she would be free to choose her own destination and, her destiny. She was guarded about both during her conversations with Hayes, but he didn't press her. He knew what an ordeal she had gone through, or at least he said that he did.

It was two days from the time that Hawk shot Brock until Hawk saw her again. She sought him out in the hospital tent. But she did not have to search the interior. Hawk and Beckwith were seated upon the charred ground in front of the big tent, pale but fast recovering. Hawk had a bandage on his head and wore a clean uniform. Canlon was there too; it was his loud and boisterous voice that led her to the men. Hawk looked up at her when she stopped and stood before him. Everyone fell silent. Hawk slowly got to his feet and they faced each other a bit longer without speaking.

"Want to go for a walk?" Hawk finally asked. She nodded, a quick smile flashing across her face and then disappearing. Hawk didn't return the smile. Before she turned to go with him, she glanced at Canlon and Beckwith. Their solemn scowls made her shudder. She remembered the vicious monster, Brock, and imagined that they would have liked to have gone through with his plan.

They walked down toward the cove, but the path wasn't deserted now. It was much wider and marines passed them every few seconds. Her boat still lay moored beside the two sunken craft. But now, a dozen naked marines lolled upon its deck. They strolled onto a rocky promontory that was comparatively isolated, and sat down there in the soft grass.

"They're taking me to Sydney tomorrow," she said. Hawk nodded and stared at the ground. "James, I know that you don't owe me anything, and that I owe you my life...and more, I suppose. But would you tell me what happened to my brother, and Rolf?"

"Japs got 'em," he answered simply. He opened his mouth to say something else, but he controlled himself. She seemed to accept his answer.

"I know what you think of us, of me..." she began.

"I don't think nothing of it. That's the advantage of being stupid. I don't much want to talk about...any of it."

"I see," she said. He was looking out at the ocean. "James, I *did* love you, you must know that. But, they were my family..."

"We don't have to talk about it," he said sternly.

"Oh, James, I didn't want to have anything to do with the war. I don't care about who fights whom or why. I loved my family, and I loved you, and there was just no solving it. You had each picked your side and you were so sure of yourselves, I just wasn't involved that deeply in the war. James, I cared about you."

"Yeah, it was a bad situation, I guess. I can see that. But I was involved, deeply. You once asked me why I fight. I know now that it's because my friends are fighting. One of my men jumped on a hand grenade to save the others. Why? I don't know. I don't know what this feeling is, what the name of it is. But I've got it. I loved you and I guess I loved them. I've seen guys get their arms and legs blown off, their eyes blown out." Hawk looked down at the ground. "That's something, something that it keeps getting harder for me to forget."

"I understand."

"Do you?"

"Yes, James. I don't have that feeling, but I know that you do. I know something keeps you...doing this. I know that you are not a brutal man. I know that you are good."

"Am I? I don't know. Good and bad, you and the war, you and me—I can't tell anymore. Everything is mixed up."

"I know it is," she said. "It was for me, too. I didn't know what to do."

"Yeah, I don't either."

"James, can't you love them and me? Aren't they two different loves?"

"Yeah, they're different kinds of love. But they don't get along too well, not inside me anyway."

"Well, James, isn't it like politics? There are different sides, but after the speech and the election, everyone forgets what it was about and who was on which side. People go back to picking their friends individually instead of by groups."

"Yeah, I guess it is. Politics comes down to war."

"But isn't it all so silly?"

Hawk sighed. "Maybe," he said. She reached out and put her hand over his.

"I love you, James," she said. But he didn't reply. He only looked at her. "Do you love me?" she asked.

"I don't know, I just don't know yet. I can't ask you to wait for me. If you find someone else, forget about me, because I just can't give you an answer and it's nobody's fault but my own. There's no way to reason it out. It's just something I have to feel."

She leaned closer and embraced him. Reluctantly, he put his arms around her.

"There is a lot between us," he said. Her face pulled close to his.

"I don't care. I love you. You're all I have. I'll wait for you in Sydney." She put her lips to his and his arms tightened around her. "I know that you'll come to me," she whispered.

"I'll...come to you, one way or the other," he said, his brooding eyes squinting in the sun. She smiled, but he still could not.

"That's all I ask," she said at last.

Hawk did not see her again. She was taken to the other side of the island later in the day, and then flown from the captured airfield to the south.

* * *

HAWK'S UNIT required quite a bit of reorganizing after the campaign, for it had been virtually destroyed. There was a period of a month before the reorganization would permit a return to the ships. Joe Canlon knew a little bit about sailing and he volunteered to take Beckwith and Hawk for a cruise. It only seemed natural to turn the bow toward the western shore. Gretchen's little sloop could practically sail itself over there. Hawk anchored the boat in the lagoon by the waterfall. The other two marines were awed by the beauty of the spot.

"I ain't never seen nothing like this," said Canlon in his hoarse voice. "After the war, I might come back to these islands, you know? It sure beats six months of snow."

"I thought Yankees liked snow," said Hawk, firing up a cigar as he reclined upon the deck.

"No, I'm serious. Wouldn't you like to live here?" Canlon persisted. Beckwith nodded, draping an arm over the gunwale and into the clear water. But Hawk shook his head.

"Naw. I think I've had enough of these islands," he answered, his voice softer and weaker than usual.

"Well sure, we ain't exactly seen 'em at their best," said Canlon, expanding on his dream. "But I mean after the war, a man could really settle down in style here."

"They'll probably settle you down about six feet," Hawk responded grimly. Canlon's enthusiastic face went white. The deck creaked prophetically. The fragrance of the tropical flowers was overpowering.

"Where you reckon we're headed next?" Canlon asked, his tone now more subdued. Hawk's tragic eyes watched as a peaceful breeze lifted the dark green treetops against the deep blue sky. Wherever they need men that are all guts and no brains, he thought.

"I don't know. Just the next worthless island," he finally replied.

A LOOK AT BOOK TWO:
THE RETURN OF SGT. HAWK

OUTLAW MARINE!

The U.S. Army has invaded the Japanese-occupied Philippine Islands, and on their heels are the Marines. Right away, Sergeant James Hawk is assigned to a division recapturing the Philippines from the Japanese. But as an inter-service rivalry develops, Hawk finds himself smack in the middle.

As the Marines are driven from the town of Liloila, Hawk meets an American girl—who becomes stranded there. Against direct orders, Hawk's unit launches an ill-fated attack on the town, prompting the Army to proclaim him a renegade criminal to be shot on sight!

Will Hawk survive multiple attempts on his life in an action-packed fight to the death?

AVAILABLE JUNE 2022

ABOUT THE AUTHOR

Patrick Clay was born a fifth generation Texan, in Galena Park, Texas, and went to a Catholic elementary school there. He attended St. Thomas High School and graduated fifth in his class. Patrick also received a scholarship to the University of St. Thomas and graduated cum laude from there. He then graduated magna cum laude from South Texas College of Law, where he was fourth in his class and a member of the law journal. While attending law school at night, Patrick operated his own locksmith shop. During the time he waited for the bar results, he began writing fiction. He began his second novel, *Sgt. Hawk*, in February 1977, and finished it in six weeks. Patrick had a well-known agent, who tried to sell it to major publishers and television. It was finally sold to Leisure Books in 1978, and by that time, Patrick had finished *The Return of Sgt. Hawk*, which was published in 1980. *Sgt. Hawk Under Attack* and *Sgt. Hawk Tiger Island* followed in 1981 and 1982, respectively. The titles of the latter two books were selected by the publisher, Leisure Books, as they originally had different names. *Sgt. Hawk and The Firebolt* was written in 1982 when Leisure Books went bankrupt, returned the rights, and never fulfilled distribution. Patrick had by then begun a solo law practice and gave up writing. He worked in a poor neighborhood, with plenty of wonderful clients, but not much compensation. So,

Patrick became a captain in the Civil Air Patrol and was Houston chess player in 1990, more for his tournament directing ability than playing skills. After fourteen years, he gave up the private law practice, and worked as an attorney for the federal government for the next thirty years. The podcast, *Paperback Warrior*, rekindled his interest in *Sgt. Hawk*.

Patrick met his beautiful wife at Astroworld in Houston, the first year that the amusement park opened. When he began writing in 1977, he had no children, and by the time he stopped writing in 1983, he had three daughters; he now has nine grandchildren. His father, a disabled veteran, and six uncles served in the South Pacific during World War II. Patrick was named after one of them, Patrick Clay, who was on a U.S. Navy ship with four battle stars. Another one of Patrick's uncles was at Pearl Harbor when it was attacked.

33108763R00161